Toro

An International Thriller

Len Camarda

authorHOUSE®

AuthorHouse™
1663 Liberty Drive
Bloomington, IN 47403
www.authorhouse.com
Phone: 833-262-8899

Published by AuthorHouse   03/31/2022

ISBN: 978-1-6655-4963-9 (sc)
ISBN: 978-1-6655-4962-2 (hc)
ISBN: 978-1-6655-4975-2 (e)

Library of Congress Control Number: 2022901554

This book is a work of fiction. While there are references to actual places and organizations, they
are used to establish credibility for the storyline. Other names and characters, while associated
with actual places, organizations, authorities and countries, are a product of the author's
imagination and are used fictitiously. Any resemblance to actual persons, living or dead is to be
construed as totally a work of fiction and not related to their actual beliefs, policies nor activities.

Print information available on the last page.

Any people depicted in stock imagery provided by Getty Images are models,
and such images are being used for illustrative purposes only.
Certain stock imagery © Getty Images and licenses from Adobe

This book is printed on acid-free paper.

Because of the dynamic nature of the Internet, any web addresses or links contained in
this book may have changed since publication and may no longer be valid. The views
expressed in this work are solely those of the author and do not necessarily reflect the
views of the publisher, and the publisher hereby disclaims any responsibility for them.

Strangers on a Train. Movie produced and directed by Alfred
Hitchcock, 1951, Translantic Pictures, Warner Brothers.

The Sun Also Rises. Novel by Ernest Hemingway, 1926, Scribner publisher

The Gambler
Words and Music by Don Schlitz
Copyright © 1977 Sony Music Publishing (US) LLC
Copyright Renewed
All Rights Administered by Sony Music Publishing (US) LLC, 424 Church Street, Suite
1200, Nashville, TN 37219 International Copyright Secured All Rights Reserved
Reprinted by Permission of Hal Leonard LLC

For my son-in-law Bob, who had absolutely nothing to do with the development of this novel, but whose marriage to my daughter 'George' (who was a major contributor to this novel) is full of love, happiness, and fun, which makes a father grateful.

"The greatness of a nation and its moral progress can be judged by the way its animals are treated."

—Mohandas K. Gandhi

Chapter One

Alejandro de Portillo, one of the most prominent and influential impresarios of bullfighting in all of Spain, slowly awakens from a drug-induced slumber. There is darkness all around him as his eyes try to focus. He is on the ground—somewhere. As he moves to an awkward sitting position, trying to remain erect with his right hand and arm, he senses he is on dirt—soft, sandy dirt. It is night, as he sees stars in the sky and a slim, crescent moon. He thinks, *what is going on?* —as he struggles to regain his senses. There is enough ambient light for him to recognize a structure in the distance. *A wall, a building*, he thinks as he moves his head, which aches tremendously. Now bracing himself with both arms extended to the ground, he senses that this structure is all around him.

He realizes he is still in the clothes he was wearing last night—dark suit, shirt, and tie—when he had dinner at El Bodegón in Madrid. *Was it last night? Was it tonight?* The fog and pain in his head continue to blur his thoughts. *What happened after dinner?* He tries to get up, pushing first with one arm and then the other, but his legs tremble at the effort and he remains sitting in the dirt. A small beam of light suddenly illuminates him, blinding him for a moment. Then, another beam of light from above illuminates an area of the structure he has perceived. He quickly realizes he is sitting on the

1

ground in the center of a bullring as he recognizes the *barrera*—the wooden barrier encircling the ring—and the alcove for one of the gates.

A short blare of a trumpet pierces the night, accompanied by the opening of the gate immersed in light. Then, a bull emerges, taking a few running strides before sharply halting, spraying dirt in front of him. Stopped, he moves his head left and then right, then pausing, staring straight ahead at the circle of light thirty meters away. The bull lowers his head, scrapes the ground with one hoof, then the other, twice, and then bursts forward like a run-away locomotive.

At first, de Portillo is mesmerized by the sight of the bull emerging from the wooden gate. Fear, like he never felt in his life, drives adrenaline through his body, overcoming the debilitating effect of the drugs in his system. He rolls to his knees and then rises, trying to run, but just stumbling forward, away from the beast that is no longer illuminated by the light. He cannot see it but feels the thunder in the ground. If he can make it to one of the *burladeros*—the wooden shields positioned at the barrier—he could slide behind it and be safe, the way a matador does. But he is only able to generate a few erratic strides before the bull reaches him. At full speed it lowers its head and thrust into the body of de Portillo. As luck would have it, the head of the bull catches de Portillo at his backside, and with an upward thrust of its head, the stumbling man flew at least five meters into the air before crashing to the ground. Sprawled on the arena sand, de Portillo realizes the bull's horns missed him completely, going on each side of his body without damage. He hurt but felt relief, a reprieve, but that sensation ended quickly. The bull skidded, turned, and stopped, looking toward the man who was trying to get up, before charging again. This time, de Portillo took the full brunt of one of the horns in his left side, bursting bone, tissues, and organs in a torrid thrust. De Portillo's body is now impaled on the bull's horn, and with every shake of its head, the man was savagely ripped apart until he was again sprawled in the sand, all life gone.

The body now laid outside the circle of light that continued to illuminate the center of the bullring and the bull, *Tormento*—Storm, continued to pummel the man, rolling him over and over with relentless attacks. Then, *Tormento* stopped, looked around and in a slow, trotting gait moved along the perimeter of the ring, near the *barrera*. The gate from where he emerged was closed, so he continued to circle the ring, not returning to the ravaged body he had destroyed. Overall, not more than two minutes had transpired from the moment *Tormento* had entered the arena. He continued trotting around the bullring, around and around, and then stopped, and just laid down with his head erect, staring at the light that illuminated the gate. Not tired, just bored.

Chapter Two

Inspector Jefe—Chief Inspector—Mercedes Garcia Rico of the Spanish *Cuerpo Nacional de Policia* (*CNP*)—National Police Force—was in her office in Madrid that morning. She had recently cut her hair short, full but short, a substantial difference from the raven-hair, below-the-shoulder length she had worn for many years. She still fidgeted with the hair at the back of her neck, but she could no longer twirl it as she did before when she was locked in thought. At forty years of age, with crystalline blue eyes and a lithe figure on a five foot-six-inch frame, she remained extremely attractive. She was engrossed in reviewing a watch-list of potential terrorists in each area of the country. This kind of surveillance had taken on a new level of importance following the devastating attack on commuter trains entering Madrid on the morning of March 11, 2004. Some fourteen explosive devices were placed on four trains detonating at, or just before, Atocha Station in the heart of the city. Almost two hundred people died and another eighteen hundred were maimed and injured. Moroccan terrorists were identified and eventually brought to justice, but just as 9/11 took the United States to a whole new global reality, 3/11 did the same for Spain. The CNP was ever alert and watchful, and thus far successful in keeping Spaniards safe from the terrorist acts occurring throughout Europe and still, on occasion, in the USA.

At around the same time, an entirely different plot emerged following the killing of a young American woman. This brought then-Lieutenant Garcia, stationed in Granada, in contact with Gene—Gino—Cerone, an ex-USA Secret Service agent and brother of the deceased woman. With no leads as to why Gina Cerone was murdered and the investigation essentially shutting down, Gino Cerone left his position as Attack on Principal Trainer with the Service, moved to Granada, to continue the derailed investigation on his own. Embarrassed by their lack of progress, as potential leads kept dying under suspicious circumstances, Garcia was assigned to work with the American— a saving face gesture. The two eventually uncovered an unfathomable conspiracy, dating back more than five-hundred years when the last vestige of the Moors' occupation of the Iberian Peninsula, the Kingdom of Granada, surrendered to the Spanish in 1492. The conspiracy was a methodical re-conquest of the country, but by economic means, with the goal of returning Spain to an Islamic monarchy, which was thwarted by Cerone and Garcia. Consequently, both moved to Madrid, Garcia promoted to CNP headquarters and Cerone assisting the government in untangling the vast network of conspirators.

Then, last year, the two again worked together after a Spanish girl and her American friend were kidnapped from the University of Madrid. That investigation led to their uncovering a plot affecting the best and brightest women—leaders amongst their peers—in universities across Europe. Partnering with Interpol, Garcia and Cerone's investigation eventually took them to the kingdoms of the Middle East, where the abducted women were located and eventually rescued and returned to their homes. That earned Garcia the promotion to *Inspector Jefe* of the CNP. The close working relationship between Garcia and Cerone grew to a romantic one over the years and the two were eventually married, with Cerone taking a position with Interpol, based in Madrid, focusing on human trafficking.

"*Inspector Jefe*," Garcia's administrative assistant excitedly exclaimed, "I have two detectives from the Madrid Police Force that need to see you immediately."

Putting her papers off to one side, then taking a quick sip of her coffee, Garcia replied, "Send them in Rosa, I need a break."

"*Inspector Jefe*," a man just short of six feet tall with a full, black moustache, in a nicely tailored gray suit, said, extending his right hand, "I am Detective Lieutenant Antonio Alvarez, and this is my colleague"—pointing to his left—"Detective José Luis Luna." Both men shook hands with Garcia as she rose and leaned over her desk. Sitting again, she resumed sipping her coffee.

With an exasperated expression on his face, he said, "We have an unimaginable tragedy on our hands, *Inspector Jefe*. This morning, Alejandro de Portillo, one of the most important bullfighting promoters in all of Spain, was found dead in the bullring at Las Ventas. Not only dead but decimated by a bull who was found resting not twenty meters away from the body."

"What? How did this happen?" Garcia exclaimed, spilling some coffee as she returned the cup to her desk.

"No idea yet, Inspector. The body was found by a security guard early this morning, who was subdued, somehow, late last night."

"The guard was apparently drugged," said Luna. "He is being screened and tested as we speak. He remembers absolutely nothing, as does another guard, who was found unconscious by the first officers that arrived, just after dawn. There will be a full toxicology screen on both, and we will know more later this morning."

"It's a horror," added Alvarez. "We got a call just as we arrived at the precinct from the first officers at the scene, but nobody can do very much until they get the bull out of the arena. Our observations were made from the perimeter wall. With today's environment regarding animal rights, there is no way we could just shoot it and move to the body. We called our superiors and were told to bring CNP into this. That is why we are here. Las Ventas management was informed, and they are arranging to bring in some matadors if needed to move the bull out of the ring. They also thought about bringing in some cattle from the pens below the stands to coax the bull into one of the gates, the way they do in *corridas*, when they want to remove an underperforming bull from the ring."

Just then Alverez's phone rang. He apologized but said it was from one of the officers at the arena. He listened for a moment and then said, *"Bueno, gracias."*

"Management at Las Ventas used the cattle and were able to get the bull out of the ring. He is back in his pen below the stands. We can now get to the body of Señor de Portillo."

"I'm not sure I would have wanted to have a bunch of cows running around the crime scene, Detective," commented Garcia, "but I understand the need to get the bull out of there. One question. If you could not get to the body, how could you identify it as Alejandro de Portillo?"

"The guard who discovered the body," Alvarez pausing and looking at a notepad he pulled from his jacket, "Tito Suarez, recognized him, despite the distance from the body and despite the destruction caused by the bull, whose name is Tormento, by the way. Suarez kept circling the arena from the perimeter wall until he was able to make out the face."

Just then, Alvarez's cell phone rang again. Rolling his eyes, he rose from the chair in front of Garcia's desk and excused himself. He listened and then said, *"Gracias."*

Turning back to the Inspector, he said, "It is confirmed. It is de Portillo. Our forensic people are there as well as the medical examiner. They were able to confirm the identification from his wallet, despite his clothes in tatters, as Alejandro de Portillo."

"I know de Portillo, not personally," Garcia commented, "and as you said, he is one of the most prominent promoters in the country. He organizes most of the events at Las Ventas, not only bullfighting, and is very renowned."

"That is why we were asked to meet with you, *Inspector Jefe*. While we have secured the scene, we know this is no accident. The Madrid brass wants CNP's expertise on this, not only for the forensics but for the investigation as well."

"I agree. I expect I will be receiving a call from my superiors momentarily. This will be all over the press throughout the country. In the meantime, no press at the scene. I do not want to see photos of this in *El Pais* or any news organization. Instruct your men at Las Ventas to lock it down while I organize a team to get over there. Total lockdown Alvarez. *Claro?* —Clear? And make sure nobody there uses their cell phones to take pictures. Check cell phones from everybody there."

"*Claro, Inspector Jefe*, it will be done," replied Alvarez, with Detective Luna nodding in agreement as they rose and departed.

Chapter Three

Inspector Jefe Garcia called out to Rosa to come in. "Rosa, call Paloma and José Maria to join me immediately—Paloma Retuerta and José Maria Duarte being the two most experienced forensic investigators in the Scientific Police Division. Also see if Miguel Alonso and Conchita Verdura are here. If you can track them down, we'll meet in my conference room in fifteen minutes."

It took no more than ten minutes for Garcia's team to start to arrive. Paloma, a petite, attractive woman in her early fifties with black hair, showing a few strands of gray, pulled into a bun, was the first to arrive. Less than a minute later, Duarte entered the conference room. In his late-thirties, Duarte was a head taller than his boss, Paloma, with thick black hair and a full beard and moustache, making him look older than he was. They took their usual seats at the right of Garcia's chair.

It took a few more minutes to locate Inspector Alonso and Sub-Inspector Verdura, who were having their morning coffee in the cafeteria. Alonso was about fifty years old, as tall as Duarte, but much thinner with no facial hair and almost bald, save the short brown hair around the sides and back of his head. Conchita Verdura was in her late thirties, about as tall as *Inspector Jefe* Garcia but a little rounder, all around. She had a pretty face, framed by black, curled, shoulder-length hair and black, trimmed eyebrows above dark-brown eyes. Verdura and Alonso had been partnered together for three years and were the best investigators in Garcia's unit.

The four investigators began chatting amongst themselves when Garcia entered from her adjoining office. Alonso and Verdura sat to Garcia's left, each with a notebook in front of them. Retuerta and Duarte favored iPads.

"*Buenos días todos*—Good morning, all. Have any of you heard the news about Las Ventas today?"—Las Ventas being the largest and most prestigious *plaza de toros* in all of Spain.

The four shook their heads no, glancing towards each other. Garcia then went on to explain the information she obtained from the two Madrid detectives. "Further, I received a call a few minutes ago from the *comisario general*—general commissioner—that the CNP will take full responsibility for this investigation, led by this unit, coordinating as necessary, with the Madrid Police Force."

"Is that all we have so far, *Jefe*?" asked Paloma. "Nothing more than what you presented?"

"That's it," Garcia replied. "I have ordered the scene, essentially the whole facility, to be locked down. Madrid has crime scene investigators there now, but I want you, Paloma, and José Maria to take charge of that. Their medical examiner is on the scene also, so get everything you can from her—*Doctora* Cervantes—and determine if we need to bring in someone from CNP.

"This is an enormous crime scene, so set up a plan of what you need to fully investigate. You will need toxicology analysis from the guards, but I have been told that Madrid has already set that up, and make sure they do de Portillo as well. He could not have just walked into that arena on his own. You will need to re-interview the guards. Madrid talked to them this morning but who knows how clear their heads were at that time?" Looking at Retuerta and Duarte, Garcia kind of shook her head and said, "Fingerprints will be an interesting task. Get them from the guards, and then think of how far do we go? The perimeter wall of the bullring, the pen that held *Tormento*, the gate to the arena? Must be loaded with prints from the workers, the matadors, and God knows who else? Then who do we print to crossmatch what we get? Paloma, think about this and discuss it with the Madrid CSI people and come up with a recommendation. And how close do we analyze *Tormento*? I can't imagine we'll get anything from that, except that its horns and body is coated with the blood of de Portillo." The four simultaneously rolled their eyes upward and nodded affirmatively.

"Miguel and Conchita, find out all that you can on de Portillo. Where was he yesterday, and particularly, last night? Talk to his office. And we need to figure out the logistics of this assassination—that is what it was, no? How did Portillo get into that building? How was the bull released? This was an ingenious plan. How-the-hell did they pull it off?

And most importantly, we need to identify who would have wanted to do this? What enemies did de Portillo have? Check for any social media activity. Someone in his position had to have created some animosities. Other promoters, the management of Las Ventas and other arenas he has worked with, the matadors and their squads, from *picadors, banderilleros*, arena employees—anyone who had contact and did business with the man. A monumental challenge, no?"

"Are you kidding?" said Alonso. "A crime scene involving the largest bullring in Spain, where last night, more than twenty thousand spectators watched three teams of matadors do battle with six brave bulls. The place probably wasn't cleaned up until after midnight. The window to get to de Portillo in there, unseen, would be quite small."

"You know, we have to consider looking at the animal rights groups in Spain. The whole issue of sending these magnificent creatures to slaughter is always front and center for those who want to bring an end to bullfighting," added Conchita Verdura.

"That's a very good point," said Garcia. "The fact that the government has now classified bullfighting as part of the Spanish culture enraged many of these groups. I'll put Francisco Prida on that. He's one of our best analysts and no one is better than him in sitting behind a computer console and digging out things. Miguel, I will get him started on that and he will report to you. God knows there will be dozens of these groups, and we will have to talk to all of them. You will also have to get to de Portillo's office and find out who may have contacted him regarding complaints or threats associated with his role in this." She paused, then asked, "Any questions?"

Everyone had some questions, and after another fifteen minutes of discussion, they were sent on their way. *Cristo*—Christ, Mercedes thought. *What a mess.*

Chapter Four

The toxicology screens were completed later that day. Both guards tested positive for sevoflurane, a popular anesthetic used in surgery. They remembered someone coming up from behind them and spraying something in their face. Both recalled a cloth being placed on their face and being eased to the ground as they lost consciousness.

De Portillo was drugged with Rohypnol—flunitrazepam—a drug commonly associated with date rape. He would have been quickly rendered unconscious and then transported to the bullring. How and when the drug was administered remained a mystery. Then investigators at the scene believed there was some indication of his being dragged into the arena as they discovered evidence of deep grooves in the sand, but much of that evidence was erased by the charges of the bull and the attacks on de Portillo when he was on the ground. Later, the use of cattle to coax *Tormento* back through the gate, erased any of the remaining grooves in the sand, but one of the detectives from Madrid did take some photos with his cell phone.

That made them think that there had to be at least two people to be able to drag the drugged de Portillo into the ring. He weighed about ninety kilos—two hundred pounds. Cause of death was clear. Massive trauma with tissue and organ destruction from the attacks by the bull. The victim's blood and tissue were all over the horns, head, and legs of the animal, based on visual examination only. At some point there would be a physical examination of the bull, but for the time being, *Tormento* was left alone in his pen.

"Why was the bull still in the facility after the *corrida* the previous afternoon? The bulls were all killed in the ring by the matadors after the six *corridas*," asked Garcia after Paloma reported her preliminary findings.

"They always have an extra bull or two on standby in case one of the bulls in the *corrida* underperforms, showing little interest in fighting. That happens sometimes. When that occurs, they call a halt to the spectacle, bring in a group of cattle—non-fighting animals—that parade around the arena with the bull eventually joining them, and they leave through the same gate they entered. That bull is eventually killed below the stands and slaughtered. A new bull is then brought into the ring and the *corrida* begins again. *Tormento* was one of the standby bulls but was not needed yesterday as the six bulls performed as expected. He was to remain in his pen overnight and would have again been standby after six new fighting bulls would be brought to Las Ventas. Of course, that won't happen today as all *corridas* are cancelled until further notice. At this point," continued Paloma, "I'm not sure what happens to *Tormento*. That will eventually be my call, but he is both a perpetrator and a witness to what happened, but obviously, he isn't talking. There is no way we can get any prints from the animal—not while he is alive and not tranquilized—but logically, it would be unlikely that anyone physically touched its horns. There are prints all over and around the pen he was in, all the pens for that matter, but that is largely from the people that work in the stables. We will print them all and go through the comparison process but expect nothing to come of that.

"Oh, and de Portillo had a cell phone on him, but it was beat to pieces, I doubt that we will be able to get anything from it. Now one, perhaps two interesting developments. We discovered two lights were on when we were there, mounted on simple tripods in the stands. Battery powered, we calculated that one was aimed at the center of the bullring and the other at the gate where *Tormento* emerged. They were still on, undoubtedly used last night—or this morning—when de Portillo was brought in."

"So maybe, three people," speculated Garcia. "Two down below with de Portillo and one in the stands managing the lights."

"Maybe," replied Paloma, "Maybe," trying to picture the scenario in her mind. "Alonso and Verdura will nevertheless try to find out who sells such units and see what turns up."

"And the second interesting development?" asked Garcia.

"We found a white feather in the bullring. Pristine, perfectly white from *una paloma*—a dove. It looks like it was cleanly cut, so it could not have fallen from a circulating bird."

"*Bueno*, interesting but probably of no consequence. Let's keep that quiet. We will need to brief the media later today, but no mention of the feather. We will have to tell the press that perhaps two or three people may have been involved, but we will parse out any details gradually until we determine what we want to release to them. I'll talk to the commissioner and see how far he wants to go. He will likely do the briefing."

* * *

Inspectors Alonso and Verdura ascertained that de Portillo had dinner last night at about ten o'clock at El Bodégon. Miguel called *Inspector Jefe* Garcia and brought her up to date. "He was alone and left after midnight," he related. "The staff believed he came and departed in his own car, a white BMW sedan, which we discovered parked up the hill from the restaurant. He must have been abducted at that time, subdued, drugged, and then brought to the arena. It is quite dark in that area and people can be easily concealed."

"Did he meet with anyone there?" asked Garcia.

"No, not really. He was in a good mood, chatted with the maître d' and wait staff, but nobody else," replied Alonso.

"Find out who knew where he would be last night. His office is in the *Torre Picasso*, so get over there and talk to everyone. Find out if there were any issues lately, threats, complaints, the works. They must keep a record of these things, and particularly check into correspondence and any lawsuits from animal rights groups. Pull out everything. When you are done there, visit the offices of the *Fundación de Toro Lidia* and any other commissions or associations associated with bullfighting. The industry is highly regulated, and the treatment of fighting bulls is governed by the *Ministerio de Cultura*. Perhaps that is the best place to start."

Chapter Five

Gene Cerone, now using his boyhood name, Gino, was at home in his and Mercedes' apartment on Apolonia Morales in the Chamartín section of Madrid. He is in his fifties, an athletic five-ten with black hair, now graying at the temples. He had a Julio Iglesias CD in the stereo and was busy preparing a light dinner for two. He and Mercedes have been married for over a year now, both very busy in their new positions; Mercedes as Chief Inspector with the CNP and Gino, Detective Chief Superintendent with Interpol, based in Madrid and focusing on human trafficking. It was about nine o'clock that evening when Mercedes entered, put her handbag on a table in the foyer, removed her handgun and *plopped* into an armchair in the living room.

"Well," said Gino, *buenas tardes*," moving to her, bending, and kissing her on the cheek. "You look like you have had a busy day."

Putting her holstered pistol on a side table, with both arms now hanging down, she said, "Don't ask. Please get me a glass of wine, red, and a good one. I need it."

Gino moved to a small bar area at the side of the living room, opened the door to a wine cooler and extracted a bottle of Pesquera Ribera del Duero red wine, looked at the label and noted the 2014 vintage. "You will like this," he said, removing the cork and pouring the deeply red wine into a clear glass goblet and bringing it to her.

Taking the glass in her right hand, sniffing, and then tasting the wine, she said, "Very good. Maybe this will be my dinner. Just the wine."

Gino laughed. "I thought I had a hectic day, but it looks like your day topped mine."

Mercedes sipped more of the wine, sighed, and then gave Gino a run-down of the killing of Alejandro de Portillo and the enormous complexity of the organization and direction of her team's investigation. "I assisted the commissioner in a press conference late this afternoon, and as you can imagine, the journalists were ravenous for information. It was a mad house. It will undoubtedly be on the eleven o'clock news tonight."

"Then we have to watch. It sounds fascinating. I'm sure it is not very often when your murder suspect is a one-ton animal."

"Not exactly a suspect, Gino. Cut and dry as to who did the killing, but how and why? That is the dilemma. But enough. I need to wind down," and took another gulp of the velvety wine. "Tell me about your day."

"It was a good day, a really good day. You remember we were tracking the activities of a group out of Nigeria, suspected of smuggling Africans into Europe. Interpol—primarily my unit— and police operations from Spain, Portugal, France, Holland, and Germany have been working for six months now in tracking this gang. They are responsible for smuggling more than one thousand people—mostly women and even some children—into Spain, primarily through Catalonia, but also through Andalucía. From Spain, these poor people are distributed throughout Europe, mostly to France, Belgium, and Germany. With the European open borders, all they need to do is get these victims into one country—in this case Spain—and from here, it is easy to take them anywhere.

"It's such a travesty. These people *pay* these smugglers to get them to Europe in hope of a better life. It's not like they are abducted, as was the case of those women taken from European universities last year. No, they want to come here for work of any kind, hopefully in the hospitality industry or in domestic service, but the women often end up as prostitutes, forever in debt to the traffickers who finance their travel, arrange for housing and provide documentation."

"It's an industry unto itself, isn't it, Gino?"

"A big industry, Mercedes, with many different organizations involved, dominated by Nigerians, Romanians and more and more, Chinese. The Chinese bring them in through former Soviet countries, but also through Lithuania, Turkey, and Greece. Very big, highly organized, and ruthless in that they recruit, transfer and exploit people from their own countries."

"How much do these people pay these traffickers?" asked Mercedes.

"It's all over the lot. Some are recruited via ads in local newspapers or through travel agencies and recommendations from unscrupulous acquaintances, and fees can run from €500 to €30,000. Debts that large can never be repaid and interest charges keep these people in some form of bondage forever."

"Interest charges? They charge interest on their fee?"

"Yes, just like a loan. Very sophisticated and of course, very corrupt."

"And today you took down one of these rings, Gino?"

"Yes, a Nigerian group responsible for bringing in more than one thousand people, largely from Nigeria, Somalia, and the Sudan, with others from other West African countries as well. Barcelona and Cádiz police arrested fifteen traffickers, including their boss in Catalonia. A victory, but there are many more groups out there, increasingly coming into Spain through Morocco. My unit is tracking three of these gangs whose victims are primarily destined for work in Spain, mostly in hostess clubs—a more sophisticated term for prostitution—and the lucky ones get to work in private homes. Granada—your old station—and Sevilla police are working with Interpol as well as a CNP unit responsible for crimes of this type."

Mercedes finished her wine, held up her glass for Gino to refill and said, "I thought my investigation was—as you Americans say—a can of worms, but you are trying to save humanity. I surrender to you. Now, what did you make for us to eat?"

Chapter Six

By early afternoon of the next day, Garcia's team of investigators—all eight of them—began a morning of preliminary contacts with several of the most active animal protection organizations in the country. These contacts were not formal interviews but more of a feeling out of the impressions of these groups to what had happened. Alonso and Verdura's visit to Portillo's office produced an avalanche of letters and petitions from both organizations as well as private individuals, demanding the cessation of bullfighting. Two cartons were filled with these communications from Portillo's files and Portillo's secretary—Carmen Ordoñez—promised to compile a list of E-mails they received as well.

Their visit to the *Ministerio de Cultura* yielded an even greater number of complaints, particularly after the ministry declared bullfighting as part of Spain's culture. While officially responsible for the protection of bullfighting—responsible for the rights of all involved—it declared that bullfighting is an artistic discipline and cultural product, assuming responsibly from the Ministry of the Interior. It, in essence, is charged with the protection of the tradition, which was a clear affront to all those opposing its cruelty to animals. The Ministry was reluctant to release these petitions and letters to the CNP, but Alonso and Verdura were permitted to go through the files and take note of anything of interest.

While this was happening, Francisco Prida started an online search, identifying organizations dedicated to the prevention of cruelty to animals, focusing, where possible, on those most opposed to bullfighting, and he fed these names to the investigators, logging who was going to contact each one. Prida was also tasked with looking into where light stands, like those used in Las Ventas, might be sold.

Returning from the Ministry of Culture, Alonso asked *Inspector Jefe* Garcia to set up a meeting with all the investigators to gather their findings and set up a more organized and focused investigative plan. It was good to start to get some preliminary readings on this angle of the investigation, but because of the scope of players possibly involved, he knew Garcia would want to tighten things and set priorities.

At three in the afternoon, eight investigators and Francisco Prida arrived at the conference room adjacent to Garcia's office. Rosa had set up a few whiteboards and Prida intended to use his laptop to project his preliminary findings.

"Buenas tardes, todos"—Good afternoon, all—began *Inspector Jefe* Garcia as she walked into the room and took a seat at the head of the table. "Miguel, bring us up-to-date on where we are."

"Sí, Jefe," replied Alonso. "Our visit to de Portillo's office this morning indicated that his secretary, Señorita Ordoñez, knew of his dinner plans, having made the reservation at El Bodégon. That's it, they have other staff at the office, but none were around that afternoon. Portillo lives alone, so there is no family to question. However, we retrieved two cartons of petitions and complaints, even some threats—although it is unclear how serious these threats

were—relating to his involvement in the promotion of bullfighting. I've asked sub-inspectors Ambrosio and Leal to return to the *Ministerio de Cultura*, where Verdura and I were this morning, to record all the complaints and petitions they had received relating to their support of bullfighting, despite it being banned in some regions of the country, like Catalonia. If there is time, I would like them to return today. The staff at the ministry would not release these documents to us but agreed we could have full access to their files. Ultimately, what I suggest we do is crossmatch the information from the ministry's files, Portillo's files, with the list of animal rights organizations that Francisco Prida has compiled from his online search."

"I may be able to help you with those ministry files. I'll come back to that," then looking at Prida said, "Francisco, I see that you have some data you want to share with us."

"*Sí, Jefe*," replied Prida, as he opened his laptop which had been connected to a projector. "As you will see, there are dozens of organizations actively opposed to bullfighting, most are local to Spain, but there are a large number of international organizations most active in this mission, opposing any kind of cruelty to animals, including the brave bulls of Spain and in several Latin American countries as well." Prida flashed page after page of organizations. "The most prominent of these entities is PETA—People for the Ethical Treatment of Animals—world-renowned and opposed to bullfighting, horse racing, dog racing, animal experimentation, and anything that endangers or mistreats animals of any kind. Whaling and the fur industry are ongoing targets of PETA, but they are active here as well. There is also the International Movement Against Bullfighting, CAS International, Animal Equality, Humane Society International, ESDAW—European Society of Dog and Animal Welfare. The list goes on. I've cited most of them here, with names of directors and locations for each.

"Closer to home is *Partido Animalista*, a Spanish political party, *Derechos para las Animales*, *Alternativa para la Liberación Animal*, *AnimaNaturalis*, *Salvan Los Toros*, Animal Liberation Front (ALF), Animal Guardians, and as you can see, two more pages of groups. Again, I have listed office locations—many are not based in Madrid—and directors where they were listed. I have hand-outs for everyone, but we need some priorities, or a lot more investigators to follow up, or both."

Garcia slumped back in her chair and emitted a sigh. "And we don't know how many others that might come from Portillo's files or those of the ministry."

"No," added Miguel Alonso. "This will be a massive data dump to go through and we don't even know if this is the right direction to pursue."

"Okay," replied Garcia. "Here is what we will do, understanding that there will be pressure to identify the perpetrators of this," she paused, "assassination. CNP hierarchy and all levels of government will want some conclusions fast. Alonso has a point, but we will focus on the animal rights groups, as we have no indication—so far—of any other motive to kill Portillo. I have asked the forensic accounting group to go through all of Portillo's financial information, accounts, holdings, the works, just in case a motive can be found there. But our priority will be Prida's list, focusing first on the local groups. Leal and Ambrosio, you will be responsible for going through the ministry's files, compiling a list of the organizations and individuals who have petitioned the ministry since their ruling on bullfighting."

"That could be several years of complaints," interjected Detective Leal.

"It could," answered Garcia, "but organize your list to highlight the last twelve months. It would not hurt to get everything in their files, but we will focus on only the last twelve months. I will get the commissioner to call the minister himself to have those files released to us. I'm sure he can make that happen. Francisco, I want you and your analysts to work with Leal and Ambrosio on how best to organize the information. Working from here will speed things up.

"Miguel, I want you and Conchita to stay with de Portillo's files. Two cartons are not a lot to go through. Again, Francisco, give them some guidance on the best way to organize this, preferably using your laptops to log the information. As to the rest of you, I want you to continue making preliminary contacts as you have done this morning. Divide up the list Francisco has distributed. Understand their reaction to Portillo's murder, sense their passion on this issue. Ask about the number of members to their organization—if you can get a list, so much the better. But keep this as a friendly inquiry for now, not an inquisition. We can go back again if and when appropriate.

"Lastly, Francisco, I suggest your analysts start to profile these organizations and their leaders. Get all the background you can, including finances.

"*Claro?*" she asked. "Questions? Good, then let's start. Leal and Ambrosio, you should be able to get back to the ministry this afternoon before everyone goes home. The commissioner should open the door for you, but bring some cartons and if you need assistance, recruit some of the uniformed CNP officers. *Va*"—Go.

Chapter Seven

Francisco Prida lingered in the conference room until the others left.

"Francisco," Inspector Garcia asked, "you have something you want to talk about?"

Prida stood quiet for a moment and then said, "*Sí, Jefe*. You know this has been a very depressing project. In looking for animal rights groups, I came across a lengthy list of activities and festivals in Spain, some going back to the Celtic period. It seems that upwards of sixty thousand animals are tortured and killed each year in Spain, sixty thousand! Largely those are related to festivals, most of which continue today. From tearing off the heads of chickens and geese, throwing goats off a village bell tower, tormenting donkeys in the streets, terrorizing wild horses—not including the terror the horses of picadors go through in the bullring. Using greyhound dogs to hunt wild game and then hanging the dogs at the end of the hunt, catapulting baby quail into the air, and then shooting them as you would with a skeet disc. When it comes to the bulls, bullfighting seems tame by comparison. One festival uses pitch and tar on a bull's horns and then sets them on fire while it is tied to a post, and then releases it to run through the streets with its head on fire. Another town releases a bull in the street and then chases it until it runs off a pier and into the sea. Dogs being illegally used for research. This is terrible, *Jefe*."

Garcia contemplated the young man, seeing the anguish in his eyes. "I know, Francisco, but many of these festivals have been outlawed now, but you can understand how these animal rights groups are outraged by these torturous activities. On the other hand, the torture and killing of *Señor* de Portillo is unspeakable cruelty against a human being. Does he deserve such a horrible fate for being an impresario of bullfighting? I think not, and it is our job to find out who is behind this. Will you be able to continue in our investigation of this crime, Francisco?"

"Of course, *Jefe*. I just never gave much thought to the cruelty of this sport—if you really can call bullfighting a sport—but just seeing how many groups are dedicated to protecting these animals—all animals—this whole thing takes on a new perspective. I have no doubts we will eventually find out who is behind this, but the list of people and organizations that care, really care, is daunting, and I can understand their passion."

"But not to kill people, Francisco. That we cannot permit to go unpunished."

"No, *Jefe*," replied Prida, as he gathered up his notes, disconnected and closed his laptop. "No, we can't," and he started to leave the room.

"Oh, I almost forgot," he added. "You asked me to look into those light stands used in the bullring. Investigators at the scene said that they were not new and were of the type used for minor road repairs in the evening. There is a large supply of them at warehouses of the city Department of Transportation. I'm not sure they even maintain an inventory of them. They can also be acquired at the various flea markets in Madrid, like El Rastro and the Mercado de San Miguel, and new ones may be available at select hardware stores. They are really not very unique."

"Thank you, Francisco. I'm not sure I want to use a lot of manpower chasing around flea markets and hardware stores, but we'll hold off on that for now. We may want to look into this later." She then patted Prida on his shoulder. "You are doing fine work Francisco, keep on it."

* * *

It took another two days to assemble, profile, crossmatch and develop a priority list of contacts for follow-up. The first wave of organizations who were the most active anti-bullfighting groups which had frequently petitioned Alejandro de Portillo and organized demonstrations were:

- International Movement Against Bullfighting
- League Against Cruel Sports
- Animal Guardians
- Animal Equity
- Salvan Los Toros
- Derechos para los Animales
- PETA
- AnimaNaturalis
- PACMA—political party
- Partido Animalista de Bilbao

In addition, six hundred individuals who wrote more than one letter to de Portillo, the Ministry of Culture, and the Ministry of the Interior, made the list. Letters to the Editor in leading newspapers across Spain, and in particular the Madrid dailies, were scrutinized and cross-matched against other sources. Lastly, the Spanish television stations were approached to provide tapes of talk shows, interviews, panel discussions regarding the drive to outlaw bullfighting. Many of those participating in these televised discussions were associated with at least one on the animal rights groups and seeing the passions of how they argued their points was deemed to be of interest. As these were public forums, warrants were not required to release the tapes.

Uniformed officers of the CNP did most of the follow-up with individuals who had written or complained—at times even threatened—to either de Portillo directly or "those responsible for animal abuse." The detectives of Garcia's unit divided up the tier one groups of organizations and started interviewing. Alonso and Verdura were charged with viewing the television station tapes as they might be important in strengthening profiles of leaders or the more active members of these associations.

Two groups stood out amongst the priority groups profiled. "The Partido Animalista de Bilbao," reported Alonso to the team again gathered in Garcia's conference room, "is a semi-political party in the Basque region, and Salvan Los Toros, based in Madrid. The Animalist Party warranted further scrutiny because their demonstrations often led to violence. There were frequent arrests and at times injuries associated with their activism. Gorka Mendoza was president of the Animalist Party of Bilbao, with Estebe Zubin, Joseba Aguirre and Nikola Ibarra, his command unit officers. All from prominent Basque families, who years before probably were fighting for Basque independence from Spain. Joseba Aguirre had been arrested a few times stemming from demonstrations that got out of hand. Many of these demonstrations were in Pamplona during the Feria de San Fermin and the running of the bulls. The group has about one thousand members and had—thus far without success—tried to gain seats in the parliament of the Basque Autonomous Community."

Conchita Verdura then rose and addressed the gathered group. "The other organization that warrants a second look is Salvan Los Toros, a small but vocal and active rights group based in Madrid. What made Salvan Los Toros so interesting is that their leader, Victoria Valenzuela, is related to one of the most popular and respected bullfighting families in Spain, as well as one of the finest fighting bull breeding ranches in the country—*Ganaderia VV de los Toros Bravos.*

"Victoria's father, Victor, and grandfather, Valerio, were bullfighters of great renown. Victor, at one point was dubbed '*El Matador*' because of his prowess and grace in the ring. He was one of the most popular matadors of his time."

"Yes, I know of him. I even had a poster of *El Matador* in my bedroom when I was a kid," interrupted Sub-Inspector Leal. "He was killed in the ring."

"Yes, I have heard, but he was very popular," continued Verdura. "Valerio, on the other hand, left bullfighting early to build one of the finest breeding ranches of *toros de lidia*, the most important breed of fighting bull, known for its combination of aggression, energy, strength and stamina. So, how is it that someone whose blood is rich in the Spanish bullfighting culture became a leading advocate against it? We want to understand more."

"Indeed, there seems to be more to learn about Victoria Valenzuela," added *Inspector Jefe* Garcia. "Conchita, you work with me tomorrow. We'll pay a visit to Salvan Los Toros. Miguel, you, Leal and Ambrosio will travel to Bilbao and visit, hopefully, with Gorka Mendoza. I'd like for you to also chat with Joseba Aguirre and get a feel for his aggressive nature. We won't call ahead, just drop in."

Chapter Eight

It is almost four hundred kilometers by car from Madrid to Bilbao, so Garcia authorized her three agents to fly. Iberia had discount flights for the CNP and round trip would cost no more than €90. Not wanting to alert anyone at the *partido* of their visit was a risk of wasting the money, but one of the staff did call ahead inquiring if the office was open.

Salvan Los Toros was located in San Agustín del Guadalix on the N-1 highway, north of Madrid. The office was in a roadside strip mall along with a branch of the Bank of Santander, an accounting office, and several small restaurants. Very understated and non-descript. It took less than an hour to get there from the CNP offices in Madrid, and Garcia and Verdura arrived at ten the following morning.

The office was small, with an open area upon entering with two women at desks, in front of computer monitors. There was an office in the back adjacent to a closed door that may have been a conference room. There were several tables off to the side of the open area with literature and pamphlets, relating to their cause, along with some printers and copiers. Posters on the wall were of *toros bravos* grazing in fields or full-size photos demonstrating their beauty and strength.

"*Buenos días,*" said the woman to the right. She was somewhere in her thirties, had long black hair, large brown eyes, and a welcoming smile. She rose and approached the two women. "I am Martina Muñoz; how can I help you?"

Removing her identification from her handbag, Garcia said, "I am *Inspector Jefe* Mercedes Garcia from the CNP, and this is Sub-Inspector Conchita Verdura. We are here to see Victoria Valenzuela."

"Oh, the CNP. I hope there is no problem."

"No, none at all," replied Garcia. "We just want a few minutes of Señorita Valenzuela's time."

"*Bueno*, just give me a minute," and she turned, moving to the office in the back, where another woman could be seen through the half-glass door. Pointing to the woman at the other outside desk, she said, "This is Luz Sánchez, can she get you something?" Sánchez, lithe and athletic looking as she rose from her chair, was probably in her late twenties, with black hair pulled back into a bun. Attractive, as was Muñoz.

"No, nothing, but thank you."

Less than a minute later, Muñoz returned followed by Victoria Valenzuela. She was maybe in her early forties and striking. Trim, about five-foot-six with short but full black hair, jet black and shiny. Two other features defined her uniqueness. She had a pure white patch of hair at her forehead, just above her left eye, an inch or so deep, and more surprising, she had slight Asian features with jade-like green eyes. *Eurasian?* Garcia thought. She was dressed in slim fitting black jeans, short, black leather boots, and a white, man-tailored shirt. The black and white motif suited her well.

"*Buenos días*, Inspectors. What brings two officers from the CNP to our modest offices?" Valenzuela said.

"I am sure that you have read about the death of Alejandro de Portillo," Garcia began. "I would like to speak to you about that."

"Why don't we go into my office?" Victoria Valenzuela offered. "It will be more comfortable, but I don't know how I can help you."

Garcia and Verdura followed Valenzuela into her office where they settled into two chairs in front of her desk. There were more posters of bulls inside as well as a poster advertising "El Matador," Victor Valenzuela, Victoria's father. There was an awkward silence for a few seconds as Garcia and Verdura unconsciously stared at the woman across the desk.

Victoria smiled and gave a short laugh. "Okay, let's deal with the two hundred kilo gorilla in the room. Victoria Valenzuela is Asian, you are thinking?"

"No, no, forgive me," replied *Inspector Jefe* Garcia, "but you are right. You do not often see Asians here in Madrid, or in Spain, for that matter, much less with a name like Victoria Valenzuela."

"My mother, Kim Watanabe, is Japanese. She was assistant General Manager at the Kyoto Palace Hotel in Madrid after its acquisition and renovation by a five-star Japanese hotel chain. My father, Victor Valenzuela," pausing to turn and point to the poster on the wall, "went there for a dinner one night. He stopped, asked for directions to the restaurant from a woman behind the reception—my mother—and a romance began. Two very different cultures, Japanese and Spanish, and my father a bullfighter, no less. Many challenges, but they made it work. And my hair? No idea how that happened. So, all that is off the table and we can talk about *Señor* de Portillo."

Smiling, Garcia asked, "What can you tell me about him?"

"One of the most successful promoters of bullfighting in Spain. A man who controlled everything from the selection of the bulls, the teams of matadors, arrangements with the facilities—the bullrings—involvement with all the regulatory groups, associations of bullfighters, picadors, everything. Successful and ruthless in his drive to make the most money possible and protect the sport. We did not like him and we constantly petitioned his office, to no avail, of course. But he is not alone, there are many other ruthless promoters of this cruel sport and it is an abomination that the government has now declared bullfighting as part of our cultural heritage."

"But it is part of your own cultural heritage as well, no?"

"My family? My father's family? Without question. I spent many years at the family's *ganaderia*—breeding ranch—in Extremadura. I was constantly around these magnificent animals. I even like the art and pageantry of the *corrida.* It is magnificent, but not to kill the bulls. When I was young, I participated in training the young bulls, wearing the matador's suit of lights, and working the bulls with different capes. Exhilarating, but they should not die for being who they are. Their lives are tranquil, grazing out in the field, but when they come to the bullring, they are tortured by the *picador*s, by the *banderilleros* and ultimately the matadors who slay them. And then the animal is dragged around the arena by a team of horses. What a horrible end to its life."

"So, you shed no tears for Señor de Portillo?" asked Garcia.

"Tears? No. It was a terrible thing that happened to him, but one less tyrant in the world is not such a dreadful thing."

"And where were you the night that Señor de Portillo was killed, Señorita Valenzuela?"

"Ah, you think that I could do such a thing?" replied Victoria. "Far away from Madrid. I was in Extremadura, visiting my grandfather, Inspector Garcia. I got back yesterday."

"It would be good if you could verify that," stated Garcia.

"Easy. My tickets and boarding passes are right here in this drawer," opening the drawer to her right and extracting Iberia ticket stubs from Sevilla.

Garcia examined the documents and handed them back to Valenzuela. "One last thing. and I hope it does not upset you, but I understand that your father died in the bullring. Some people say that this may have been deliberate on his part; that he went into the bullring to die that day. Is it true?"

Sadness immediately appeared in Victoria Valenzuela's eyes, and she then turned to face the poster of her father on the wall. "Who is to say? I know he was not happy. Some years before he was unable to make the kill of a bull, a magnificent animal from my grandfather's ranch, *Gladiador*—Gladiator. The sword would just not go in and my father continued to fight the bull with the *muleta* cape, pass after pass, without the sword. It was an amazing display of artistry and grace, and my father then demanded that Gladiador not be killed. It would be spared. But all the traditionalists thought he had failed, and they booed him. The bull was regarded as the hero and my father a failure. After that, it was difficult for him to get *corridas* in the more important bullrings. He was relegated to smaller towns and cities, far from the prestige of Madrid or Sevilla. People still loved him and praised the courageous battle he had with Gladiador, but he was shunned by the great impresarios."

"Like de Portillo."

"Yes, like de Portillo."

Chapter Nine

Thirty Years Ago

Victor Valenzuela was one of the most successful matadors of his time. He was so successful and revered, he was called *"El Matador,"* an accolade that infuriated Miguel Benitez Perez—*El Cordobés*— the charismatic and acrobatic contemporary of Valenzuela. Toward the end of his career, as chance would have it, a set of bulls was drawn from the *Ganaderia VV de los Toros Bravos* for a *corrida* in Las Ventas, the iconic plaza de toros in Madrid. Valenzuela fought the third bull of the afternoon and was awarded an ear for his magnificent performance. He was also scheduled to fight the last—the sixth bull that evening.

Bulls are given names at the ranches where they are bred and each comes to the arena with a set of traits he has acquired during the breeding and training process. Skittish, pulls to the left, very aggressive, somewhat slow, terribly fast. Bullfighters generally do not have knowledge of these traits, but when the bull enters the ring, and the younger matadors of the team—his *cuadrilla*—work with it using the large *capote*—cape, the bullfighter, studies these tendencies before he gets into the ring. Valenzuela was aware that the bulls that day came from his family's VV ranch, but was stunned when he saw the name, *Gladiador*—Gladiator. His daughter, Victoria, loved the majestic animals at the VV ranch and while she understood that they were bred to fight and die, she was totally opposed to the *corrida*. But *Gladiador* was her favorite. She felt there was a kinship between them.

When the bulls were young and in training, they were kept in corrals adjacent to the training bullring. Victoria would often wander near the fence housing the bulls and talk to them. Still ferocious animals, and not in any way tame or friendly, *Gladiador* would come up to the fence and Victoria would chat, saying how beautiful this shiny, black bull was, how brave he is, anything that would come to her mind, and the bull would just stand there, his nose just inches from her. Perhaps it was also the patch of white he had on his forehead, not unlike the patch of white in Victoria's hair. Victoria loved *Gladiador* and despite her numerous protestations, he was still destined for the bullring, somewhere.

Eventually *Gladiador* entered the bullring. The younger matadors worked with the large cape, pass after pass, while Valenzuela studied its tendencies from behind the *burladero*—perimeter wall. The bull was indeed aggressive, and when Valenzuela entered the ring he completed his passes elegantly, despite the anxiety he felt, performing the two-handed *veronica* and other flourishing passes. He ended with a *media-veronica*, in which the full swing of the cape is cut short, forcing the bull to turn quickly, and bringing it to a stop, causing the spectators to cheer—*Olé!* Valenzuela looked away when the picadors arrived. Mounted on heavily padded, robust horses, they began pushing the short, broad knife at the end of their lances into the muscles of *Gladiador's* neck, to bring the bull's head lower, making it easier for the matador to achieve a clean kill with the sword. After three forceful charges at the horse, the matadors enter the ring again and, with flashy passes with the large cape, luring the bull away from the departing picadors. The *banderilleros* followed, placing the short, decorated barbed darts in the bull's withers, behind the area that the picadors had ravished, weakening the great neck muscle even more.

Victor was now in the ring again for the *faena*, the conclusion of the contest, this time with the short red cape—the *muleta*—and a slightly curved sword. But he was not the same *matador*. He was tentative, anything but graceful, and the crowd, at first bewildered, began to boo their longtime hero. When it was time for the *coup de grace*—the moment of truth—peering over the cape, sword raised to shoulder level pointing at the bull, the great matador trembled, his legs were weak and perspiration dripped into his eyes. Gladiador stood there and despite the wounds in his neck, blood covering his shoulders, he raised his head, pawed the ground, first with one hoof and then the other, and then charged.

Victor's first attempt at the kill went badly. The sword bounced off bone and almost flew out of his hands. *Gladiador* turned, threw his head up high and again faced his adversary. Victor inched closer, the small red cape in front of him and again the sword held high. "*Toro, e toro,*" he called to the bull, continuing to close the gap between them. Again, *Gladiador* charged with his head lowered to strike the matador, and again Victor's thrust struck bone and this time, the sword flew out of his hand. He continued to make some passes with the *muleta* as *Gladiador* charged, turned, and charged again. This time, Victor's passes with the small cape were *El Matador* of old, elegant, graceful, daring, with the bull brushing against him at each pass. He performed passes named after and attributed to the great matadors of old, the *Manoletina, Arruncina,* and *Dosantina,* with majesty. Now, Victor's *traje de luces*—suit of lights—was covered in blood and soon the two stood facing each other, only meters apart, exhausted. The sword remained on the ground, but Victor moved closer and placed his hand on the forehead of the wounded warrior in front of him. *Gladiador* moved his head slightly upward but made no move to charge.

The spectators were divided in their reaction. Some still booed the failed attempt of the kill. Others began to applaud, mostly for *Gladiador*. Victor removed his hand from the bull, turned with his back to the animal and slowly walked to the barrier. Alone, in the center of the ring, stood Gladiador, head held high, turning left and then right, blood covering his shoulders and legs. The spectators now stood and applauded the courage of this magnificent creature. Victor called over the promoter and said, "This bull does not die. I want the medics to cleanse his wounds and give him something for the pain. He will be returned to the VV ranch, surgically repaired, and cared for. This bull does not die." Totally unprecedented, but he was still *El Matador* and his directions would be heeded. The president of the *corrida* raised an orange handkerchief granting the petition.

The papers the next morning were also mixed in their reaction. The bullfighting journalists, experts at all the traditions and requirements for the *torero* to complete, were harsh to Victor Valenzuela Ordoñez. He had failed. The public, however, had a new hero, *Gladiador*. "*El ganador, Gladiador*"—the winner, Gladiador, the headlines read. El Pais, the city's major newspaper, devoted columns to the magnificent bull whose life was spared. They were less harsh to Victor and praised his bravery, but the cadre of traditionalists, journalists that live and breathe the fine points of the *corrida*, were writing off *El Matador* as weak and past his prime. *El Cordobés* would be their new hero.

Chapter Ten

The three detectives from Madrid arrived in Bilbao on time at nine-thirty in the morning. Rosa had arranged for one of the uniformed officers from the Bilbao office to meet them and serve as their driver for their visit to the *Partido Animalista de Bilbao* headquarters, located off the Plaza Nueva on Foru Kalea. This location bordered on the historic old quarter, dating back to the sixth century and was very popular for walking tours. Today, the streets of the old quarter are lined with shops, restaurants and many specialty stores offering all varieties of tapas, pastries, and chocolates.

Bilbao is a city of about three hundred and fifty thousand inhabitants, in the north-central part of Spain, but the great metropolitan area has a population of more than one million, the fifth largest urban area in Spain. Heavily nationalistic in their pride of their Basque heritage, so much so that its football club—*Atletico de Bilbao*—is comprised of only Basque players and is one of the most successful clubs in Spanish football history. The Basque Nationalist Party remains the most powerful political party in the region, although their drive for a separate, Basque autonomous state has diminished now that ETA—*Euskadi ta Askatasun*—is no longer an activist, violent movement. But the Basque culture remains ingrained in the citizenry. Forty years ago, eighty percent of the population could

41

speak and understand only Spanish, with less than eight percent able to speak and understand both Basque and Spanish. Today, that figure is thirty percent with fifty percent only able to understand and speak only Spanish.

The Guggenheim Museum, the work of Canadian architect Frank Gehry and inaugurated in 1997, has done much to transform Bilbao into a more cosmopolitan center where tourists flock to see not only the important artwork therein, but to see the unique architecture of the building itself. Inspector Alonso asked his CNP driver to pass by the iconic museum as the morning sun always created an inspiring image with light blazing off the metallic structure.

In short time they were at the *Plaza Nueva* and in front of the PAB headquarters, a nondescript building at street level with *Partido Animalista de Bilbao* engraved in gold letters above the door. Alonso, Ambrosio, and Leal alighted from the car and entered the office. A man greeted them and they identified themselves as CNP inspectors and would like to speak with Gorka Mendoza. The man excused himself for a moment, returned and led them to Mendoza's office in the back. They passed tables full of literature associated with the group's movement.

"So, what have we done to warrant the visit of three CNP inspectors, traveling I understand all the way from Madrid?" Mendoza said as he moved around his desk to greet the CNP officials. He was a small, lean man, perhaps in his forties, with a full beard, black with some gray starting to appear around his moustache. He was bald on top but had long black hair flowing over his ears and beyond the collar of his shirt.

"Nothing, we hope," replied Alonso, "but with what happened in Madrid a few days ago, we think it prudent to meet with the more aggressive animal rights movements in the country. We'd like to get a better idea of your objectives and how you hope to achieve them."

"Ah, you are referring to that pig de Portillo. Someone should get a medal."

"So, his death is something you welcome, Señor Mendoza?" asked Alonso.

"Don't get me wrong, Inspector. We are a peaceful movement totally opposed to animal cruelty of any kind, and the tormenting and torture of our Spanish bulls is high on our list of atrocities. So, to see one less of these affluent, arrogant promoters is essentially a good thing, but not something the *Partido Animalista de Bilbao* would ever be involved with. We want to influence people, influence the government and its archaic regulators, but again, we are a peaceful movement."

"It is interesting that you say that" added Leal, "with one of your officers being arrested on many occasions related to the violence of your demonstrations."

"Passions get out of hand at times, on both sides, but pushing and shoving is all it ever amounted to, and if you are referring to Joseba Aguirre, he was never convicted of anything. Arrested, released and nothing more to it. You met Aguirre when you entered, does he look like an assassin? Joseba, come in here please."

Aguirre left his desk in the open entry area and joined the group in Mendoza's office. He was taller than Mendoza, also in his forties, with gray hair and a trimmed beard and moustache. He wore black slacks with a black shirt that had a PAB logo on his breast pocket.

"Joseba, these officers of the CNP are concerned with violence that has occurred during some of the demonstrations that you have led."

"Hardly violence, I assure you," began Aguirre, "and it is something we never provoked. Those addicted to the violence in the bullring are the ones that want us to be quiet and go away. Yes, that is where the violence is, in the bullring. We are essentially pacifists. We respect life, all life and particularly the life of our majestic fighting bull."

"And where were you on the night of de Portillo's killing, if I may ask?" said Inspector Leal.

Smiling, Aguirre responded, "Spending the night in jail in San Fermin. We had a demonstration that afternoon about the famous running of the bulls, that hideous Pamplona spectacle. We were blocking traffic, as was our intention, parading with banners condemning the event. We do this on an ongoing basis, always trying to bring attention to this tragic *feria*, that people from all over the world come to see. Horrible how these magnificent creatures are treated."

"Yes, I can see your point, but how do you expect support from this community when economically, it means so much to them?" asked Alonso.

"True," replied Mendoza, "but the more noise we make, the more we can influence the young people of this community. They will be the ones that drive the change and come up with new ways to bring economic benefit to the area."

"Spoken as a true idealist," lamented Alonso. "Not so easily achieved."

"Absolutely, but does that mean we stop trying? Hopefully one day we can establish the *Partido* as a true political party and make ourselves part of the governing authority. The world has changed and more and more people recognize the cruelty we bring to innocent animals. They will begin to vote with their hearts. That is what we want to achieve," added Mendoza.

"One last thing. We will of course check on your stay in the San

Fermin jail, Señor Aguirre," said Alonso. "And Señor Mendoza, we would appreciate a list of all your *Partido*'s members.

"If a judge authorizes the CNP to have such a list, we will comply, but not without a judge's order. So sorry," said Mendoza.

Smiling and rising, Alonso ended the meeting and thanked Mendoza and Aguirre for their time and cooperation.

Outside, they waved the waiting CNP officer to bring the car around. "Not sure we got anywhere this morning," said Ambrosio.

"No," added Alonso. "They had all the right answers and Aguirre just doesn't look like the kind of guy who would pull off what happened in Madrid. I think we must keep looking. I'll meet with Garcia when we get back and fill her in."

"But why don't we stop first at the *Casco Viejo*—Old Quarter— for some pastry and a coffee before we head to the airport?" asked Leal.

"*Bueno*"—Good—responded Alonso, and he instructed the driver bring them closer to the old town walking district. "I know just the place."

* * *

Back at the office, Garcia's team met again to go over the first significant contacts with activist groups of interest. "We didn't get much from the *Partido Animalista de Bilbao* interview," began Miguel Alonso. "Passionate about what they do and certainly no tears for de Portillo. We were even able to talk with Joseba Aguirre, supposedly their most aggressive activist, but he was in a San Fermin jail the night of the attack, so clean alibi. Got the feeling they aren't likely to take their mission to the point of killing one of their perceived bad guys." Ambrosio and Leal nodded in agreement.

"Conchita and I had a very frank and open discussion with

Victoria Valenzuela," began *Inspector Jefe* Garcia. "She certainly was more forthcoming than I thought she would be. Like the *Partido* group, de Portillo's death was regarded as somewhat well deserved. They too are very passionate about changing the culture in Spain to respect and save the Spanish bull from the torture of the *corrida*. But the woman is certainly an enigma, with her family deeply entrenched in the breeding of these fighting bulls as well as a history of successful matadors, most notably, her father, Victor Valenzuela. At one point he fell out of favor with the bullfighting traditionalists and impresarios, and if there was ever a motive for what happened in Las Ventas, Victoria certainly has a particularly good one. As I said, she was very frank and open with us and made no attempt to obfuscate her feelings. She was in Extremadura the night of the attack, but that doesn't mean she wasn't involved in some way. We will keep *Salvan Los Toros* high on our list of groups of interest and we will talk again with her. In the meantime, we continue to examine the most interesting of the activist groups and whittle down to the most promising suspect organizations and individuals."

Chapter Eleven

Claude Le Clerc, one of, if not the most successful horse trainer in Europe and beyond, slowly awakened from a drug-induced stupor, not knowing where he is, with darkness all around him. He realizes he is on the ground and tries to right himself to a sitting position, his hands feeling dirt, and *what is that—hay?* He then smells the unmistakable odor of horse manure. He spent his life around horses and senses he is in a stable somewhere. He hears panting, huffing and the movement of hooves, stroking the ground, close to him. A horse? One of his? *Mon Dieu,* —My God. *What is going on?* he thinks, fear suddenly causing nausea within him, and his lips begin to tremble.

A bright, pinpoint light suddenly strikes the eyes of the horse in the stall with Le Clerc, suddenly spooking the animal. He rears up, trying to escape the dreadful, blinking light that blinds him. He moves from one side of the stall to the other, pounding his hooves and continuing to rear up. Le Clerc then hears thunder and the light directed at the horse continues to blink on and off, giving Le Clerc a flickering image of the terrorized animal. *Thunder and lightning? A storm?* he senses. *I'm in the middle of a storm with this animal?*

The horse, *Ameer Sa Hraá,* known as Desert Prince in racing circles, now goes wild, its eyes wide with fear, and he more violently pounces and runs within the confines of the twelve meters by twelve-meter stall, striking Le Clerc repeatedly, as the man rolls and tries to avoid the pounding of the terrified horse, but to no avail. He is struck over and over again. His arms, trying to cover his head, offer little protection as lightning and thunder continue to enrage Desert Prince. Soon, all is quiet as the light and the noise stop and the horse begins to calm down. Claude Le Clerc, curled up in a corner of the stall, is battered, bloodied and lifeless, as a white feather flutters down beside him.

* * *

The next morning, Gino Cerone receives a call from Klaus Schickhaus, his superior at Interpol headquarters in Lyon, France. "Gino, my friend, I'm glad I caught you in. I want to personally congratulate you on bringing an end to the human trafficking operation in Spain. I meant to call you yesterday but was caught up in the never-ending mass of paperwork we generate here."

"*Merci*, Klaus, but the credit has to go to the Spanish police in Cadiz and Catalonia. They made the arrests and closed it down."

"Yes, I know. I saw your report, but it is gratifying when Interpol and local law enforcement work so well together. But I am also calling you about an unusual incident that took place at the Saint-Cloud Racecourse outside of Paris. One of the most successful thoroughbred trainers in Europe was trampled to death by one of his horses that was there to compete in the upcoming *Prix de Saint-Cloud*. I saw the report on the news this morning and know little more than that, but it brought to mind the incident in Madrid a few weeks ago, when a prominent bullfighting promoter was killed by a bull in Las Ventas."

"Mercedes is leading the investigation of that horror and we have, of course, talked about it, but why your interest?" asked Gino.

"Well, it may be absolutely nothing, but I thought, *how coincidental*? A prominent bullfight promoter killed in a bullring in the middle of the night and here, an important horse trainer trampled to death by one of the horses he trains, in its stable, also in the middle of the night."

"You know how I feel about coincidences, Klaus, don't really believe in them, but why are you discussing this with me?"

"I'm sending one of our investigators to Paris today to get more details from the Paris police. Depending on what he finds out, I wonder if these killings are linked in any way. If we determine they are related, it makes a cross-border crime and something that Interpol may need to be involved with."

"I can see your point, Klaus. Some similarities, but what do you want me to do?"

"Nothing, for the moment, but you are in a good position to assess both incidents with Mercedes heading up the investigation in Madrid. I know there are outcries in Spain to solve that heinous crime and I am sure we'll be seeing the same thing in France, especially from the whole horseracing community, if indeed it is a criminal act. Very prominent figures in their sport, killed by the animals they are most associated with. This can become a hot political issue quickly."

"It already has in Spain. Mercedes is feeling pressure from government, the industry and of course, the public."

Gino, you have closed the human trafficking case and this could open some time to look into these incidents. Interpol has the resources to support such an investigation, and depending on what I find out from Paris, I'd like for you to head this up."

"That's fine with me, and coordination with Madrid—and Mercedes—will be a plus for the investigation. We need, however, to learn a lot more regarding what happened at the Saint-Cloud Racecourse."

"I'll get back to you once we get more details on the circumstances there. The investigator I am sending is French, so that should ease communication. As soon as we hear from him, I will call you, either way."

"Okay, I'll wait to hear from you, and I'll book a flight to Paris for tomorrow, just in case."

"Good, Gino, we'll talk later."

Chapter Twelve

The Saint-Cloud Racecourse is located on a picturesque hillside overlooking the Western side of Paris. It is one of the most highly regarded racetracks in France and the *Grand Prix de Saint-Cloud* serves as a trial for the most prestigious horse race in the country, *The Qatar Prix de l'Arc de Triomphe*, which is held a few months later.

Claude Le Clerc had entered Desert Prince in the *Grand Prix de Saint-Cloud* with an eye to compete in the *Qatar Prix de l'Arc de Triomphe* at the Longchamp's racecourse in the Bois de Boulogne, also just outside of Paris, so the death of Le Clerc would rattle the entire international horseracing community.

Lieutenant Louis Gérard took a call from one of the local *gendarmes*—officers—who had responded to contact from the Saint-Cloud Racecourse regarding the death of Claude Le Clerc, trampled to death by one of his horses in its stall. Briefing his superior, Capitaine Vivienne Cousteau, he reported, "Le Clerc's body was discovered early this morning by one of the grooms in his organization. Le Clerc is a renowned horse trainer and was here to compete in a race at Saint-Cloud in a couple of days."

"I know of Le Clerc. He's a pretty famous trainer; and he is trampled by one of his horses?" Cousteau asked.

"Apparently. Desert Prince, the same horse entered to race.

The groom approached the horse's stall, as he does every morning, preparing for the morning's workout. Desert Prince was standing calmly, looking over the half door of the stall. As the young man began to greet the horse and pet its nose, he saw a crumpled body in the back of the stall. Enough morning light was brightening the area for him to see that the body was quite bloodied. He immediately used his cell phone to call Le Clerc and was stunned when the ring tone came from the body. He then called Mark Jordain, one of the assistant trainers. When Jordain arrived, he directed the groom to lead Desert Prince out of the stall and he went inside, identifying the body as Claude Le Clerc. He immediately called his on-site veterinarian, who confirmed Le Clerc was dead. That is when they called the police."

"Considering the notoriety this will generate," responded Cousteau, "let's get over there."

By the time Gérard and Cousteau arrived from their headquarters, things had taken an ominous turn. Jordain and the local *gendarmes* discovered two security guards—part of Desert Prince's standard security detail—unconscious behind the stable area, their faces covered with a surgical mask.

"Call headquarters," instructed Cousteau to Gérard. "I want the medical examiner and a full forensic unit out here immediately. And have that stall taped off. I want no one in there. We have a crime scene on our hands."

Doctor Julian Benoit, Chief Medical Examiner of the Paris Prefecture, arrived shortly along with a crime scene investigative unit.

"With the horse out of the stall, one of the assistant trainers and a veterinarian checked on the body before we got here," Cousteau advised the forensic team. "They felt they had to check on the victim, and I can understand that, but there is now some contamination of the crime scene. They assumed it was a tragic accident until the unconscious guards were discovered."

"We'll do our best," replied Benoit, donning plastic booties, lifting the tape, and entering the stall. "This incident would be suspicious anyway, considering that Le Clerc was intimately familiar with the horse, working with it every day. Such an attack would have been very strange indeed.

"Severe trauma, apparently from the horse's hooves," called out Benoit. "Marcel"—Benoit's assistant— "find out where they brought the horse. I want its hooves examined for blood traces and samples taken. I do not think there is any doubt about what happened here, but we must do a complete examination. And make sure nobody washes that horse!" Looking to Capitaine Cousteau he said, "I only need another minute before the forensic group gets in here. We will do a full tox screen once we get the body back to the morgue and possibly know more."

Soon Benoit lifted the crime scene tape and emerged from the stall. "That horse had to be severely spooked to do such damage. Extensive wounds all over the body, especially his hands and head. Probably was trying to protect his head from the onslaught, but he had little chance of surviving this. Let the forensic unit in there now. Not very optimistic considering the dirt floor and hay scattered around, but hopefully something will turn up."

"*Merci*, Doctor Benoit. I'll instruct the forensic investigators to also dust the gate and other surfaces for fingerprints. From Mark Jordain we'll find out who has access to this stall and have them printed for comparisons, but this is a very unusual crime scene. Before you go, however, I understand the security guards are conscious now.

I want blood drawn for tox screens as well as swabs taken from their face and nostrils. And test those surgical masks, of course."

"No problem. Marcel will do this immediately," replied Benoit.

* * *

Omar Saliba and Ibrahím Khan were both Emiratis and had been assigned to Desert Prince for some time. They and two other security guards traveled with the horse to all events and were employed directly by Sheikh Abdul bin Sa'id, part of the Dubai royal family. Both men had regained consciousness and were sitting on a bench about thirty meters from the stable area. They were still a bit woozy but said they were able to speak with investigators.

The men said that they saw Le Clerc earlier that evening walking around the stable area. This was not unusual as he routinely checked on his horses himself even at night. They knew he was something of an insomniac, so seeing him strolling at night raised no alarms. Last night, he was walking with another person. Given the darkness of the evening and their distance from the men, neither could describe the other person. Le Clerc was easily identifiable with his silver hair shining in the ambient light.

"We came on duty at eight o'clock," explained Omar Saliba. "We don't sit in chairs next to Desert Prince's stall, but constantly patrol the area, separately. At one point," Saliba said, "I had this uncomfortable feeling and then heard and felt, spray to my face." He remembered the hissing sound and nothing after that.

Ibrahím Khan said basically the same thing, being in the back of the stable when confronted with a hiss, a spray to his face and nothing until a little while ago. Both men were visibly distraught, with Saliba constantly wringing his hands. "Has anyone advised Sheikh Abdul of what happened?" he asked. "He is in Dubai but must be informed. He will be very upset."

"I doubt anyone here has informed your boss, the sheikh, but I suggest you do that immediately. He will be even more upset if he hears of this on a television report or in the newspaper. He undoubtedly pays you to protect Desert Prince, and indeed the horse is safe. That is the good news. Unfortunately, he probably won't be racing this week."

Leaving Saliba and Khan to think about what they were going to say to the sheikh, Cousteau and Gérard then went to talk to racetrack officials. They learned that Saint-Cloud employs a private security firm to police the large facility. They are not armed and are minimally trained, more akin to the type of security you see at a shopping mall. Men—and some women—with gray uniforms who walk the facility. As there are rarely any incidents, boredom invariably creeps in. That night, one of them passed the area where Desert Prince is stabled, saw nothing and continued his patrol. They were aware that the owner of Desert Prince provided his own security.

"So, what do we have, Louis?" asked Cousteau. "A quiet night with nothing suspicious seen by Saint-Cloud's security. Le Clerc seen in the area with an unknown person—man or woman we do not know—leisurely walking around, and then the horse's Emirati guards subdued by a chemical of some kind, possibly chloroform, and then Le Clerc's body discovered by a stable boy, trampled to death by the very horse he trains. That's it."

"We'll see what we get from the toxicology analysis. Le Clerc was probably drugged as well," added Gérard.

* * *

The forensic unit found nothing out of the ordinary at the crime scene. It will take a while to compare all the fingerprints they have, but given the stealth operation, they had little hope there. Strange was the discovery of a white feather on the ground in the stall. Not far from the scene they found a metal sheet, less than one meter long and about a half-meter wide. If one shook the metal sheet, it sounded like thunder, something that could have agitated Desert Prince and possibly set off the frenzy. Unknown, but a possibility. No prints were found on the metal sheet and no one had ever seen it before.

When the sheikh brought his horses to race, he commandeered the whole wing of the stable. His horses were in the center stall and all adjoining stalls were empty, so there were no other animals near the crime scene. That area of the stable was for Desert Prince only, and the sheikh paid handsomely to ensure that privacy. Desert Prince was a little skittish, so the trainers made sure there were no distractions that could bother the horse. That did not work last night.

"Next step, Louis, is to talk with and profile all members of Le Clerc's team. Here and at his office, which I understand is in Paris. Someone engineered this killing, and we need to know who likely suspects might be. What enemies does he have? Also, get the analysts to do a financial check on Le Clerc. Who does he owe money to, and what kind of threats or complaints are there against him? The works."

Chapter Thirteen

The initial profiling and background check of Claude Le Clerc showed he was in the business of horse racing for more than thirty years. Handsome, in his mid-fifties with a full head of impressive silver hair, he worked with a handful of owners, and the horses he trained have won important races throughout Europe as well as in the desert kingdoms of the Middle East where, increasingly, members of royal families had become very active in the *sport of kings*. Amongst his more prestigious wins were the Longines Dubai Sheema Classic, the Epsom Derby in Surrey, England, as well as capturing the *Qatar Prix de l'Arc de Triomphe* twice at the Longchamp's Racecourse in Paris. One of the wins had Saudi ownership and the other, the most recent, was by a French conglomerate.

"Yet," reported Lieutenant Gérard, "all Le Clerc's successes were not without controversy. He was constantly running afoul of various regulatory agencies and animal rights groups. He had been fined and one horse was disqualified after a win in Italy. Predominately he was accused of using prohibited performance-enhancing drugs with some of his horses. Muscle relaxants, sedatives, anti-inflammatories, lidocaine, and other potent pharmaceuticals, legitimately used to treat ailments such as ulcers, lameness and inflammation were, at times, associated with animals that had no apparent symptoms. He had accumulated more than thirty drug violations, yet the charismatic trainer somehow avoided serious scandals and he continuously entered the winner's circle with great accolades. His 'Hall of Fame' credentials continued to grow, but animal rights groups like PETA as well as international and local humane associations constantly targeted Le Clerc and monitored his activities."

"How does Le Clerc maintain this stellar image of one of the best trainers in the world, with such a record of abuses?" asked Cousteau.

"I don't know, but somehow he managed to avoid such damaging notoriety. Good-looking guy, personable and articulate, he had an extraordinarily strong and loyal following," replied Gérard.

Just then, Doctor Benoit poked his head into Cousteau's office. "I just got the toxicology results," he said. "Here are the reports, but do you want a preview?"

"Absolutely," Cousteau replied.

"Well, as we thought, Omar Saliba and Ibrahim Khan have indeed been subjected to an inhaled anesthetic—sevoflurane—and the surgical masks that covered their noses and mouths had also been soaked with the drug."

"They wanted to be sure they remained unconscious for a while," commented Gérard.

"Without question," said Benoit. "Le Clerc's tox screen was somewhat different, however. We detected scopolamine, which can produce a zombie-like effect."

"What do you mean, zombie?" asked Cousteau.

"Well, one of its effects can make a person very docile, ambulatory, but without free will."

"So, when he was seen walking with that other person, he could have been under the influence of the drug," commented Gérard.

"Absolutely, but it had to have been a low dose, as it could also render a person unconscious for up to twenty-four hours. Somebody knew what they were doing. We also found a trace of sevoflurane in his system."

"Why both?" queried Gérard.

"I'm speculating now," replied Benoit. "It could be that the scopolamine was used to keep him ambulatory, but he probably had no idea of what was going on, being under the control of this other person. That person could have directed him to where he wanted him to be—inside Desert Prince's stall. Easier to walk him there rather than trying to carry an unconscious body around. Thereafter, a small dose of sevoflurane would render him sedated and at the mercy of the agitated animal. That's all a guess, however," Benoit concluded.

"That sounds like a very reasonable scenario," added Cousteau. "Walk Le Clerc to the stall, sedate him and then agitate the horse to the point where he tramples him. I've been told that the horse is somewhat skittish and care had to be taken to keep him calm and focused. May not have required much—maybe that sound of thunder—to rile and excite him. You have been very helpful, Doctor."

"You're welcome. I also brought the forensic report, which added little to the investigation. Le Clerc was dressed in his typical black trousers, a white, button-down shirt, and a black jacket with the Le Clerc logo. Nothing garnered from his clothes as they were badly torn from the horse's hooves. An odd thing they reported was the presence of a white feather, a dove's feather, alongside the body. It is not likely that it had fallen from a bird as the end of the feather had been cut cleanly. No idea what that tells us. The fingerprint analysis will take much longer to process."

* * *

Schickhaus's investigator from Lyon was able to glean the key points of the Paris police investigation at the scene without causing conflict with the detectives. He reported that the discovery of the unconscious guards made it clear that this was no accident, instead a very diabolical way to kill Claude Le Clerc.

"I hope you have your plane ticket, *mon ami*," were the first words Schickhaus said when Gino answered his phone. "There is no doubt that this was a planned assassination of Claude Le Clerc, and considering the circumstances associated with Alejandro de Portillo, we have the makings of some kind of cross-border conspiracy." He gave Cerone the information he had received from the Interpol investigator.

"It certainly feels that way, Klaus, and yes I have my ticket and even booked a hotel. Wouldn't hurt if you put in a call to someone at the Prefecture, letting them know we are going to begin an investigation and try to determine how the Paris incident relates to what happened in Madrid."

"I plan to call the commandant of the Command Corps as soon as we hang up. He is Armand Dupont and we have worked together before. A Capitaine Vivienne Cousteau is heading the investigation and she reports to Dupont. They will undoubtedly be intrigued to find out if these cases are indeed linked."

"Mercedes had a dossier prepared for me regarding the Madrid incident. They are still knee-deep in their investigation but are leaning towards looking closer at the anti-bullfighting organizations in Spain. If the French haven't started down this avenue yet, I'll recommend they do the same thing, looking at the animal rights groups involved in protecting racehorses."

"Is that where the CNP is focusing now?" asked Schickhaus.

"Not entirely, but de Portillo had received thousands of

complaints—even some threats over the years, from those opposed to bullfighting. It is a massive effort to try and cull out legitimate suspects, but that is what they are concentrating on now," replied Gino.

"It sounds daunting, and to think they may have to follow a similar path in Paris depresses me."

"Hey, I'm just getting into this. Got to keep a positive attitude. And get some of our analysts to get me a synopsis of the horse racing industry in France and what is going on regarding the protection of these animals. A major issue in the country? Mercedes has included the same thing for me regarding the anti-bullfighting groups."

"Sounds like you have some reading to do before you meet with the French. Don't let me keep you then. *Bon chance*"—Good luck.

Chapter Fourteen

By the time Gino landed in Paris and made his way to his hotel, he had an E-mail from Lyon, with what looked like a sizeable attachment. After checking in, he made his way to the Business Center and printed out what Interpol had sent him. A helpful attendant at the Center even put the papers into a spiral binder. Before contacting the Paris police, Gino wanted to get a perspective of the environment he would be working in, so he started to read.

France passed its first animal protection law in 1850, primarily relating to the public cruelty towards domestic animals. Interestingly, bullfighting and cockfighting were and are exempt from Penal Code application. Force feeding geese and ducks to produce *fois gras* is also exempted from animal cruelty legislation, and by law, *fois gras* must come from force-fed animals. *So their animal protection regulations seem a bit flexible*, thought Gino.

With regards to horse racing, France is part of the International Federation of Horseracing Authorities, with the EMHF—European and Mediterranean Horseracing Federation—the major watchdog group in France. Gino noted that it looked like there are more owner and breeder groups, like French Galop and the National Thoroughbred Racing Association, active in the sport than guardian groups. All regulatory and owner associations focus on "the integrity of the sport." PETA—People for the Ethical Treatment of Animals—actively challenges that notion along with other strong advocacy groups like World Horse Welfare and the Eurogroup for Animals.

A PETA exposé published in the NY Times in 2014 showed a side of the sport that the industry has tried to shield. They concluded that there are three types of people involved in horseracing. There are the crooks who abuse their horses with dangerous drugs—performance-enhancing drugs—daring the watchdog agencies to catch them. Then there are the dupes who labor under the fantasy that their sport is broadly fair and honest. And then there are the masses, neither naïve nor cheaters, but rather honest souls who know their industry is more crooked than it ought to be, but still do not do all they could to fix the problem.

Not cited in the PETA exposé but perhaps even more important is the money involved in the sport in France. Each year more than ten thousand horse races are followed by six and one-half million bettors, wagering more than €9.5 billion Euros. Pari-Mutuel betting involves a network of more than eleven thousand points of sale in the country, governed by the state-supervised horse betting authority, *Pari Mutel Urbain* (PMU), the single largest supporter of the French equine industry, the largest pari-mutual betting operator in Europe and the second largest in the world. Times change, regulations change, animal protection activists become more organized and stronger, but the PMU has addressed these challenges to its monopoly by globalizing its scope in a growing global economy. This led to the creation of the French Regulatory Authority of Online Gaming (ARJEL) which operated in a complex array of tax revenue streams, but attempted to address fraud, consumer protection and money laundering, in sync with EU regulations but in reality, more time and energy was devoted to this large betting pool than the integrity of the sport and animal abuse.

With France as the home to the most active horse racing industry in Europe, the PMU was constantly fighting challenges while creating new opportunities—many via partnerships in broadcasting and licensing—to protect its immense betting pool. Argentine races, for example, could be offered in the late evening and winter in France when local races may not be available. The PMU has truly globalized the French horseracing industry.

Gino tried to digest the profile of the horseracing industry in France, where revenue is at the top of its goals. Regarding the treatment of the racing thoroughbreds, he learned that top-tier horses are treated like pro athletes, *not unlike Desert Prince*, he thought. Some horses have spa-like facilities at their training center and fly first class. In many cases with Middle East owners, they fly in their own private plane. Yet many of these horses are mistreated and abused. Performance-enhancing drugs are used, often compounded by administering phenylbutazone—Bute—an anti-inflammatory drug often allowing injured horses to race, but later weakening bone, tendons, and muscles, destining them to the glue factory.

Wow, thought Cerone, leaning back in his chair. *With so much at stake, it is no wonder that Le Clerc's indiscretions have been largely overlooked, as winning, and preserving that global betting pool is paramount above all. The bullfighting industry is small change by comparison.*

* * *

In the afternoon, Cerone made his way to police headquarters on Rue de Lutèce in the fourth *arrondissement*—district—in the center of Paris. It was within the impressive *Palais de Justice* overlooking the pedestrian-only street. Upon entering, he was met almost immediately by Capitaine Cousteau. She was a tall woman, lean, reminiscent of a biking enthusiast or even a model. Somewhere in her thirties, her good looks were only slightly marred by a nose just a little too big for her face. *Just a little*, Cerone thought. After a few minutes of pleasantries—she spoke excellent English with a lovely accent— Cerone said, "I never realized the importance of the horseracing industry in France. The money earned by winning—to the owners and the trainers—is nothing compared to the revenue generated by betting with the government earning a big part of that pool."

"Yes, and Claude Le Clerc was an important part of that revenue stream," replied Cousteau.

"I can see that there has to be tension between the business of the industry, or sport, and the groups so opposed to the mistreatment of these animals. With Le Clerc, despite dozens of drug violations, he basically had his wrists slapped."

"He, of course, is not alone, as the international advocacy groups are constantly documenting these abuses, in France, Europe and the United States. Chief Superintendent..."

"Gino, please call me Gino."

"*Bon*, Gino. As to this murder, we know the *what* and the *how*, but finding the *who* will be a challenge. It sounds, however, that you are leaning towards these animal rights groups as potential suspects."

"Based on the investigation in Madrid, and with what little I understand of the situation in France, leaning is a good description. We think that the large, international organizations, like PETA, are clean, but a closer look at local organizations is warranted, trying to uncover who might have a strong motive. Can Interpol provide you with any assistance in identifying and looking into these groups? Analysis is one of our strengths."

"Maybe," said Cousteau, "but we have a team of investigative analysts already looking into such groups and preparing profiles of the organization, their leaders and members. It is an enormous undertaking, but at this point, we may be in the best place to manage it."

"I read that your forensic people found a white feather at the crime scene. The CNP never made it known, but a white feather was also found in the bullring with de Portillo. This is no coincidence."

"A calling card perhaps?" Cousteau asked.

"We don't know, but it is likely important, particularly now that we know the perpetrator may have multiple targets. Abuse of Spain's fighting bulls and abuses against France's racehorses are somewhat related. Once you have your list of organizations, Interpol can cross-match the most suspect organizations and individuals across both countries."

"Sounds like we have a plan," Cousteau added. "Give us a few days to whittle this down."

"Good, but I'd like the full report from your medical examiner and the forensic unit. I want to compare them to the Madrid reports."

"No problem. I'll have copies made for you now."

* * *

As was the case in Madrid, there were both international and local animal rights groups actively addressing the abuse of racehorses. The international organizations are the most organized and active, primarily via investigative reports and publications documenting their findings. The local groups in Spain, and the public at large, seemed to be more involved particularly since the government had decreed bullfighting as a cultural part of Spain's heritage. For a while, newspaper coverage was constant and prominent. In France, the local groups tended to be more active in letter-writing to regulatory authorities, small demonstrations at racing events, distributing their written materials, especially regarding the rampant use of performance-enhancing drugs with these magnificent animals. They were, for the most part, relatively small groups with leaders holding full-time jobs in unrelated industries. They were predominantly non-violent. Confrontations with police involved dispersing gatherings if they blocked traffic flow within the racecourse parking facilities, for instance.

Nevertheless, the Prefecture's analysts identified nine groups as subjects of interest. They were:

- *D'Argent Hospital de Equin* (D'Argent Horse Hospital)
- *Institut de Equin Bien-être* (Equine Welfare Institute)
- *Quatre Lancer de Fer à Cheval* (Four Horseshoes)
- *France Cheval Sauver* (France Horse Rescue)
- *Le Traitement Humain des Animaux* (The Humane Treatment of Animals)
- *Se Sentir du Cheval* (Horse Care)
- NOT The Sport of Kings (the only English named group)
- *Association du Cheval de France* (French Horse Association)
- *National Pur-Sang Trust* (National Thoroughbred Trust)

Profiles indicated that only the National Thoroughbred Trust has headquarters with full-time staff, as did the D'Argent Hospital with its team of veterinarians dedicated to horse recovery. The others were smaller, often run out of their leader's apartment or home, with a network of resources they could call upon as needed. Two organizations, NOT the Sport of Kings and Four Horseshoes, had relatives previously employed in the horseracing industry. Cousteau and Gérard had their investigators meet with these groups, albeit in a somewhat unofficial manner, just to talk.

Chapter Fifteen

A team of six investigators, including Cousteau and Gérard, set out to contact the groups, getting additional background information from their web sites. It was too early to label anyone a suspect, far too strong a word to describe these groups as many were doing really heroic things to make life better for these animals. The D'Argent Equine Hospital—founded by Doctor Victor D'Argent—was just that. A veterinary medical facility to treat and rehabilitate horses abused by owners and trainers. At times, the hospital was able to get court orders to actually take these animals away from their abusers. The staff at the hospital saw the worst effects of these abuses: lame animals, bodies weakened from illicit drugs, and often, horses abandoned in the countryside, searching for food and water. They had a real reason to resent those perpetrators of cruelty.

Cousteau and Gérard visited the hospital and were impressed with the work the veterinarians were doing, many volunteers, with their work supported through donations. Victor D'Argent, founder and president of the organization, was an elegant-looking man, probably in his seventies, sporting a well-trimmed moustache and goatee. Maybe short of six feet tall, he stood straight as a ramrod, looking very professional in his white lab coat. Now semi-retired, he still ran the business of the hospital, focusing on securing donations and government subsidies.

It was hard not to respect the work D'Argent was doing and Cousteau wanted to pick his brain regarding the most abusive owners and trainers, the ones who repeatedly flouted the rules. She also hoped to gain some insight on which animal rights groups—he knew them all—might be predisposed toward violent action against the abusers. The most prolific abusers were easily identified by D'Argent, but he was reluctant to identify anyone or any group that would go to the extreme of violence against the abuser.

"Le Clerc was a superstar in the sport," he noted, "but his animals were generally well cared for, notwithstanding the use of performance-enhancing drugs that he apparently used frequently. It was a travesty that he would be allowed to continue in his profession, a profession that is always talking about maintaining the integrity of the sport," he bellowed, waving his hands. "And Le Clerc should have never risen to such fame and fortune, but his horses did win, didn't they?"

Cousteau and Gérard left the hospital, turning back to really appreciate the complex. A pristine white building with adjacent corrals and stables where the horses would be sheltered and rehabilitated. They had a better understanding of the abuses this facility had to deal with but gained no insights that would help their investigation.

They had made arrangements that afternoon to visit NOT the Sport of Kings. From their web site they ascertained that Alaine Chapelle ran the group out of what turned out to be a modest chalet in the commune of Gentilly, just South of Paris. Being only four kilometers from Paris City Center, Gentilly was well situated for commutation and communication.

Chapelle greeted the detectives and led them to a back room that served as the office for NOT the Sport of Kings. In his late thirties, Chapelle had thick black hair starting to gray around the temples, and a square jaw with the popular five o'clock shadow. About five-foot-ten, he seemed well fit and relatively muscular. Reaching the office, Chapelle introduced the visitors to two of his collaborators, Camille Beaumont, and Juliette Jordain. Cousteau explained that the police just wanted to chat, get some perspective of their organization and the things that they do.

"Well," said Jordain, "if that is all you want you could have gotten that from our web site."

"*Touché, Mademoiselle*. To be honest," said Cousteau, "we are talking with many animal rights groups around Paris, as we'd like to get to know the players a bit better."

"Because, of course, of what happened to Claude Le Clerc," added Chapelle.

"Yes," said Cousteau. "What happened at Saint-Cloud was no accident, but a planned murder. Therefore, we'd like to exempt as many people and organizations as possible, that we can from subjects of interest, so we can concentrate on the criminals behind this crime."

"Fine, you know I am Alaine Chapelle. I am a private investment counselor from a family that has done very well for themselves. My parents sold their consulting firm—Chapelle and Associates, where I began my career—a few years ago and are now retired in Nice. Juliette?"

Juliette rose from her chair. She too looked to be in her thirties and had short black hair, worn close to her head with bangs to her eyebrows. Pixie-like face, pretty, relatively fit and tall, she wore a snug, beige, short-sleeved sweater and a brown, suede mini-skirt. "Juliette Jordain," she began. "I work as a fashion consultant for

Galeries Lafayette Haussmann and Le Bon Marché. Previously, Printemps and Le BHV Marais were among my clients."

"A prestigious group of stores," remarked Cousteau.

"Yes, very," remarked Juliette.

"*Alors*—So—it is now my turn," said Camille Beaumont, smiling broadly and glancing at her comrades. In her late twenties, somewhat shorter than Jordain, she had blond hair worn in a ponytail, an incredibly smooth and flowing complexion and penetrating blue eyes. She wore a blue sweater over leotard-like blue tights, and like the others looked very fit and athletic. "I work as a salesclerk in one of Juliette's former clients, Printemps, also one of the finest stores in the city, and as one of their senior sales representatives, they allow me flexible hours, very convenient for our work. I've been there almost four years."

"So, I see three attractive individuals, somewhat affluent or at least economically comfortable, but dedicated to making the lives of French racehorses better. How did that come to be?" asked Lieutenant Gérard.

"Well, my father worked in the horse racing industry most of his life," replied Camille. "He worked with various trainers over the years, caring for their horses and preparing them to race. I grew up around horses and race tracks all my life. Some years ago, however, working for Maxim Moreau, a successful trainer, one of Moreau's horses, in a race at Deauville-La-Torques, tested positive for Lasix, a powerful diuretic, a legitimate drug to treat high blood pressure. The horse had placed third in the race, but had no history of high blood pressure, and was eventually disqualified. Moreau claimed he had no knowledge of the administration of the drug—which was a lie—and cast the blame on my father. The authorities had been placing more and more scrutiny on the use of performance-enhancing drugs and chose to make an example of my father. He was dismissed by Moreau, his reputation in ruins, while Moreau got only a modest fine, in addition to losing the third-place winnings. My father has not been able to work in the industry since, and he currently works as a janitor at Printemps. That got me involved in the issue of doping and the abuse of these animals and knowing her since her time as a consultant to Printemps, I got Juliette to become involved in this issue. A footnote to this is that Moreau has moved to Australia, working as a trainer there."

"And hearing about the efforts of Camille and Juliette—there was a newspaper article about these ladies of high fashion trying to take on this powerful industry—and looking for something constructive to do with my life, I approached them and together we founded NOT the Sport of Kings," added Chapelle.

"A very worthwhile mission," said Gérard, "but I must say, Camille," turning to look at her, "you obviously harbor some harsh feelings about this issue, particularly with your father being cast out of the sport."

"Of course, I do, and that is what drives me, and us, to get this sport to change its ways."

"And, if you will forgive me," continued Gérard, "where were you the evening when Le Clerc was killed?"

All three of the subjects glanced toward each other and smiled. "We, all three of us were in Deauville, in the Normandy area, two hundred kilometers from Paris, demonstrating at the Deauville-La Torques Racecourse. We were there two days and then paid visits to a few breeders. That area is the main horse breeding region in France and home to numerous stud farms. We were trying to recruit some of the breeders to commit, officially, to the cause. They breed these magnificent animals and should care deeply about what happens to them. We were also trying to secure some donations to NOT the Sport of Kings. We spent two days in Deauville before returning home."

"And you can prove this?" asked Cousteau.

"Of course," replied Chapelle. "We can show hotel receipts, and three breeders can confirm our visit. Plus, the Deauville police can attest to our presence as they asked us to move our demonstration as cars began arriving for the afternoon races."

"Well, I must say that *Mademoiselle* Beaumont has motive to want some of these trainers punished. Moreau is no longer in the country, but we know that many others continue to abuse their horses with performance-enhancing drugs. It appears, however, that you have an alibi for that night, although I need to see those hotel receipts, and we will talk to the Deauville police," said Cousteau.

Chapelle was able to get his hotel receipts and the two women said they would E-mail them to Cousteau directly.

"One last observation. All three of you seem incredibly fit. Do you all work out?"

Juliette laughed. "I run. I run every day, early in the morning regardless of the weather."

"I run," said Camille, "but I am not as dedicated as Juliette. If it is raining—and it often is in Paris—I stay home, but Alaine has a little exercise room in the basement. A bicycle and some weights. I often go there—Alaine has given me a key—to exercise and keep fit."

Then added Chapelle, "I'm in the exercise room every day working with weights and a half-hour on the bike. It is amazing. The bicycle has software that allows you to bike all over the world if you like, increasing tensions for hills. I've biked through Paris, Central Park and even the rolling hills of Scotland, all from my little room. It's a marvelous piece of machinery."

"Well, it seems to work for all of you. Makes me feel a little guilty," commented Cousteau.

The two detectives then thanked the group for their cooperation, wished them good luck with their endeavors and left the chalet.

Outside, Gérard said, "I started to become a little excited when Camille was telling us about her father. She was very forthcoming, clearly making herself a prime suspect for retribution, but their alibi looks solid."

"Yes, they would have to drive about two hundred kilometers, in the middle of the night, to get to Saint-Cloud, organize an extraordinarily complex operation, and then get back to their hotel before morning. Possible, but highly unlikely," commented Cousteau. "We'll keep NOT the Sport of Kings on our radar, Louis, but I think we have more looking to do."

* * *

Back at headquarters they went over their findings with the other investigators, who reported on the other groups contacted. None of the other groups of interest showed any promise. "We profiled nine groups and it looks like we got nowhere," said Capitaine Cousteau. "I think we have to move to the next tier of possibilities and begin again. Nothing else in Le Clerc's history—no money problems, no jealous husbands, nothing—indicating a motive for murder. We have to stay with these animal rights groups and dig further."

Chapter Sixteen

After two days in Paris, visiting the crime scene, talking with Le Clerc's staff, meeting with forensic investigators and Saint-Cloud officials and a brief *adieu* with Capitaine Cousteau, Cerone returned to Madrid, somewhat depressed about the state of the horse racing sport in France.

"You know, Mercedes," I learned a lot about the situation in France, but I don't think I know enough about bullfighting and the whole start-to-finish process, especially with regards to where it begins. Do you think Victoria Valenzuela could arrange for us to visit her family's ranch, see how the entire process works?" Gino asked. "Besides, she intrigues me, and I'd like to maintain contact."

"That's a good idea, Gino. From what you told me, Interpol gave you a very comprehensive profile of the horse racing industry in France and we should—both of us—have a better understanding of how the breeder to bullring process works here. It would also be useful to speak with the people out there regarding their take on the de Portillo murder and maybe glean a little more about Victoria and the family's attitude towards her. I'll call in the morning."

* * *

Victoria Valenzuela was extremely cordial and almost excited that *Inspector Jefe* Garcia and her husband—an inspector from Interpol—were interested in visiting her family's ranch. "Why, of course," she responded when asked by Mercedes. "I think you will find it fascinating. Let me call one of my uncles and he'll set something up." Within an hour, Victoria called Mercedes. "My uncle Vergilio will be happy to show you around our *ganadería*," she advised. "We can do it the day after tomorrow, which will give you time to arrange flights. The ranch is in the South of Extremadura, so I suggest you fly to Sevilla. Once you have flight details, it will be arranged to have you picked up at the airport by one of our ranch hands and taken to the ranch. We think that a full day will provide you with a good insight into what we do. A late afternoon or early evening flight back to Madrid should work out fine. Get me your flight details and everything will be taken care of." She also gave Mercedes her uncle's cell phone number in case anything came up.

"That was easy," Mercedes said to Gino. "I don't know, but she seemed very enthusiastic about our visiting her family's ranch. Kind of proud about what they do, despite her misgivings about the sport itself."

"I really would like to meet her," said Gino. "She remains an enigma to me. Loves the bulls, loves how they are bred and cared for but hates the *corrida* where they are eventually killed. Yes, an enigma."

* * *

Mercedes and Gino departed Madrid on Iberia 8560 at 7:40 AM, getting to Sevilla at 8:40 AM. The return flight was on Iberia 8567, leaving Sevilla at 9:30 PM and arriving in Madrid at 10:25 PM. They booked a later flight to make sure they had enough time at the ranch, depending on Uncle Vergilio's itinerary. It will be a full day, but undoubtedly there would be a substantial lunch sometime during the day.

Arriving at the *Aeropuerto de Sevilla* on time, they were met by Manolo in a green Land Rover with the VV logo in white over a black silhouette of a bull in profile, on each of the two front doors. The distance from Sevilla to the VV Ranch was about eighty-five kilometers, and in less than an hour, they were at their destination. They passed through an archway of timber, with a large wooden sign above stating, *"Ganadería VV de los Toros Bravos,"* to an open area of hard-packed dirt, surrounded by a number of buildings, all white, stucco construction with terra-cotta tile roofs. Off to the left they saw what appeared to be a bullring with a small viewing area, and adjacent to it, small corrals of black bulls.

Pulling up in front of the larger of the white buildings, they were immediately greeted by a weathered *vaquero* about sixty years old, slim, and medium of stature, dressed in jeans, boots, white shirt and leather vest. On his head he wore the traditional, Andalusian, flat-brimmed, leather sombrero—the *cañero*, or Cordoba hat.

"Bienvenidos. Yo soy Vergilio Valenzuela," Victoria's uncle greeted them, reaching out to shake hands with his visitors as soon as they emerged from the Land Rover. *"Bienvenidos a la Ganadería VV de los Toros Bravos,"* he continued with a welcoming smile. The conversation proceeded in Spanish with Gino managing to comprehend—barely—and Mercedes adding an English translation when he looked perplexed.

"My father, Valerio, acquired the ranch in 1965 and over the years added adjacent properties," sweeping his arm across the horizon, "to where we now are almost one thousand hectares in size. Not the biggest by far, but a good-sized ranch with more than five-hundred animals, known for the quality of the bulls that we breed."

He pointed out that the large building in front of them was their office and the smaller building closer to the corrals was the veterinary center, where they employed five full-time veterinarians as well as housing the all-important breeding analytics laboratory. The veterinarians arranged for all the necessary vaccinations and behind it was a clinic where animals could be treated for any ailments.

"That large hacienda off to the right is the residence of my father. My mother, Maria, passed away some years ago. We, my brother and sister, have residences a little further down that road," pointing to the right where more buildings could be seen, all white with terra-cotta roofs. Victoria, my niece, and her mother also have a small hacienda here for when they come to visit. Victoria's mother, in fact, is here this week for a board meeting we just recently had. Kim is quite a talented business-woman, and even though my brother Victor passed away many, many years ago, she still maintains an interest in the ranch, and in this day and age, her financial skills are invaluable."

Vergilio asked if Gino and Mercedes would like a coffee before they began their tour and both readily accepted. Given the early departure of their flight to Sevilla, coffee and some pastries were welcomed, especially to Gino, who was starving. After their refreshments on the veranda of the administrative building, Vergilio directed the visitors back to the Land Rover with Gino and Mercedes in the back seat, Vergilio in the passenger seat and Manolo still doing the driving.

"I thought you might like to see our bulls in their natural environment. The cows are kept in separate grazing pastures. The animals are free-range, foraging for their food in these grassy fields. Everything organic," he laughed. They drove down one of the roads leaving from the entrance area and into the countryside. There were heavy fenceposts and rails on both sides of the road, and they could see the bulls, leisurely munching on grass or lying down, resting.

"These bulls are what is called the Miura breed, or *Toro de Lidia*. The Miura ranch, near Sevilla, really developed this line of bulls back in the 1800s. The family is truly responsible for the line of fighting bulls recognized as the best and most aggressive animals in the world today, and is the only breed sanctioned by the regulatory authorities to fight in the official *corridas*. You may not know, but the fighting bull can be traced back to the arena games of the Roman Empire, and even as far back to Greek mythology, where the minotaur—the so-called monster of Crete—was said to have the body of a man with the head of a bull. But the Miuras gave us the breed we have today, and their ranch is still fully operational and still managed by the Miura family."

As they drove, Mercedes remarked, "These animals are truly majestic, beautiful in a foreboding way, but to look at them now, so peaceful and seemingly docile, it is hard to imagine their destructive capabilities."

"*Sí, Inspector Jefe* Garcia..."

"No, Señor, please call me Mercedes," and pointing to her right, "and he is Gino. No inspectors here today, just tourists."

Laughing he said, "*Bueno*, Mercedes, and I am Vergilio. But yes, you don't see it now when they are grazing, but these bulls are carefully and scientifically bred to be fierce and cunning with strong, oversized muscles at their neck and shoulders. Those that do not make the grade are in butcher shops. The cost of raising a bull to maturity—about four years of age—is up to five-thousand euros. Much of that is recovered, sometimes more, when one of our bulls is sent to the *corrida*, especially to one of the more important bullrings.

If we must send a bull to the slaughterhouse, we are likely to receive only ten percent of that cost. So, you see," and he waved his arm across the horizon, "we must constantly strive to raise the best, most aggressive bulls with the highest stamina."

"But isn't there intense pressure on you in light of the pressure to prohibit bullfighting, as they did in Barcelona?" Gino stammered in his Spanish.

"Every day," replied Vergilio. "There were more than thirteen-hundred official breeding ranches of fighting bulls in the country, but that is much diminished now. That, in fact, is how my father was able to grow, acquiring the land and livestock of struggling *ganaderías*. So there has been much consolidation, but many bankruptcies as well, with slaughterhouses benefiting from their demise. The fact is that there are about one-half the number of *corridas* that there were fifteen years ago, about fifteen hundred now. But the big arenas like Madrid, Sevilla, and Pamplona continue with great popularity. And now that the bullfighting is recognized as a vital part of the culture of Spain, we have hope—the breeders, the matadors, the picadors, the banderilleros, the municipalities that own the bullring, the people and the vendors working there—we all have hope that the industry will survive, but it will not be easy. Our lives will be increasingly difficult, but this is who we are and what we do. The onslaught, however, of the animal rights groups is relentless."

"Like your niece, Victoria," said Mercedes.

"Ah yes, our beloved Victoria, and I say that sincerely. She is unique, in many ways with the spirit of her father. She loves the bulls, loves the ranch and the time she spent here, but does not want the bulls to die. Except, of course, that is what they are bred for. To perform valiantly and bravely, but then to die at the hands of a skilled matador. Without that spectacle, they would just be meat on our plate to eat."

After the tour of the pastures with the grazing bulls, Vergilio directed Manolo to return to the ranch. He brought them to the area behind the administrative building, to the bullring. "This is where we evaluate and train bulls for the corrida. We also train young matadors, *novilleros*, who build their skills with young bulls. You probably don't know this, but one of the most important things we do here is evaluate the cows. At two years of age, they are brought here to face matadors working with the large cape, to test their bravery, aggressiveness and whether they would be suitable for the breeding of our brave bulls. These characteristics come from the mother so this is most important for our future. Here, at the *plaza de tientas*, where we assess and probe for these traits, the future of the bloodline is established. We do, however, also bring in young bulls, some of them are in the bullpens over there," pointing to the corrals where the young bulls waited. "We test their bravery and decide if they will be good enough to bear the VV brand. They are also used to train the aspiring matadors."

It was time for lunch and they ventured to a separate low, open structure behind the administrative building. It was clearly a cafeteria for the workers, and there was a separate room off to the side, where Gino, Mercedes and Vergilio went. Kind of a rustic, executive dining room. Of course, the entrée was rare steak, with a green salad and a side dish of eggplant and tomatoes. "The vegetables are from our garden," Vergilio said with some pride, "behind this building. It is quite prolific and we have to use netting above it all to soften the sun we get here in the summer."

"I feel a bit guilty eating this steak," said Mercedes. "This obviously comes from an animal that did not make the grade."

"You are quite right, Mercedes. Those that do not show the characteristics we require are destined for the slaughterhouse and become food—necessary food—for the nation. Some bulls, however, particularly good ones, can also find themselves in a situation of luxury. While not groomed for the bullring, they can be even more valuable as *sementales*—stud animals—mating with the highest quality cows we select from right here." Gino followed the conversation, but was far more interested in the huge, medium-rare piece of meat on his plate.

After a sumptuous lunch—it was now well into the afternoon—the group wandered over to the corrals where the young bulls and cows were—never together. They could get relatively close to the animals, behind heavy timbered posts and rails, Mercedes could understand Victoria's feelings about these majestic animals. Then she had a thought. "Vergilio, you said that Victoria's mother was here. Do you think that we might meet with her? I have been very impressed with her daughter and would like to tell her that."

"I can't see why not," replied Vergilio "Why don't we walk over to her hacienda," over there he pointed, "and knock on the door? She is a very charming lady. It is a shame my brother could not enjoy a lifetime with her."

And so, they did and were greeted by a diminutive, attractive, Japanese woman, also probably in her sixties. She too was dressed *vaquero*-style—*I guess in Rome...* thought Gino—with dark gray hair worn to her shoulders, luminous green eyes, and a smooth face devoid of wrinkles except for a few creases at her eyes. Introduced by her brother-in-law, who then departed, she led her visitors to a nearby sitting area with brown leather chairs and sofa.

"I spent some time with your daughter *Señora* Valenzuela and just wanted to tell you how impressed I was with her," began Mercedes.

"*Gracias*," the woman replied. "I am very proud of her for her courage and independence to do what she thinks is right, despite growing up here," opening both her arms and looking toward a window by the front door.

"So, Victoria spent a lot of time here at the ranch?" inquired Gino.

"Yes, she did, especially in her early years when her father was traveling. When she started school in Madrid, we lived in an apartment there, but spent many summers here, except when we went to Japan. I still have family there, in Kagoshima, and she studied Japanese martial arts during some summers. In Japan martial arts and here, she fought bulls," she said with a laugh.

"Fought bulls?" Mercedes asked.

"Oh, yes. She was barely nine years old when she went into the bullring over there," pointing in the direction of the *plaza de toros*. "She started with young calves, dressed in jeans, but soon, seeing how well she worked with the bulls, we dressed her as a *matadora*, complete with the traditional suit of lights. She liked blue. Soon, with tutoring from her uncles, as she grew older, she graduated to young bulls, some up to one-hundred and fifty kilos, and she was brilliant. Using the large cape, she turned and swirled with grace and beauty. She showed no fear when she worked with the *muleta*, the small red cape. Of course, I was nervous, but her father and her uncles just marveled at her courage. It was like she was born for this.

"As the bulls she worked with grew larger, it became clear—to me—that she started to use some of the martial arts strategies she learned in Japan. Most of the martial arts taught in Japan for centuries were geared toward battle, confrontation with an enemy. That is why so many of the techniques dealt with the use of the sword, but others focused on the mind. She was drawn to *aiki*, epitomized by the notion of joining physically and mentally with an opponent to overcome the will of the adversary, redirecting their will and intent. It may be used to defeat an opponent without harming them. Very esoteric, no?" she asked.

"Very," said Gino. "Sounds quite complicated."

"Yes, it is, and it requires great commitment and confidence. I do not fully comprehend how it works when confronting a fighting bull, but at times she would just stare at the animal, looking deeply into its eyes before making any motion with the cape, and the bull would hold its ground, staring back. I don't know, but it seemed she was able to get closer to the animal, making many daring, flourishing passes with the cape. The concept of defeating the bull without doing any harm appealed to her and she never, never brought a sword into the ring. Doing battle without killing inspired Victoria.

"How incredible she looked, in her suit of lights, with the family and spectators cheering her every move. And she never worse the matador's cap, remaining bareheaded with that shock of white hair blazing in the sunlight. Maybe it was the hair that mesmerized the bull, who knows, but everyone came to call her *La Pluma Blanca*— The White Feather."

At the phrase, *La Pluma Blanca*, Mercedes and Gino quickly glanced at each other. "*La Pluma Blanca*," murmured Mercedes.

It was getting late and Gino and Mercedes rose from the sofa and thanked Señora Valenzuela for her time, leaving and looking for Vergilio.

"Did you enjoy yourselves today?" he asked.

"Wonderful," replied Mercedes. "What an incredible operation you have. It was an education."

"I am glad. We work very hard here to continue to be the best and not let the challenges wear us down." He then looked at his watch and said, "You know, if you wish, Manolo can drive you to the airport now. I know you have a nine o'clock flight tonight, but you might be able to catch something earlier if you leave now."

"A very good idea," said Gino, a bit tired from concentrating on the Spanish conversations all day.

They said their good-byes, with Mercedes getting a kiss on each cheek from Vergilio and Gino getting a strong hug—very Spanish amongst friends—and then joining Manolo in the Land Rover.

"*La Pluma Blanca*," said Mercedes softly once inside.

"*La Pluma Blanca*," repeated Gino. "Oh boy."

* * *

On the plane, an earlier flight leaving at 7:10, the two talked.

"I definitely have to meet the lady, Mercedes," said Gino. "The enigma has just become even more of an enigma."

Mercedes laughed. "Definitely. She could not have been more gracious in arranging this visit and it seems the family holds no animosity towards her. They like her. They are proud of her, even though she wants to end what they do."

"Not exactly, breeding these animals and killing them are two distinct processes. The animals, however, die one way or another. Off to the slaughterhouse to provide meat for the public, or by the matador's sword in a spectacle of courage, bravery, skill and, yes, cruelty. But dead one way or another," said Gino. "I'm gonna take a little nap."

Chapter Seventeen

After their return from Sevilla, Gino, Mercedes and Capitaine Cousteau had a conference call, first to establish connection between the Madrid and Paris investigators, and then to bring everyone up to date. Ongoing conversations with animal rights groups in both countries had failed to yield any promising leads. The two primary subjects of interest, *Salvan Los Toros* and NOT the Sport of Kings, had to be dismissed because of solid alibis by the key parties in each organization. Pressure kept building, however, in Madrid and Paris to solve the murders, but both police units were at dead ends.

"We know, or strongly suspect, that both incidents are related, but Interpol's analysis, cross-matching groups and individuals in both countries, has not revealed any associations, but there has to be a connection," began Gino.

"I agree," said Cousteau, "but there is no evidence to substantiate this."

"No, none," added Mercedes, "and the political pressure is increasing every day. There is the media, the ministries, and now associations like Bullfight Organizers and Event Organizers, the business interests in the sport, are demanding a resolution."

"I have the same in Paris," said Cousteau, "even stronger

considering the role the government plays in assuring the lucrative betting pool from horseracing is not jeopardized. It is a quagmire."

"Maybe we can do a better job in profiling members of these groups, especially the leaders; deep profiles, deeper than we have done, to see if we missed something or a red flag shows up," said Mercedes.

"Let me give that challenge to Lyon. That kind of penetrating analysis is one of their strengths," replied Gino. "Both of you need to get to me a comprehensive list of the individuals, many of whom have been interviewed, but I agree Mercedes, we need to go deeper. Okay?"

"Agreed," both women replied. "You'll have our list by tomorrow morning," said Mercedes.

"Yes, by tomorrow. I'll E-mail the file," added Cousteau.

Gino and Mercedes looked at each other, each thinking the same thing. They did not mention *La Pluma Blanca* and the white feather found at each crime scene. Gino wanted to meet with Victoria Valenzuela first.

* * *

Mercedes called Victoria and thanked her for arranging such a wonderful day at the family's ranch. "It was very impressive, Victoria. Your uncle Vergilio was extremely gracious. I will have to send him a note of thanks."

"I'm so glad. It is a splendid operation and they all work so hard."

"We also saw your mother yesterday. She happened to be out there for a board meeting and we just stopped by to make her acquaintance. Lovely lady," added Mercedes.

"Thank you. She called me last night and mentioned meeting you and your husband. She was a little curious why an Interpol Agent and a Chief Inspector of the national police were out at the ranch, but I explained it was for background information relating to the whole bullfighting industry, and I was just helping you."

"That is true and she too was very gracious to us," said Mercedes.

"Thank you. I am very fond and proud of her. We both live in Madrid, but we do not see enough of each other. Her work at the ranch, her various charities, occasional consulting with the Kyoto Palace group, keeps her very busy. Her family controls a number of high-end hotels in Japan, and the hospitality industry is in her blood. Busy lady, but we do try to meet for lunch and dinner from time to time."

"Before I go, I'd like to ask another favor of you. My husband, the Interpol agent," and she chuckles, "would like to meet with you. You are an enigma, you know that, and Gino would appreciate some time to get more of your thoughts."

"I don't mind," replied Victoria. "We are at a quiet point right now, so anytime this coming week will be fine."

"Great, I'll have him call you to set something up. I hope *Spanglish* will be okay. He is American and has been here a few years, but his Spanish is still developing."

The next morning, Gino drove out to San Agustín del Guadalix for a ten o'clock meeting with Victoria Valenzuela.

"*Buenos días*," Gino said to the two women—Martina and Luz— as he entered the office of *Salvan Los Toros*.

"*Buenos días, Señor Cerone*," Martina replied, with Luz smiling brightly—he was still a handsome man— "Victoria is expecting you," leading him to her office in the rear.

Like his wife, he was immediately taken aback by the beautiful woman with Asian features and of course, the patch of snow-white hair at her forehead. The two exchanged pleasantries and Gino did accept an offer of coffee.

"The enigma is here to give you any information you require," Victoria began with a big, broad smile.

"Oh, my apologies. Do I have to thank my wife for mentioning that to you?" said Gino, taken a little off guard.

Victoria laughed. "Yes, you do, but I take no offense. I certainly do not look like a Victoria Valenzuela should look and my work is a 180-degree departure from my family and upbringing. Okay, I am an enigma."

"I know Mercedes mentioned to you that we met with your mother last week. Enigma or not, she speaks very highly of you and is very proud of your achievements."

"And I bet that she talked your head off about my time at the ranch and my days as a *matadora*," Victoria said, again laughing.

"I must say that she did, but all of it was fascinating, including how you employed a form of Japanese martial arts when confronting the bull." Gino chose not to bring up *La Pluma Blanca*.

"I tried," Victoria replied, "but it was not always successful. Regardless, I loved my time in the bullring, loved the skills my father taught me, and I love the art of the battle, often a battle of wits—yours and the bull's—which is exciting."

"Do you do that anymore?" Gino asked.

"No, no. Not for a very long time. With my father's passing I lived in Madrid with my mother, going to school here and getting out to the ranch on some weekends and in the summer. My mother actually was out there more often than me as a member of the Board of Directors, and the fact that we both have a personal stake in the business, a legacy from my father."

"You mentioned school. What did you study?"

"Well, I spent a good deal of time studying. After high school, I entered the Complutense University of Madrid, which essentially brought an end to my *matadora* days. The university is just west of Madrid in the *pueblo* of Alarcón. Not far from the city but I stayed at the campus of Somosaguas rather than commute. As my life was totally involved with the raising of the Spanish Fighting Bull, I studied what you would call animal husbandry, a mix of agriculture and veterinary science. It dealt with the production and care of domestic animals, especially those used in the production of food—meat, eggs, dairy. After that I went on to a graduate degree in veterinary medicine."

"So, you are a veterinarian?" asked Gino.

"Technically yes, but I never went into practice. It was about that time that I became involved in the anti-bullfighting movement and spent some time understanding the industry itself. I knew breeding and bullfighting, but the business of the sport—if you can call it a sport—I only knew at a cursory level. In between the raising of the bulls and the eventual *corridas*, there is the whole unsavory business process. The promoters, the event organizers, the regulatory associations, the role of the national government—which could change depending on what political party is in power—and the municipalities that own the arenas. Who are the players, the rule makers, the money dispensers? Who are the workers that operate and perform—the employees of the bullring, the picadors, the banderilleros, the matadors and their — *cuadrillas*—the matador's team—and the associations that are there to protect them, like workers' unions."

"I can understand what you are talking about. I just spent some time learning—trying to learn—about the horse racing industry in France, which is quite complex, also with many vested interests, as well as the presence of a strong animal rights movement."

"Because of the Le Clerc incident?" Victoria asked.

"Yes, to be honest. It is remarkably similar to what happened in Madrid, so it warrants a comprehensive investigation."

"I can imagine. Whatever I can do to help, please call on me. We are committed to protecting and saving animals, but such violence is not who we are."

Satisfied with this visit, Gino thanked Victoria, bid *adios* to Martina and Luz and made his way back to Madrid. *Probably not going to get a profile better than that*, thought Gino. *She is quite impressive, but still an enigma.*

* * *

At their apartment on Apolonia Morales, Gino and Mercedes discussed his meeting with Victoria Valenzuela.

"That whole *La Pluma Blanca* things bothers me a lot," he said. "But she is so forthcoming. I cannot believe she is involved in this."

"That's because you think she is so beautiful, that anything nefarious cannot be attributed to her," commented Mercedes.

"Well, I'll give you that. She is absolutely stunning, with that little Asian touch making her look quite exotic."

"So, she is infatuating, is that what you are saying?"

"No... yes," laughed Gino. "Yes, her beauty is disarming, but so is her demeanor. It looks like she has absolutely nothing to hide. She tells you everything about her past, even those areas that give her motivation for what happened to de Portillo. But she was hundreds of kilometers away when that bull destroyed him. Motive? Possibly, but no opportunity. We cannot ignore that. If she wasn't there, she couldn't have participated in the killing. No?"

"I know," sighed Mercedes. "Your Asian beauty has a rock-solid alibi, so she could never be charged with anything, except not liking the victim. Undoubtedly, there are dozens of people who did not like the man."

"The only beauty I am interested in is that raven-haired, blue-eyed, Spanish chief inspector that I am married to," said Gino. "You can keep Victoria on your persons of interest list if you want, but I am moving on, *La Pluma Blanca* or not."

"Okay, you move on. See what France turns up. I understand you have a person of interest there as well."

"Yes, sort of, but again, rock-solid alibis. You and Cousteau have to keep on digging."

Chapter Eighteen

Doctor Arnold von Beek, fifty-nine-year-old Director of Orion, a primate research facility, finds himself tied to a chair. The Orion facility outside of Amsterdam is more than fifty years old and is now used as a satellite to a newer, more modern research center in Utrecht, in the center of the little country. All is dark, but he realizes he is in one of his facilities as he hears and smells the creatures he breeds and cares for before they are requisitioned for use in some experiment or research study. He does important work, for the benefit of humanity, but it is very controversial. And tonight, as he struggles to come out of the fog his mind is in, he begins to fear what might be happening. *Where are the security guards?* he thinks, as he begins to regain some of his senses. He also smells something else, something sweet, and a weight on his lap. *Could it be bananas?*

Then he senses someone walking and he sees a beam of a flashlight moving toward the cage areas. Two sets of primates are housed in large, open cage-like structures. Rhesus monkeys are in a chain-link structure because of their small size. It is a large space, fifteen meters wide, seven meters deep and fifteen meters high. There, thirty-five monkeys are kept, with all sorts of ropes and tree limbs to allow them to cavort as they wish. There is also a separate, glass-enclosed nursery in the back for pregnant and newborn monkeys. The adjacent structure, a little larger, houses chimpanzees, with thirteen male chimps, who are much larger. The structure is barred, not enclosed with chain-link, and similar ropes, limbs, even tires are there for the amusement of the animals.

The beam of light moves to the chimpanzee cage and von Beek can make out a hand with a key being inserted into the lock of the door housing the chimps. He hears a click of the lock opening and the light allows him to see the door made slightly ajar. The person and the light beam then move quickly across the open area and a door is heard to open and slam shut. It is now totally dark again and von Beek can hear the clever and industrious chimps moving about excitedly. Then the squeak of the cage door opening and the almost deafening, excited clatter of its inhabitants filling the room, causing the Rhesus monkeys to join in the auditory melee. Soon there is movement all around him. He is poked, touched, and pushed. The chimps all know him and he is never cruel to them, but he is their jailer. They find the bananas and now, more high-pitched squealing assails his brain. He begins being hit with bananas, almost to the point of unconsciousness. Then he is covered with the weight of several chimpanzees, pounding, biting, and killing him.

* * *

The following morning, the two, armed security guards of the facility begin to regain consciousness, apparently incapacitated during the night. Totally confused, they rise and groggily make their way inside the building. Opening the door to the caged area, they are greeted by rampaging chimpanzees and can detect a body lying in a toppled chair amongst the animals. The door is quickly shut and a call is immediately made to the police and a patrol car is dispatched to the scene. Talking to the guards and assessing the situation, one of the officers immediately calls their station, and detectives Guus Arden and Bibi Van Amstel from the Amsterdam-Amstelland Regional Unit of the Netherlands Police Force, soon follow.

"You can't go in there," advised Gijs Cruyseen, the constable at the scene. "It is full of chimpanzees running amok and there is a body in there."

Diverted, the detectives approached the two security guards, sitting on the front steps of the facility, near to the patrolman. "We were gassed," one of the guards said. "I'm still a bit woozy, but I can't imagine what happened in there. Doctor von Beek came by last night, about one o'clock, and said he had to check on the Rhesus monkeys, born yesterday. That is all I remember. He disarmed the alarm system with the keypad, went in, and the next thing I remember is waking up in the foyer. That's got to be von Beek inside."

"Well, how do we get in there?" Inspector Arden asked.

"We have to call our center in Utrecht. Speak with Doctor Kuiper. He is the assistant Director. He'll know what to do," the guard—Loek Koopman said.

"Well, make the call and explain the situation to Kuiper," Arden directed. He then called Hoofdininspecteur—Chief Inspector—Aaldenberg and summarized the situation. "This is a mess and we'll need some back-up here."

Two more patrol cars arrived at the scene, followed by Chief Inspector Aaldenberg. "What do we have here?" he asked Inspector Arden.

"A body inside, presumably Doctor Arnold von Beek, who is the director of Orion, a primate research facility. This building is a smaller satellite of their main center in Utrecht. He's in there with I don't know how many chimpanzees, loose and running around. We can't get in there. Called the Utrecht center for some help. And there are two security guards, incapacitated somehow, who were just waking up when we got here."

"What did you get from the guards?" asked Aaldenberg.

"Not a lot. We are waiting for them to get their heads a little clearer. They were unconscious for some time, but it is probably okay to talk to them again now. They're over there," pointing to the men sitting on the front steps of the building.

Koopman and the other guard, Willem Borst, told the same story. Doctor von Beek showed up some time after midnight, saying he had to check on the newborn monkeys. He disabled the alarm system and went inside. "We continued with our rounds and at some point, each of us was sprayed in the face with something that made us pass out," Borst said. "We were outside, but I guess we were dragged into the entrance there," pointing behind him, "'because that's where we woke up, with a surgical mask on our faces."

"We'll need a forensic unit here," said Aaldenberg. "Arden, make the call, and when the doc gets here, have him check out the guards immediately. We'll need some blood work, swab for chemicals on their faces and have those masks placed in evidence to check back at the lab."

"The Crime Scene Unit won't be able to get inside," said Sergeant Van Amsel. "We have to wait for the Utrecht people to get here.

About twenty minutes later, a blue van with the Orion logo on the side pulled in front of the building. A middle-aged man in a white lab coat emerged with five others, dressed in blue overalls with long sleeves. Each came with heavy gloves, a plastic face-shield, hard construction hats, and each was slipping on plastic booties.

"I'm Kuiper," the man in the lab coat said. "These are some of our animal handlers who will try to get the chimpanzees back in their cage. If that doesn't work, they'll have to be tranquilized...or worse." One of the men carried a large black case, presumably with the tranquilizing equipment. The men cautiously opened the door and quickly entered.

After almost an hour, one of the handlers emerged. Taking off his gloves and face-shield, he said to Kuiper and Aaldenberg, "Done. They are back in their cage and the cage door has been secured. Someone, inexplicably, left it open. You can go in now."

"More likely, someone opened it," said Aaldenberg, almost to himself. "We'll take a peek from the door to the caged area, but no one goes inside until the doc and the forensic team get here."

Shortly thereafter, the forensic unit arrived, led by Doctor Wouter Van Dijk, a tall man in his fifties, clean-shaven and a full head of gray-blond hair. Van Dijk and his three forensic investigators entered inside, first crossing the foyer-area and then to the door to the caged area. All but Van Dijk toted a large, leather case. "Holy shit," the detectives heard one of the crime scene investigators say. "I don't know what we are going to get with this."

Indeed, the large room was a mess. Debris, feces, banana peels and all sorts of objects and notebooks pulled from shelves. Plus, five animal handlers spending almost an hour in the crime scene. Sticking his head out the door, Van Dijk said, "To say that the crime scene has been compromised is an understatement."

First priority was to examine the body, still tied to a chair with nylon rope and on its side. The person in the chair was terribly ravaged and clearly dead. Bite marks on his face and neck, as well as his arms and legs as evidenced by the tears in his clothing. There was blood on his face and blood stains on his clothes, but not a lot of pooling on the floor. Bruises could be made out on his face and most likely on his body. "He took quite a pounding," Van Dijk commented to one of his colleagues. "Look at them," pointing to the cage where the chimps had been returned to, "some are a meter and a half tall and weigh close to sixty kilos." He then walked to the door and called out to the detectives.

"We'll bring the body to the morgue now and do a full examination there—autopsy, toxicology and DNA screens, the works. I'll bet the center has DNA records of all the chimps, so we likely can determine which ones of them did the most damage, as if that matters. The CSI team will continue here, dusting for fingerprints on the chair, cage and all doors including the storage area in the back. It looks like the bananas came from some stalks they have in the back. They will look, but not sure what else they will find in this mess. They'll let you know when it is cleared for you to enter."

As Van Dijk was departing with the body, and biding their time until they could enter, the detectives exchanged thoughts with their boss. "The guy apparently walked in here but didn't tie himself to that chair. Like the guards, he had to be incapacitated, and then someone let the chimps out," said Sergeant Van Amstel.

"Apparently," said the chief inspector, but what worries me is that the news of this is probably leaking out right now. We are going to have reporters here in the blink of an eye, and other than the obvious—man killed by chimpanzees—we are not going to have anything concrete to say for a while, at least until Doctor Van Dijk completes his analyses, so you guys say nothing to nobody. All communication to come from me and our press people." He then noticed that Doctor Kuiper was still there with the animal handlers.

"Doctor Kuiper, I just informed my detectives on the importance of controlling communication to the press. Considering who Doctor von Beek is, or was, and all the controversy about animal research, there will be a clamor for any tidbits of information, and you will be sought after. Please limit your remarks to the basic facts that apparently von Beek was killed by chimpanzees that escaped their enclosure. That is it, and communicate that to all your people, especially the handlers that got the chimps back in their cage. That's all you know, the police are investigating, and that is that. Can I count on you to do that?"

"Yes, and we have a public relations department that will issue a statement to that effect, referring inquiries on the investigation to you," replied Kuiper.

While they were talking, Inspector Arden received a call and looked exasperated when it concluded. He quickly sought out Aaldenberg. "Chief, our crime scene is kind of expanding. I sent a unit to von Beek's residence—he lives in Hilversum—to do a cursory check there. The guy lives alone, his wife divorcing him years ago because of the harassment from the animal rights groups, but I found out the center also keeps a security guard at his residence. When our guys got there, they found the guard unconscious—lying behind shrubs near the front door—and like the ones here, with a surgical mask on his face. The front door was closed but unlocked and von Beek's car was still there."

"So, he was kidnapped at his home, drugged or disoriented with something and brought here," said Aaldenberg. "We need a crime scene unit over there also. Advise the constables there to close the scene and wait for the forensic people."

Some time passed and the crime scene investigators emerged from the cage room. "You guys can take a look around now," one of them said. "Better put some booties on as there is all sorts of shit on the floor—literally. We've collected what might turn out to be evidence, but we're not very hopeful. Interesting thing. I found this right inside the door," holding up a clear plastic evidence bag with a white feather inside. "How it got there is curious. Certainly, no birds inside and it looks like the feather was cut off, not plucked, or fallen from a bird. We'll check on what kind of bird when we get back to the lab, but *interessant*—interesting—no?

"Also found that they have a closed-circuit TV system here, both inside and outside. You can see the cameras there in the ceiling," pointing to several locations around the cage room. We located the recording equipment and it had been turned off and no tape—really a disc—in the machine. There were some discs on a shelf, likely those from a previous period, and we took them with us, but I think what we had hoped to find is gone."

* * *

Little by little, pieces started coming together and at the police station, Inspector Arden and Sergeant Van Amstel brought Chief Inspector Aaldenberg up to date on the von Beek murder. "Latest news on the cause of death, sir, cardiac infarction."

"Heart attack? He died from a heart attack?"

"Doctor Van Dijk confirms that from the autopsy. While he was severely beaten by the chimpanzees, including being bitten numerous times, he died from a heart attack. Apparently, he had a history of heart disease. That's why we did not find great pools of blood around his body. He died, and the heart stopped pumping. The next important thing is that they found scopolamine in his system. This is an interesting drug in that it could make him subjected to direction from others. The person could be ambulatory, but not operating on his own free will. This is not a drug that is easy to obtain, and it has some legitimate medical uses, but its effects are quite strong. Doctor Van Dijk said it is reported to have been used by governments as a truth serum during interrogations—black-ops interrogations. Anyway, it was administered as a powder, inhaled by von Beek.

Traces were found in his nasal passages. Very unusual drug in that it can turn individuals into zombies—those are Van Dijk's words—and whoever administered it knew what they were doing, because it can also create unconsciousness. It has no use as a recreational drug, so it is not readily available. I'll come back to this again when we lay out what probably happened."

"Bibi," Arden said, nodding for her to continue.

"The tox report of the security guards, including the one at von Beek's residence in Hilversum, confirmed they were subjected to the anesthetic sevoflurane, sprayed into their faces and also on the surgical masks placed on their face."

"To make sure they stayed unconscious," said Aaldenberg.

"Exactly," replied the sergeant. "So, with that understanding, we tried to build up the sequence of events that led to, what is essentially an assassination."

"The whole thing started in Hilversum," began Guus Arden, "where somehow the security guard was incapacitated by the same anesthetic spray and Doctor von Beek was essentially kidnapped. The front door was opened and not broken in, so somehow, perpetrators got him to open the door and then he was subjected to the scopolamine. Doctor Van Dijk said that via inhalation, the drug works relatively quickly, but he is going to check further on what exactly happens. Our scenario is that he was taken to the research facility—his car is still at his residence—and while being transported directed to carry out a number of activities."

"When he arrived at the building," picked up Van Amstel, "he walked to the entrance, barely greeting the guards and telling them he had to check on the nursery. The guards thought he was kind of wooden and distracted—their words—but they attributed that to the lateness of the hour. He went to the keypad that disabled the alarm system, opened the door, and went in. That's where their memory cuts off, other than remembering a hiss and a spray to the face. We believe von Beek went directly to the CCTV unit and turned it off. The discs the crime scene unit reviewed showed nothing of the events of that night. Those discs are now here, but of little use. The perpetrators took anything relevant with them."

"The rest is pure speculation," continued Arden. "One, or more than one, individual entered the building and tied von Beek to a chair. Whether he was in some kind of a stupor, we don't know, or he was just docile enough to let that happen without resistance. Thereafter, the chimps were let out."

"Why were there still chimpanzees in this research facility?" asked Aaldenberg. "I remember the Netherlands outlawed the use of these animals in medical research years ago."

"That is true," Arden replied, "but a little history first. Doctor Kuiper told us that this was the main primate research center until about fifteen years ago. Two things were happening then. First, Orion was planning a new and more modern facility for some time as this building is about fifty years old. Doctor von Beek was the main planner of this move and that was when Doctor Kuiper came on board. Then, as you mentioned, the Dutch government outlawed any medical testing using chimpanzees. The trials that were underway were allowed to continue, but Orion had to cease any further research using chimpanzees. A number of the animals here were transferred to zoos—the ones that had never been involved in any research or medical trials—others to a sanctuary, but the Dutch government allowed Orion to continue to keep and care for chimpanzees that were not able to be relocated. Orion was not allowed to ship any chimpanzees to other countries where they were still used for research. Some of the remaining chimps were old and a few, too aggressive and were allowed to live out the rest of their lives in the cages here. Not very humane, but at least they were free from any further experimentation. Research using Rhesus monkeys was allowed to continue and Orion used this facility for breeding of these monkeys."

"It is of some relevance," added Van Amstel, "that these researchers, primate researchers, are under constant threat from animal rights groups, those opposed to using any animals in research testing. That is why there are guards permanently stationed these facilities. The Utrecht center has a major security force there, given the size of the center and its prominence. Von Beek, Kuiper and a few others also have guards at their home."

"Last point," added Arden, "there are only five workers as full-time staff here, primarily involved with Rhesus monkey breeding and the feeding and care of the remaining chimpanzees. Not knowing what occurred, they showed up for work on the day of the incident and of course were barred from entering. The employees were interviewed, fingerprints taken, and each is being investigated as subjects of interest until we know differently. They bitched and moaned at not being allowed to enter the building, as they needed to tend to the newborn monkeys in the nursery and of course, to continue to feed the chimps. Forensics said it was okay, but we maintain police supervision of that building for now. We were also assisted by the Utrecht Regional Unit to do the same with the employees there and of course, we have probed into all aspects of von Beek's life but have no leads from that. His ex-wife, who fled from all the notoriety associated with his work, now lives in England and is not a subject of interest."

"And the chimps?" asked Aaldenberg.

"Tough call," answered Arden. "Kuiper said that it was unlikely that all the released chimpanzees were engaged in the attack on von Beek. He estimated that no more than three or four were involved, and we now have DNA evidence that backs that up. Plus, the fact that the chimpanzees actually did not kill von Beek is a little wrinkle. They undoubtedly caused the heart attack, but they did not kill him. What happens to those chimps remains under discussion with Kuiper and the government agencies that regulate these things. From Van Dijk's DNA analysis, we know the animals that engaged in the attack, but are they to be removed and euthanized? *Should* they all be removed and euthanized? One way or another that will also involve dealing with all the anti-animal research groups, both locally and the large international ones, before a decision is made."

"As we search for motive and opportunity," said Aaldenberg, "we cannot lose sight of the fact that many of these animal rights groups are very vocal and aggressive. The threats against these researchers need to be thoroughly investigated. Have a team go through any files at the Amsterdam facility and of course, the Utrecht Center, and start to compile and profile groups and individuals that exhibit the most aggressive actions and threats, against von Beek personally and against Orion in general. This was an extremely well organized and well executed plan, and it is unlikely a single nut could have carried this off. There is some deep animosity here against the use of animals for research, by many parties, and we will have our hands full to sort this out."

Chapter Nineteen

Interpol maintained a small office in Madrid, with Gino Cerone as the Senior Detective Chief Superintendent. Two detective inspectors were assigned to him, Antonia Juanes, and Rolando Gonzalez, both recently promoted because of the work done in shutting down the human trafficking ring operating in Spain. Elia Castilla was a detective constable, serving as office administrator, as part of her development program. Juanes and Gonzalez were in their late thirties and Castilla in her late twenties.

The Interpol office was located on the eleventh floor of a twenty-two-story glass edifice on Paseo de la Castellana, near Plaza Cuzco. Its layout was simple, three cubicles for Juanes, Gonzalez, and Castilla, with an enclosed office for Cerone in the rear, overlooking the wide, tree-lined Paseo de la Castellana. A small conference room was adjacent to Cerone's office containing an oval table seating six and a working area opposite the windows. Here there was a whiteboard wall, three meters wide and two meters high with wood panels that could slide over the whiteboard, shielding its contents when required. A cabinet was mounted on the wall adjacent to the whiteboard containing erasers and an array of colored markers that Gino was fond of using. The board included a list of key issues and questions regarding the de Portillo incident on one side and Gino

106

had already started to do the same for the Le Clerc attack. *La Pluma Blanca*/white feather was listed on each side of the whiteboard.

"*Jefe*," called out Elia Castilla. "A news alert is coming through about a terrible incident in Amsterdam. The director of an animal research center—Orion it is called—was killed during the evening by chimpanzees they housed at one of their centers. Not a lot of details yet, but the story does mention the highly active anti-primate research groups in the Netherlands, citing a history of extremist group attacks on researchers in the past. This looks nasty."

"Get me everything you can on this, Elia. I'm going to check with Lyon if they picked this up," said Cerone.

Klaus Schickhaus answered his phone by saying, "I guess you saw the news."

"I did, Elia just alerted me. No real details released yet, but this is an ominous sign," replied Gino. "Another country, another cruel incident potentially related to the animal rights movements. The report doesn't use the word 'accidental' or anything like that, and I am guessing that this might be another murder of an individual on the other side of the issue."

"I wouldn't doubt that, Gino. I'm going to call the chief commissioner, Pieter Quelhorst. We are old friends. I will hear what he has to say and give him a summary of our theory of these events being connected, at least between Paris and Madrid, and find out who is running the investigation in Amsterdam. I'll advise him that you are our chief superintendent dealing with these events and get his agreement to have you involved immediately."

"I assumed as much," answered Gino. "Gonzalez has just started an investigation with the Guardia Civil here regarding a new immigration issue that may be tied to trafficking, so I'd like to take Juanes with me. If these atrocities keep occurring, we'll need all the resources we can get. Let us try to get ahead of this and keep your analytical group on standby, no better yet, have them start digging into the anti-animal research movement in the Netherlands, particularly those that have employed extreme or radical measures against companies or individuals involved in the issue of biomedical research."

"Good idea. I'll call Quelhorst and get back to you."

Gino then advised Juanes that they might have to travel to Amsterdam. "And Elia, start looking for flights to Amsterdam for tomorrow."

In short order, Elia reported that there was a flight with vacancies tomorrow at 8:45 AM, arriving at Schiphol airport at 11:25 AM. "There is a later flight in the afternoon at 15:45 PM, arriving in Amsterdam at 18:25 PM. Two hours and forty minutes flight time either way."

"We'll want the morning flight," Gino said, "assuming Schickhaus gives us the green light after talking with the Dutch police. Book the morning one, just in case."

An hour later, Schickhaus called. "Quelhorst is incredulous that this could be a coordinated and planned plot but welcomes our input. If you can get there tomorrow, that would be fine. Let me know your flight schedule so I can advise him. A Chief Inspector Aaldenberg of the Amsterdam-Amstelland regional unit is your contact and he said he would send someone to pick you up. I checked and we have a special discount at the Radisson Blu Hotel in the city center, so have Elia book you there. It's not far from Aaldenberg's station."

"I love it that you always watch the budget," laughed Gino.

* * *

The Iberia flight to Amsterdam arrived early at 11:20 AM and Cerone and Juanes were met at the baggage claim by Sergeant Van

Amstel. "We'll check into our hotel later," advised Cerone. "Let's go directly to your headquarters so we can start on this."

Bibi gave them a summary of what they found, while en-route.

Chief Inspector Aaldenberg greeted the Interpol agents in his office and after an offer of coffee—the Dutch love coffee—which they both accepted, they moved to a conference room. Inspector Guus Arden was already there, and Sergeant Van Amstel joined them. Gino then gave the group a synopsis of the Madrid and Paris as background as to why Interpol was here. Then, the two detectives gave the details—at least what they had so far—of the attack on von Beek. Commissioner Quelhorst joined them shortly thereafter.

"I guess it was a good thing that von Beek died of a heart attack. It spared him some terrible trauma," said Antonio Juanes, after Arden and Van Amstel recounted the details of what they found at the scene.

"I suppose," offered Aaldenberg, "but he suffered a terrible ordeal, nevertheless."

"I can imagine," said Cerone. "One question. Was a white feather found at the crime scene?"

"Why yes," answered Arden, with a surprised look on his face. "We don't know what to make of it."

"Shit," said Gino. "Well, we now know this incident is connected with Madrid and Paris. A white feather was found at each of the other scenes."

"So, we have some kind of plot, relating to the abuse of animals, to murder prominent figures involved in such abuses," offered Aaldenberg.

"The short answer is, yes, and from our investigations in Paris and Madrid, we are focusing on animal rights groups as potential suspects. However, the abuse of racehorses, cruelty against the Spanish Fighting Bull, and now the use of animals in biomedical research, involves three totally distinct groups of activists. While there are major international and European organizations engaged in this movement—animal rights of one kind or another—we don't believe they are behind this. We believe we must look at local groups, the most aggressive, extreme, radical ones, to find those responsible."

"But you say that these events are connected. It is only the larger organizations that span interest in all these abuses. Do the anti-animal research groups care about the cruelty in bullfighting?" asked Quelhorst.

"You make an excellent point, Commissioner," replied Gino. "The emotions of these groups, their passions about the atrocities, however, seem to be the highest within local groups, and from what little I know, these are the kinds of groups that are the most aggressive in The Netherlands. I read a report on the plane citing attacks on researchers—both physical and emotional—as well as on their facilities and any companies reaping the benefits of biomedical research. Arson, destruction of property, personal threats, probably cannot be laid at the door of PETA, for instance. But somehow, someone seems to be coordinating the activities of these radical, local groups. I think it is locally where we must start to get answers."

"How many individuals or organizations are committed to end the use of animals in medical research?" asked Arden rhetorically. "Dozens, if not more, and then there are splinter cells within such groups that carry out the assaults you referred to. Some activists, we know. Some have been arrested and imprisoned, but it is like a hydra with many heads."

"Then we have to get started weeding them out. I have directed the Interpol analysts to investigate this and we need to coordinate Lyon's efforts with your own. However, while we all start to collect this data, I would like very much to visit the crime scene as well as the research center, did you say in Utrecht?"

"Yes, Utrecht. Orion has a major center there, working with all kinds of animals—monkeys, pigs, rabbits, rats, guinea pigs, birds, whatever. It is an enormous and modern facility, including large outside pens for some of the animals. On the surface, it looks very humane, but the ultimate destiny of the animals they house and breed is torture, nevertheless," said Aaldenberg. "Sergeant Van Amstel will take you to both facilities, and in Utrecht, I'll arrange for you to meet with Doctor Hans Kuiper, who is now Acting Director of Orion."

"Thank you," said Gino. "And again, I want to emphasize that Lyon's analysts and computer systems are second to none, and between your work to identify suspect organizations and theirs, we should be able to map out and prioritize those groups and individuals we'd like to speak with. This part is critical, as is your knowledge and experience on the lay of the land."

* * *

The visit to Orion, Amsterdam, was interesting as well as depressing. The chimpanzees were still in their cage—all thirteen of them—and the Interpol agents could not help but wonder which ones of the chimps were the attackers. Looking at them, they appeared docile, curious, and somewhat subdued. The Rhesus monkeys, on the other hand, looked active, happy, and playful, making all sorts of screeches. The newborns in the nursery looked nothing short of adorable. Gino thought that Mercedes would have loved to hold and cuddle one of them. Hard to imagine their ultimate fate, although you cannot discount the benefit they have brought to biomedical research. HIV and Hepatitis are two deadly diseases, thought incurable, which would have never generated the life-saving treatments and cures without them. Chimpanzees especially contributed to these breakthroughs, saving millions of lives. *But God, they are cute,* thought Gino.

The visit to Utrecht with Doctor Kuiper was more than interesting. Scientifically, it was a marvel of what was being achieved, collaborating with pharmaceutical companies and research laboratories all over the world to find treatments and cures. The facility itself was very impressive, nothing like the cages in Amsterdam, and Kuiper went out of his way extolling the benefits of the work they do there. He made sure to give Cerone and Juanes literature from the European Association for Animal Research (EARA), defending the mission of biomedical research in health improvement in Europe. "EARA provides accurate and evidence-based information that demonstrates the achievements made using experimental animals in biomedical research. Facts and evidence," he stressed, "not emotional arguments by those opposed to what we do."

Two sides of the coin, thought Gino, *each with compelling arguments supporting their cause. But the researchers have a little more meaningful mission that those torturing bulls and doping horses for sport.*

After the visit to Orion, Utrecht, Van Amstel brought the Madrid visitors to the Radisson Blu Hotel—she still had their bags in her car—where they checked in, noting that they would be receiving the special Interpol discount. Later that evening and after a wonderful dinner at an Indonesian restaurant—very popular in The Netherlands, as Indonesia was once a Dutch colony—the two called it a night, their minds juggling the two arguments about the use of animals in biomedical research.

* * *

By morning, Lyon had E-mailed Cerone and Juanes a comprehensive list of anti-animal research groups in The Netherlands as well as a number of individuals with a history of extreme activism. He immediately forwarded the material to Commissioner Quelhorst and Chief Inspector Aaldenberg. Bibi picked them up at the hotel and again brought them to the police station.

"If you don't mind, Guus and I will work with you today. Chief Inspector Aaldenberg said he would join us from time to time, but the commissioner will not be with us. I know he told the chief inspector that he was impressed with your insights, and we have a copy of the material provided by Lyon. I have it on my laptop but we're printing copies now."

"Please have copies made for Antonio and me—jumping to a first-name basis—we only reviewed the report on our phones, and I still like paper," pulling out a yellow marker and red pen from his jacket pocket.

Van Amstel led them again to the conference room they were in yesterday, but today, two whiteboards were set up at the end of the room and pens and pads were at each chair setting. Guus Arden was already there again, partaking of coffee from a table where coffee and pastries had been set up.

"Help yourselves to some coffee, Señores," Guus laughed.

"We are Gino and Antonio," Gino said, pointing first to himself and then Juanes. "And you are Guus, right?"

"Yes, good, and here comes Bibi with her arms full," said Guus.

"The material from Lyon is very comprehensive and has been laid out quite nicely," she said. "We haven't really read it, but we had our analysts work during the evening and we do have something we can cross match. Give me an E-mail address in Lyon where we can send our work and the two sides can make comparisons."

"Good, as we have only skimmed the material, why don't we take some time reading it, making notes, and then start to highlight what we think is important?" proposed Gino.

"I totally agree, and we have nice, hot Dutch coffee to sustain us," replied Guus.

"It is good," said Gino. "I might pick some up at the airport to bring home."

A good hour went by with sounds like, "mmm, *Dios mio*" (from Juanes), "*Mijn God*" (from Bibi), coming from the detectives around the table. Everyone made a few trips to the coffee table.

"How are we doing?" asked Gino. "Do you think you have read enough to start thinking about what we'd like to highlight?" All nodded in agreement.

"Why don't you start, Guus? This is your turf, as we say in the States."

"Yes, I can start, and Bibi, maybe you can write on the board what we think is relevant?"

"*Ja*"—Yes, she replied, rising from the chair, and moving to the end of the room, toting a coffee in her hand. "Besides, no one can read your writing," she said, looking at Guus.

He began. "We have seen aggressive, violent demonstrations—even attacks—going on for years by these anti-animal research activists. I thought we were the worst in Europe, primarily because of the primate research centers we have in The Netherlands, but there are tens of thousands of activists and organizations around the world led by the British and the Americans. From the Vegans who protest the eating of meat, those targeting the fur farms, those against the use of nets for fishing, and the animal research protestors, they are everywhere. I thought, however, it might be useful to list the most prominent organizations dedicated to this movement first, the

European and international groups, and then identify those that are the most extreme. I suggest this because sometimes there are splinter groups, or cells, like the report says, sprouting out of the bigger activist groups, not necessarily strictly local. This will give us an idea of the scope an investigation will have to take."

"Good approach," said Gino. "You start and we all can add whatever we have noted from the Interpol report."

"*In ord*"—Okay, Guus answered.

After about fifteen minutes, the white board listed:

- Party For the Animals (political party in parliament)
- Dutch Organization Animal Rights (DOAR)
- Humane Society International
- World Animal Protection
- PETA – People for the Ethical Treatment of Animals
- International Primate Protection League
- Center for Alternative Animal Testing (CAAT)

"These are prominent European and international organizations that have been active in education—including videos—literature generation, conferences, seminars and intensive lobbying to governments, all very legitimate efforts that have produced important legislation in many countries, including here. These efforts, for instance, produced legislation in Holland prohibiting the use of chimpanzees in biomedical research. That was a big victory for these groups, but I cannot say that the pressure from the radical groups did not have a role in this legislation. I also thought that The Netherlands was at the top of the list in terms of animal protection legislation, but I saw that we only earned a B-grade—signifying only moderately strong protection—in the World Animal Protection Index. I thought we'd be much better," said Arden.

"Good start," said Gino. "We took a similar approach in France in mapping out key groups, but now we get to the more extreme groups."

"Yes, but did you take notice that the British inspired many of these activists? The Huntington Life Sciences organization in Cambridge, England—a contract research organization used throughout the world—founded in 1951, started to draw the ire of activists in the UK and there was a spill-over and alliances with Dutch groups. The Stop Huntington Animal Cruelty (SHAC) group was very aggressive in their activism against this research group because of their widespread use of animals in research."

"I just noted the time," said Guus. "Why don't we arrange for sandwiches to be brought in? We can use a break." All agreed, and after lunch they turned to identifying the more extreme groups operating in The Netherlands.

After an hour of discussion, the list generated follows:

- Stop Huntington Animal Cruelty-Netherlands (SHAC-NL)
- Anti-Vivisection Coalition (AVC)
- *Anti-Dierproeven Coalitie* (*ADC*) – coalition against animal testing
- *Respect voor Dieren* (*RVD*) – Respect for Animals
- Cruelty Free International – infiltrated high-profile laboratories
- Eleventh Hour For Animals – UK spillover
- Negotiation is Over – NIO (USA)
- National Operation Anti-Vivisection (UK spillover)
- *Een Eind Makan aan Dierenproeven-Nu* – Stop Animal Research Now (SARN)
- *Dierenbevrijdings Front* (*DBF*) – Counterpart UK Animal Liberation Front

- Animal Rights Militia
- Monkeys Are Us

"We agreed to list a couple of UK and USA groups because of splinter groups and cells being spawned out of them and because of their radical inspirational leaders, like Steve Best, Camille Marino and Linda Grossman advocating threats against researcher and with convictions for their activities. Luke Steel in the UK is another convicted activist. We haven't been able to identify individuals of such an ignominious stature, certainly not as visible, but likely they are in these groups somewhere," said Bibi.

"But in Holland," started Guus, "we have seen significant violence from groups like these, including the burning of automobiles, threats to family members of researchers and employees of pharmaceutical companies."

"Home visits are another heinous activity where groups of activists gather at the home of a targeted individual, shouting their slogans, spray painting graffiti on their homes and generally terrorizing families," Bibi said. "And there are incidents of the release of animals, like rabbits and rats from research facilities, even minks from mink farms. No wonder that von Beek's wife left him."

"I made note of an organization, The International Animal Rights Conference, which brings together these activist groups to share experiences of their actions as well as better organizing against those trying to stop them. It's a networking platform for activists to hone their skills and build on their own security measures," offered Gino. "I think they meet annually in Luxembourg. We should find out when the next one is planned and try to get some of our people there."

"That's a great idea," said Guus. "We'll take on that responsibility, but for now, are we comfortable with what we have up there?" pointing to the whiteboard.

"Well, it's a start. Bibi, can you get someone to put this on a laptop and get copies to each of us? And give one to your boss, Chief Inspector Aaldenberg. He can determine what should go to Commissioner Quelhorst, although we are just at the beginning of this investigation."

At 5:00 PM, both Aaldenberg and Quelhorst joined the group in the conference room. By that time, printed copies of the lists were available and distributed.

"*Mijn God,*" said Quelhorst when he looked at the list.

"And this could be just the tip of the iceberg," offered Gino. "And to go from harassment to murder is a pretty big jump, so there is much profiling and screening to do. To sift through these groups, their leaders, and their members, will be a challenge, and much of this will fall to the Dutch National Police Force. One of the groups, *Respect voor Dieren*, RVD, is here in Amsterdam, but we haven't laid out where the other groups area. That should be in the work your analysts have completed, and then mapped out, literally."

"Well, I suspect that most of these people are not saddened by the death of von Beek, but we will start getting pressure from the other side of the coin, the research organizations, like the Association for Animal Research, the vast public relations organ for biomedical research. And we cannot forget the pressure we will receive from our ministries. I have already received a call from the prime minister."

Turning to Chief Inspector Aaldenberg, Quelhorst continued, "Karl, once you have the locations of these groups identified, including of their leaders, I'd like you to organize a teleconference with all the relevant regional unit commanders, as we are going to need their resources to conduct interviews."

"Of course, and Detective Chief Superintendent Cerone has offered to lay out a discussion guide or suggested protocol for these preliminary contacts. These groups should not be approached as suspects but more as persons of interest at this point. This was the approach used in Spain and France, and follow-up interviews followed where warranted," replied Aaldenberg.

"I'll have that for you before we leave," said Gino. "We have it in French and Spanish, but Lyon has made an English version which I tell them to send you immediately. And I would like to ask a favor. Once your people go through this list and determine there are some you'd like to talk to again—and where language isn't a problem—I'd like to sit in on a couple of them."

"Yes," said Quelhorst. "We can arrange that."

Juanes and Cerone were able to catch a flight back to Madrid that evening, using only one night of discounted rate at the Radisson Blu Hotel.

Chapter Twenty

It took more than a week to get all the details they needed. Web sites helped enormously but it was the location of the leaders of the groups that took the most time. Ultimately, addresses were in Rotterdam, Eindhoven, Arnhem, Nijmegen, Amsterdam, and Haarlem, a mix of offices and individual residences. In the end, with collaboration of other government agencies, like the Dutch Tax Administration—part of the Ministry of Finance—things came together, not unlike the interagency collaborations in Spain and France. All the groups had the potential for lone wolves, and the deeper they could get into memberships, the better. Plus, the von Beek incident likely required more than one person to pull it off.

After a round of preliminary contacts was completed, Gino received a call from Guus Arden.

"Our detectives have had discussions with all of the groups we identified, but the outcome is not promising," he began. "For the most part we have identified the leaders but getting deep into memberships is proving to be almost impossible. Plus, some individuals are not members per se, but only on mailing lists or E-mail blasts, like you might get from supermarkets. The most suspect groups are RVD—Respect for Animals, DBF—counterpart of Animal Liberation Front,

EARN—End Animal Research Now, Animal Rights Militia and Monkeys Are Us.

"An interesting discovery is that the sister of one of the leaders of the End Animal Research Now group—Jan Hendricks—worked undercover in one of the research laboratories using animals for experimentation, animals that were obtained from Orion. She apparently provided confidential information to her brother and EARN. Further, another member of that group—Niels Beekhof—is a pharmacist, working in one of the major hospitals in Amsterdam. Given the use of chemicals in the von Beek attack, this makes him a person of high interest.

"We had some other red flags with the Monkeys Are Us group and the Coalition Against Animal Testing—ADC—where the people we talked with were very uncooperative and gave us very little. Plus, our files indicate that some of them had been convicted for property damage and extraordinary harassment. We need to pursue this further," Arden concluded. "Maybe an Interpol presence will loosen some tongues."

"I welcome the opportunity to participate in some of these follow-up interviews. We would treat the sessions a little more intense, but I really would like to start with the End Animal Research Now group," said Gino.

"I thought you would. Besides Hendriks and Beekhof, there is Max De Groot, their leader, operating out of his home in an Amsterdam suburb. I'll set something up when we can get the three of them together for you."

"Set the time and date and I'll be there," replied Gino enthusiastically.

* * *

End Animal Research Now, in Dutch, *Een Eind Maken aan Dierenproeven Nu*, was a relatively small group when compared to the other of-interest groups, and besides the troika at the top, there were dozens of others on-call as needed. As-needed generally related to at-home confrontations. From the web sites of pharmaceutical companies, research laboratories and breeders of research animals, it was easy to obtain names of executives, research, and medical directors—the key players—of each organization. Then, it was not difficult to get addresses and create surveillance teams to map out when they went to work, when they returned home, and importantly, to identify family members and their comings and goings. Teams of five or six would gather a target's home, usually late at night, to create mayhem. This could include simple chanting of their slogans, like repeating and repeating "end animal research now," but it also included starting fire on the property, spraying graffiti on the house or automobiles, sometimes damaging the automobiles, and then disappearing into the evening. Jan Hendrik's sister Greta, at one point, provided EARN with names of researchers in her organization, Scion Laboratories.

An appointment was set up to meet with the leaders of EARN in de Groot's home in Amstelveen, just outside of Amsterdam proper. The group's headquarters operated out of de Groot's home. All three spoke English fluently—as do most Dutch citizens—so Cerone's participation in this round of interviews would be no problem.

Max de Groot lived in a narrow, three-story, attached brick building. There was a five-step stoop with black iron railings leading up to a double door with frosted glass inserts.

"Interpol," de Groot commented as Gino was introduced by Guus Arden and Bibi Van Amstel. "And you seem to be American. Did you travel all that distance just to meet with us?"

"No," Gino laughed, "I live in Europe."

"Well, please come in. My home is not very big, and if we are going to be six people, I'm afraid we have to climb three flights of stairs where I have a room that can accommodate us," and he led the three visitors up very narrow stairs to a comfortable-looking room on the third floor. There was an oriental rug in the center of the room, with a low coffee table surrounded by a gray leather sofa and three comfortable-looking armchairs. Two men, already in the room, were each carrying a chair to add to the grouping. All three of the EARN members were tall—typical of the Dutch—each just short of two meters and thin. Niels Beekhof and Jan Hendriks were introduced by de Groot to the visitors. Each was in their mid- to late-thirties.

Max de Groot had a full head of long blond hair, spilling over his ears and shirt collar, and a full, neatly trimmed beard. Niels Beekhof, the pharmacist, was also blond-haired with no facial hair and a neat haircut, but with long sideburns. Jan Hendricks had short brown hair, a goatee and moustache and was the only one with brown eyes, the others were blue-eyed, and Beekhof wore rimless eyeglasses.

"I know you want to talk about what happened to Arnold von Beek," began de Groot as everyone moved to a chair with Beekhof and Hendriks gravitating to the sofa. "As I told you detectives, Niels and I were at a board meeting of the International Animal Rights Group in Luxembourg—almost four hundred kilometers away—at the time of the incident, and Jan was visiting with his sister in Benidorm, Spain, so we couldn't have been involved with what happened."

"Well, that's getting to the point," commented Gino.

"Listen, it was a terrible thing that happened, but von Beek has killed, or arranged to be killed, hundreds of chimpanzees and other primates. What goes around, comes around, I have heard Americans say."

"Okay, so you are not grieving, but since you brought it up, I understand that you went over this with the inspectors when they were here and you provided proof of where you were, so that seems clear. I just wanted to get a little more insight on who you are and what you do, when you're not harassing researchers. Jan, if you don't mind, tell me about your sister's activities at Scion Laboratories."

"Well, you should know that was the reason for my visit with her in Benidorm. She was staying with our parents who now live in that area. They have been spending summers in Benidorm for twenty years, and when we were young, Greta and I were with them. They then decided to retire there a few years ago. There is a large British and Dutch expatriate community living there full time, also largely retirees. My sister went there to regroup after leaving Scion. She was a chemist there, very happy with her job, and I convinced her to do some undercover work for us. Activists are constantly doing things like that, and I put pressure on her to help us. She got us names of researchers working with animals and took a number of pictures, reluctantly doing this for her brother.

"After we carried out an 'At Home' visit to one of these researchers, and the publication of some of her photos, Greta felt very guilty and felt that she could not continue working at Scion, even though they were not aware of her role. She is a very responsible young lady. I went to visit her to make amends for using her, causing her to leave Scion. She understood our mission, but as a scientist, she was caught in the middle, so now she is without work and is very disappointed she helped me. That's the story."

"Will she return to her chosen field of work?" asked Gino.

"Yes, I am sure. Max promised to get her something with Phillips, in their research center in Eindhoven. They use chemists in their work at that facility."

"And Mr. Beekhof, I understand that you work in a hospital in Amsterdam."

"Yes, at Slotervaartziekenhuis. I've been there for six years," replied Beekhof.

"Hospital Sloter... what?" asked Gino.

"Slotervaartziekenhuis," laughed Beekhof. "I know, our six-syllable words are difficult. Anyway, before that I worked in retail pharmacy, an *apotheek*, but the work at the hospital is more meaningful than slapping a label on a box of pills."

"No doubt," commented Gino. "Are there opportunities for you to compound medications, mixing agents according to doctors' prescriptions?"

"Yes, at times, but things are more automated for efficiency and less chance of error."

"Is today one of your days off?" asked Gino.

"No, I work nights, from 8:00 PM to 4:00 AM, so basically I am just returning from work."

"You must be tired. One last question," added Gino. "Are you familiar with scopolamine?"

"Yes, of course. It is rarely used today, but I understand that it may have some benefit in irritable bowel syndrome, when traditional medications haven't worked. Otherwise, because of its side effects, it is pretty much shunned. It comes from a tree in Colombia and has been used in South America for criminal activity. It is called the Devil's Breath down there."

"You seem to know a bit about scopolamine," commented Gino.

"I am a pharmacist and I know about lots of drugs. That's my job," replied Beekhof.

"Have you ever used it at the hospital?" asked Gino.

"No, never, and it certainly is not maintained in our drug inventory."

"Who at the hospital maintains control of your drug inventory?"

"That would be Rens Roggeveen. He is the chief pharmacist, and any narcotic or psychotherapeutic drugs need his approval before ordering. I know it is not in our inventory, but you can ask him about it."

"And sevoflurane, is that used at the hospital?"

"Yes, it is one of the most common anesthetics used by anesthesiologists in surgery."

"So, this is readily available at the hospital?"

"Yes, but anesthesiologists maintain control of it," answered Beekhof.

"Thank you, Mr. Beekhof, you have been most helpful," commented Gino. "And now, just a few questions for Mr. de Groot," turning to the third member of EARN. "You work at the Phillips headquarters in Amsterdam. Is that correct?"

"Yes, at Koninklijk Phillips, NV—Royal Phillips. I started work with them in Eindhoven, in the South of the country, in its technology research center. I am an electrical engineer but was moved to Amsterdam to their medical imaging area: CT scans, MRIs, and the innovative 3D imaging equipment. Jan works there also, in the consumer electronics division."

Leaning back in his chair, Gino paused for a moment. "And you all came to abhor using animals in research. Each of you have high-tech careers—science and technology—and yet, you challenge other scientists for their use of animals for the benefit of the health and wellbeing of those suffering from disease. And you use very aggressive, some say radical means to make your point," said Gino, looking at each of the EARN group.

"Yes," said de Groot, "we harass these research organizations and their researchers, as a means to get proper attention so that laws can be created and enforced to stop these massacres. That happened with chimpanzees and the outlawing of animals, like rabbits, to be used in developing cosmetics. We—the whole anti-animal research establishment—have had some successes, but we cannot stop applying pressure to the abusers and the regulators."

"You've made that speech before," commented Gino.

Laughing, de Groot said, "Many times, but we do not kill people."

Gino rose, joined by Arden and Van Amstel, thanked each of the EARN members, shook their hands, and thanked them for their time.

Back outside, Bibi went for their car while Guus and Gino summarized their session with the EARN leaders. "Guus, get to that Sloter..., whatever you call it, hospital and check with," glancing down at his notes, "Rens Roggeveen. Find out if scopolamine was ever used at the hospital and if any inventories are kept—or have been kept. Check also on the use of sevoflurane and how its inventory is monitored."

"Absolutely, but you know that the alibis of each of them check out for the night of the attack. The Beekhof angle looks very promising, especially with his access to sevoflurane, but it still may be a dead end if they weren't there."

Chapter Twenty-One

Before leaving Amsterdam, Cerone met with Commissioner Quelhorst and Chief Inspector Aaldenberg and brought them up to date on the interviews he had conducted.

"The End Animal Research Now group has to remain subjects of interest—notwithstanding the alibis for each of the leaders. The pharmacy connection with Niels Beekhof remains troubling, as he could have provided drugs to someone else that we have not identified. However, the chief pharmacist at Beekhof's hospital said there was no missing units in the sevoflurane inventory."

"So, what are our next steps Detective Chief Superintendent?" asked Quelhorst.

"There are still a couple of other groups that your investigators haven't been able to eliminate completely. They will continue to gather more information in these instances, digging deeper into backgrounds. Surveillance has been set up as well on their key leaders to see if anything unusual turns up. They have also put surveillance on Niels Beekhof to monitor his activities and who he meets with. To be honest, where we are right now isn't very promising. I'm sorry. We will, however, continue to try to determine who might be coordinating these attacks. They definitely are connected, so someone must be pulling the strings. Interpol will pursue this vigorously."

Cerone also praised Aaldenberg and his team for the investigative work they have been carrying out, "You have an excellent unit here, Commissioner. We will stay in touch with them and share any further developments from Paris and Madrid."

* * *

Instead of flying back to Madrid, Cerone detoured to Lyon to meet with Klaus Schickhaus.

"Your analysts here did an outstanding job on profiling the most likely extreme groups to investigate," he began with Schickhaus. "It gave us a head start in Holland and helped the Amsterdam unit integrate their data in the format you provided. Please tell them that we appreciate their efforts."

'Thank you. I will pass your comments on to them, but we still are not close to finding out who did this, are we?" asked Schickhaus.

"Closer, but every lead seems to come with airtight alibis."

"Then we have to keep looking," added Schickhaus.

"Yes, and I have advised Cousteau and Mercedes to dig further. Such high profile and dastardly murders, yet we cannot pin anything down. It's frustrating, but we cannot let up. We are missing something, and we have to keep going over everything until we find it."

* * *

Back in his office in Madrid, Cerone went to the white board, erased everything there and then added.

- Victoria Valenzuela – Madrid??? Motive
- Camille Beaumont – Paris??? Motive
- Niels Beekhof – Amsterdam??? Opportunity

- Connected? – YES
  - How?
- Perfect alibis

Looking intensely at the whiteboard, Cerone thought, *Two individuals with motive, if not against the individual victims, certainly against the sport, albeit Valenzuela's motive goes back thirty years. And one individual, with no apparent personal motive but certainly the opportunity regarding access to implicated drugs. Can Beekhof get those drugs to the groups in Madrid and Paris? Key questions,* Cerone pondered.

Chapter Twenty-Two

Benny Dawson was a well-known, but universally disliked greyhound racing promoter in England. This day, he went to the Harlow Stadium in Essex County for the opening day of the greyhound dog racing season, staying for the race on Wednesday. Thursday was a day off, which he spent going over the facilities of the small venue which could accommodate fifteen hundred spectators on a good evening. He remembered going to dinner—fish and chips—but nothing else, and now he finds him lying on the ground, his mind in a fog. All is dark. It is nighttime as he can make out stars in the sky, despite the cloud cover, and he begins to awake from his drugged stupor. He can see very little but feels the soft dirt he is lying in.

He tries to sit up, but discovers his hands are tied to something—a rod or a pole—something metallic. His legs are free, as he tries to maneuver to a sitting position, but his hands are bound to this thing, whatever it is, hampering his ability to rise. In the ambient light of the stars, he realizes he is on a dog track within a stadium—Harlow, where he was today? He can now make out that fluffy thing on the rod that simulates a rabbit that half-a-dozen greyhounds chase around the racetrack. Suddenly there is the unmistaken sound of the racing call, the music that starts the race and he hears, "And they're off."

Then Dawson begins to be dragged, tied to that rod that the dogs chase after. He is pulled, bouncing, and twisting as the speed of the device accelerates down the track. He hears and feels his wrists break as he twists and turns and is pulled along the dirt track. He cries out in pain. There are no dogs, just Benny being dragged, around and around to his death.

* * *

Early the next morning, the only security guard at the Harlow racecourse—Alfie Baker, an elderly, overweight, contracted agent—woke up with a splitting headache. He remembered a hiss and something sprayed in his face, and now, found himself sitting, with his back against a wall, a surgical mask on his face. Pulling the mask down, he rose, awkwardly, and fought to suppress the impulse to vomit. *What the bloody hell,* he pondered.

The sun was just rising as he stood, bracing himself against the wall near the ticket office above the racetrack. From his vantage point, he looked around, trying to get his bearings. The stands were empty. He looked toward the racetrack and could see what looked like a crumpled sack of clothes near the starting gate. He slowly, and unsteadily, worked his way down, using the seatbacks on the aisle to keep his balance. As he reached the bottom of the steps, he could see that the pile of clothes was a body. Getting closer, he leaned over the railing, trying to identify who this was, but the face was just a raw and bloody mask. Now, he did vomit. Pulling himself together, he pulled out his cell phone from his uniform jacket and placed a 999-emergency call to the Essex Police.

The call was routed to the Force Control Room (FCR) located in Chelmsford, and a unit was dispatched to the racetrack. Upon arriving there, Detective Constable Luke Cox and Constable Gwen

Stewart were led by security guard Alfie Baker—who was feeling a lot better—to the body crumpled up on the track.

"God," said Constable Stewart, "it looks like he was tied to that mechanism and dragged around the track. Horrible."

"Horrible, indeed," added Detective Cox. Turning to the guard, he asked, "Do you know who this might be," pointing to the body.

"No way, but it looks like a man," said Baker.

"I think so," added Cox. To Constable Stewart, he said, "I'm going to call this into the Crime Division. We'll need a medical examiner and a forensic unit down here."

"Should we be putting up a crime scene tape in this area," asked Gwen Stewart, who was relatively new to the force and in training with Detective Constable Cox.

"Yes, get some tape from the boot of the car and we'll string a ten-meter by ten-meter square around here, but the crime scene could be the whole damn racetrack. The Crime Division detectives will take over and it will be their call how they want this mapped out. My guess is that they will turn this over to the Major Investigation Team (MIT), as this obviously in no accident."

* * *

The Essex Police Force is one of the largest, non-metropolitan police forces in the United Kingdom. Over the last dozen years or so, they have undergone a series of reorganizations designed to create specialized units. The Crime Division focused on serious crimes and had their own director of intelligence, a lead senior investigating officer and an upgraded information technology group that supported them. But in an effort to become more efficient, The Major Investigating Team was created, focusing on homicides, abductions, rape, and extortion. They had a similar operating structure as the

Crime Division, with a senior investigating officer (SIO), who pulls in all the resources necessary and directs the course of the investigation of each crime.

Some critics said that this fine tuning of investigative structures, with all the different operating units, led to confusion at times, but Essex's closure of cases was excellent. As one of four in the county, the MIT office in Harlow would assume responsibility for this investigation.

* * *

After Cox's call to headquarters, Senior Investigating Office Lloyd Edwards was dispatched to the racetrack, accompanied by Detective Inspector Hugh Chapman. They were shortly followed by Doctor Rhys Morgan and the forensic team, who, after donning their protective apparel, moved to examine the body, and quickly confirmed it was a man and he was dead.

After a few minutes, Doctor Morgan called out, "I have an ID, Benny Dawson. The cards in his wallet indicate he is a promoter of greyhound racing. The wallet was almost torn free from his trousers, and you can see how the body was ravaged. His clothes are largely in tatters."

SIO Edwards—whose official rank was Detective Chief Inspector—looked intently at the body from over a railing. "Looks like the was tied to the device that simulates a rabbit for the dogs to chase and was dragged around the track."

"Looks that way," said Doctor Morgan. "He likely died from the head trauma he experienced from being dragged by this mechanism. I suspect that this was the cause of death, but we have to get Mr. Dawson back to the morgue before we can confirm that."

'There was a guard on duty last night and he was drugged with something," said Detective Inspector Chapman. "He needs to be tested to see what knocked him out."

"Yes, I'll have one of the forensic investigators do that right away. They will then have to walk the entire racetrack, clad in their booties and protective gear. You can see the grooves in the dirt where Dawson was dragged, and we will have to see what may have fallen out of his clothes as he was pulled along by this device."

"This is obviously a very nasty murder," said DCI Edwards. "Someone tied Mr. Dawson to that chase mechanism bring about a tortuous death. We need to alert the Major Investigating Team, as this case will fall to them. I'll call Detective Chief Inspector Elizabeth Lawrence and get them down here. I will also alert her to get the MICAS—Major Investigative Centralized Administrative Support—Group to dig into everything they can on Benny Dawson. His finances, potential enemies, business relationships, colleagues, and all that. They can put together a deep profile on the guy."

"You know, Lloyd," said DI Chapman, that investigation will have to include all the anti-greyhound racing groups, locally and nationally. This is an extremely hot issue with the animal rights groups and that could be where you start in listing enemies."

"Absolutely. Let's also talk to our intelligence director in the Crime Division. His group may have a ready-made list and profiles of these groups as a lot of their activities would fall into our bailiwick. I'll let DCI Lawrence know. It should save some time."

Chapter Twenty-Three

DCI Lawrence arrived at the Harlow Racetrack accompanied by DI Graham Richards. Lawrence was about fifty of medium height, slightly portly, with blond—turning to gray—hair, pulled back into a bun. Her eyes were light hazel, bright and piercing. She had held the SIO position for almost five years, moving up from the Crime Division. DI Graham Richards was in his forties, tall with brown hair in a very receding hairline. Unlike Lawrence, who was dressed smartly, Richards had somewhat of a rumpled look. Gray sports coat with wrinkles at the elbows and dark gray trousers that had lost their pleat and a white shirt, unbuttoned at the neck.

DCI Edwards apprised the MIT officers of what they had so far. "I'm not sorry we are turning this over to you Liz. As you can see, the forensic team is walking the length of the racetrack to see if anything tore loose from Dawson's clothing. I'm told that this track is three hundred and fifty-four meters long, one of the shortest greyhound tracks in the country, but still a long way to be dragged at forty-five miles per hour."

"That chase mechanism moves that fast?" asked Lawrence.

"That's what the guard told me," replied Edwards. "Maybe it goes a little faster to stay ahead of the racing greyhounds. We started identifying all the relevant parties involved with the Harlow Racetrack;

owners, managers, employees, anyone who can shed some light on this. We'll turn over that list to you. I expect that people associated with this venue will start showing up for work soon. I've placed a constable at the entrance to log-in these people, who they are and what they do, but all will be kept from entering for the time being.

"Doctor Morgan is finished with his examination and is anxious to get the body back to the morgue. I've delayed that until you get to see the crime scene and then give him direction."

"Thanks." Lawrence and Richards then moved closer to where Dawson's body was and from the railing behind the crime scene tape, they looked at the devastation that once was greyhound racing promoter Benny Dawson. She then gave Doctor Morgan the okay to move to body.

"Lloyd, you set everything up nicely and that was a good call to have the Crime Division Intelligence Unit to start identifying and profiling these animal rights groups. Not too long ago there was an incident in the Netherlands involving chimpanzees killing a director in an animal research facility. From what I have heard, this is an avenue they are pursuing there."

"Do you think what happened here could be related to what happened in Holland?" asked Edwards.

"I have no idea, but let's see what our analysts turn up before we get too far ahead of ourselves, You can gather up what the intelligence group puts together and then get that to me."

"Good, will do. Now this is all yours," said Edwards, relieved he was passing this nightmare on.

* * *

Later that day, Doctor Morgan completed his examination and called SIO Lawrence. "Time of death, about three or four in the morning. Cause of death is as we expected, multiple blunt force trauma to the head. His wrists and arms were broken in multiple places as a result of the twisting and turning he endured while being dragged. Whoever did this left about eighteen inches between the rod and his tied wrists, ensuring he would be bouncing and twisting, as he was pulled along. If his wrists were tied directly to the rod, he would have been simply dragged around, probably doing nothing more than tearing up his clothes. They thought this out carefully.

"Dawson's toxicology screen revealed he had flunitrazepam in his system—the drug Rohypnol. He could have been rendered unconscious with this drug or moved to a state of disassociation, not unconscious but not fully conscious, depending on the dose. Rohypnol is that famous date-rape drug used in sexual assaults."

"We see a lot of that when investigating rapes," said Lawrence. "The victim remembers very little of the attack."

"Yes, but in this case it hardly mattered what Dawson might remember. He was dead," said Morgan.

"Anything else doctor?"

"Yes, the guard was rendered unconscious by sevoflurane, an anesthetic commonly used in hospitals in surgery. It acts very quickly and usually has a short recovery time—a benefit after surgery, but the mask on the guard also had sevoflurane present, preventing any quick recovery.

"Lastly, the forensic unit took fingerprints from the device, and there were many. You will have to print all employees that work with that chase mechanism including the control panel adjacent to it. By process of elimination, we can see if any prints do not match the employees, but undoubtedly, our perpetrators would have worn gloves.

"Oh, probably of no significance, but we found a pristine white feather at the starting gate by the control box. Took it with us and it looks like it is from a dove or a pidgeon, but the feather was cut cleanly at its end. It didn't just fall from a bird, but we placed it in evidence and have it here."

Chapter Twenty-Four

"Did you see what happened in England," Gino began his call to Klaus Schickhaus.

"Yes, I was about to call you. No question that this is another connected murder. That whole greyhound racing industry in England—and elsewhere I might add—is under constant attack regarding how the dogs are treated, including doping as we see in horseracing. But greyhound racing is much seedier. I've had our analysts start to put together a primer of British greyhound racing for you, identifying those animal rights groups most active in their protests."

"Thanks, I'll certainly need that."

"I'm also going to call the Chief Constable of the Essex police," Schickhaus added, "and find out who is leading the investigation. They have clearly delineated responsibilities between their Crime Division and the Major Investigation Team, and I sometimes get them crossed-up, but I'll find out who is running the investigation and clear the way for your involvement."

Gino got the information package from Lyon via an E-mail attachment later that day. He immediately sent Antonio and Elia copies, asking Elia to print out a copy and create a new file, "Greyhound Racing – UK."

There are nineteen licensed greyhound racing stadiums in the United Kingdom, dramatically fewer than in years past, largely attributed to the anti-greyhound racing activists—both nationally and internationally—and an increasingly sympathetic public. The sport is heavily regulated, primarily by the Greyhound Board of Great Britain, registering racing dogs and supposedly, fostering greyhound welfare and racing integrity by applying Rules of Racing to racecourse facilities, trainers, kennels, and to the retirement of racing animals.

Along with the nineteen registered racetracks, there are almost one thousand licensed trainers, four thousand kennel staff and close to nine hundred racecourse officials. Greyhound owners number fifteen thousand, with seven to eight thousand greyhounds registered for racing each year.

There is also such a thing as Independent Racing, held at three venues, where centralized registration is not required, nor licensing and no code of practice. In England, despite a national Rules of Racing policy, actual standards for racing and racing integrity are set by local governments—city or county—and there is no real governing nor regulatory authority in these instances.

How are these places allowed to operate? Gino wrote in the margin of the report.

An interesting tangent to greyhound racing in the UK is the fact that 83% of the dogs are bred in Ireland, with six thousand greyhounds exported England each year. With Brexit, it isn't clear how this exportation process will be affected. With the myriad of import/export issues surrounding the execution of Brexit—primarily dealing with goods and materials—the situation involving greyhounds was not on the list of priorities, except to those involved with the sport.

Like bullfighting, greyhound racing is usually staged by a

promoter, working with the various dog racing tracks in the country, along with breeders and trainers. As with horseracing, it is heavily driven by parimutuel betting. Bookmaking is a legal enterprise in England, with off-track betting dwarfing the money wagered at the racetrack venue, estimated to reach £1.6 billion annually. The Bookmaking Afternoon Greyhound Service (BAGS) is a powerful group organized to protect this betting pool. While allocating a share of their profits to greyhound welfare, there was no system in place to measure how this money was spent. In their most important outlay, BAGS paid almost £30 million to racetracks for rights to televise daytime races put on by bookmakers. It has been said that if it were not for BAGS, there would no longer be a sustainable greyhound racing industry in England. While attendance is down at the racetracks over the last fifty years, along with gambling revenue, it still remains a very economically viable sport, thanks to the off-track betting pool.

The primary reason for the decline in popularity of greyhound racing is the greater understanding by the public regarding the treatment of these animals. Despite UK government regulations on the care and welfare of greyhounds, abuse is widespread, giving rise to animal rights groups organized to protect them. GREY 2K USA Worldwide is the largest greyhound protection organization in the world, taking responsibility for the closing of racetracks, first in the USA, and extending to the UK and other countries. Despite retaliation from promoters and bookmakers, GREY 2K USA Worldwide continues to be a leader in documenting abuse of greyhounds.

Gino now understood that, as with the French horseracing industry, the betting pool is the most important issue associated with greyhound racing and the vested interests of those associated with the sport, despite setbacks, retain enough power to sustain it.

Gino now came to the section of the report entitled Greyhound Abuse. The most glaring abuse cited involved keeping racing dogs, for lengthy periods of time in cages at kennels, where the dogs barely fit. Horses are different because of their size. They are kept in stables and stalls, but greyhounds are held in locked cages, alone and uncomfortable and continuously muzzled. In addition, racing dogs suffer from drug abuse, both to hide injuries and to enhance performance. While the betting aspect of greyhound racing can be lucrative, the purses at racetracks are relatively small and many owners find it difficult to make money. They are driven to cut expenses and often kill the animals just to avoid the ongoing costs of feeding and caring for them.

Despite the various greyhound welfare associations and regulatory groups, greyhounds receive no adequate healthcare and are often riddled with fleas, worm infestations, malnutrition, and serious dental problems. Injuries are not always treated. Many injuries are due to poorly maintained racetracks and racing frequency can lead to muscle injuries and broken limbs, largely fatal. The industry is not required to declare greyhound injuries and their self-regulation is non-existent, with the government reluctant to act.

Gino concluded his reading quite depressed. Despite all the other abuses, he kept coming back to keeping these sleek, beautiful animals in cages, almost all the time. The bulls in Spain lived their lives in open ranges, almost pampered in their care until the last twenty minutes of their lives—when they enter the *corrida*. Horses are maintained in corrals at the breeders ranch, exercised and cared for by grooms, preparing them to race. Even at the racecourses, their stable was spacious and their grooming and proper feeding continued. But these greyhounds, in cages 90% of the time, suffered immeasurably.

Chapter Twenty-Five

Gino received a call from Schickhaus, paving the way for him to travel to England and meet with the MIT unit. Chief Constable Hamilton was intrigued by the possibility of the incident at Harlow could be part of a coordinated plot across several countries. No fan of greyhound racing, he, in fact, had rescued a greyhound some years ago at one of the many adoption centers across the country. He, however, abhorred what was done to Benny Dawson.

Schickhaus gave Gino his contact at the Essex police. Chief Detective Inspector Elizabeth Lawrence was the Senior Investigating Officer and her commander is Nigel Fox. Gino was told they looked forward to his arrival at their office in Harlow.

Elia determined it was best to fly to London Stansted Airport in Essex County, east of London and arriving midday on Iberia flight 730 arriving at 8:55 AM. This routing avoids the mayhem usually experienced at Heathrow. It was a two-hour, twenty-five-minute flight to Stansted and Gino was picked up at 9:00 AM by DI Richards, driving, surprisingly, a BMW 535.

Gino remarked that he was glad he was flying into Stansted instead of Heathrow and was surprised it was quite busy and quite large.

Richards laughed, "Stansted is one of the busiest international airports in the country."

Harlow was situated in the west of Essex, on the border with Hertfordshire and London, and the trip to the MIT office was less than twenty minutes. That didn't give the two men a lot of time to talk while on the M 11 motorway, but as they got closer to Harlow, Gino observed that the area was quite pretty.

"This is a relatively new town," Richards said. "Quite a bit of the population lives here but work in London, preferring the green, village-like setting."

As they arrived at the MIT office, Richards explained that this was one of four MIT Divisional Headquarters in Essex, the others in Brentwood, Stanway and Rayleigh. "The Essex police Headquarters is in Chelmsford," Richards added as they were alighting from the car, "only about thirty kilometers from our office. Less than a half-hour away, so coordination is not a burden."

The office was relatively small, in a two-story, Tudor-style building, and Richards led Gino to SIO Lawrence's office on the first floor. As they walked, Richards said, "MIT investigators are here on the first floor—pointing to about a half-dozen desks with men and women either on the phone or in front of their desk-top computer. Upstairs is our analytics/computer center as well as the office of Divisional Commander, Nigel Fox. In the basement there are three interview rooms as well as the lock-up section. Nobody in there right now," turning and smiling at Gino.

Lawrence greeted Gino warmly. "We are going to put you to work right away, Detective Chief Superintendent. Our commander, Nigel Fox wanted to be advised as soon as you arrived as we would like for you to give us a synopsis of the other killings that Interpol is investigating." Fox then entered Lawrence's office and greeted

Gino with a firm handshake. He was probably in his upper fifties, of medium height and bald except for the gray fringe around his ears and back of his head, very neatly trimmed and wore black-rimmed glasses. Lawrence directed Commander Fox and Gino to leather armchairs in front of her disk, and Richards moved to a chair off to the right.

Fox opened the conversation by stating, "As DCI Lawrence—our Senior Investigating Officer—has probably informed you that before we brief you on the incident at the Harlow Racetrack—which is not far from here—I thought it would be useful for you to give us a summary of the incidents you are investigating in Madrid, Paris and Amsterdam. I have been told by your Chief of Criminal Investigation, Klaus Schickhaus, that you believe they are all connected somehow."

"Gladly," said Gino. "And yes, we do believe they are connected in some kind of heinous plot." He then proceeded to give them a synopsis of each of the three murders. "We believe they are connected because of the white feather found at each of the scenes, and the fact that each of the victims had been a target—either directly or by association with animal abuse—of animal rights groups in each city."

"Doctor Morgan said the forensic team had found a white feather near the starting gate at Harlow," said DCI Lawrence.

"Damn," said Gino. "I am sure that the feather you found had been cleanly cut..."

"It was. Doctor Morgan said it could not have fallen for a bird flying in the area."

"We know that the feathers we have found were from a dove and we have started an analysis of DNA to see if was from the same bird, or different birds, but it probably doesn't matter, unless the culprit behind this keeps a dove in a birdcage in his or her home," said Gino. "We'll send you the details of this analysis and suggest you do a DNA test on the feather you have in evidence. I'll also have the full report of these murders from each of the investigating officers sent to you as well, and once we have your reports, we can add that to our analysis.

"Our frustration is that we have not been able to identify a viable suspect in each case. The most likely suspects—or at least persons of interest—are all within the animal rights movements. Anti-bullfighting activists, horseracing abuse organizations and anti-animal research advocates have become our primary area of investigation, but anytime we think we have a lead, the persons of interest have rock-solid alibis, and were nowhere near the scene of the crime. From the brief research I have reviewed, anti-greyhound racing movements, and Benny Dawson's role as a promoter in this sport, fits in with the other incidents in Madrid, Paris and Amsterdam."

"We have had our intelligence units including our Major Investigation Support Group—MICAS—start to put together a list of the anti-greyhound racing organizations in the country with profiles of the groups and their leaders, Investigators are also going through Dawson's files and computer, as well as government regulatory agencies to identify complaints or threat made against Dawson. That may even be completed by now," said Lawrence.

"After you have eliminated any persons of interest not related to animal rights groups—who knows, he may have a deranged ex-wife who hasn't received her alimony—I suggest we start down that animal rights avenue and see if your MICAS group has come up with any most likely suspects," added Gino. "I can help you with that, going over what we did in the other cases as a protocol for this investigation."

"That sound good," said Commander Fox. "I'll leave you with Lawrence and Richards to go over the incident here, and then we can start investigating the activist groups." He then rose and left.

"That works," said Gino to DCI Lawrence. "Interpol did an analysis for me on anti-greyhound racing organizations here. We can print it out or download it from my laptop or I can just E-mail it to you.now."

"E-mail it," said Lawrence, handing Gino her car with her E-mail address. "We'll make copies to work with and cross-match your data with our work."

"One thing I should add," said Gino. "In each of the other countries, there was significant public interest and outcry regarding animal cruelty. After reporting on the crime and the victim, the press published ongoing reports describing the suffering of the animals. The anti-bullfighting furor was never so loud. Horseracing in France is under intense scrutiny and in Holland, there are pickets around research and pharmaceutical organizations experimenting with animals. Not just the animal rights activists, but more of the public involved, even families with children holding plush rabbits and monkey dolls. I expect that will happen here also, so whomever is behind this, they seem to be making their point."

It took about a half-hour for Lawrence and Richards to detail the murder at the Harlow racetrack "We have interviewed all people associated with the racetrack, including employees. Trainers and Harlow officials, but we have no suspects. There is CCTV where the dogs are kept and at the ticket office, but nothing showed up. We are checking roadside cameras for traffic from 2:00 AM to 5:00 AM but haven't heard back from the camera monitors yet. The racetrack people are going nuts because we have closed them down, as the racetrack itself is a crime scene, but I expect we can allow them to resume business now," said Lawrence.

"Before you do that, I would like to visit the crime scene," said Gino. "I am curious about that device with the rabbit that the greyhounds chase."

"Sure, we can do that now," said DI Richards. "And by the way, it's not a rabbit, just a wooly, black sock, pulled over the end of the rod that protrudes into the racetrack. They did use rabbits at one time, I am told, but maybe the anti-rabbit abuse activists got the industry to change to the wooly sock," smiling as he rose from his chair.

Gino then accompanied Richards to his car and they drove the short distance to the racetrack. Calling ahead, he arranged for one of the racetrack officials to meet them at the ticket office above the starting gate, The official explained that Harlow have one of the shortest tracks in circumference in the country, 354 meters, where other tracks are 400 meters of more. The dogs can run as fast as 45 miles per hour—75 kilometers per hour—so the mechanism with the mechanical hare is set to run slightly faster, keeping the charging greyhounds at least ten meters behind it, "A typical race," he explained, "is only about twenty to twenty-five seconds long,"

"So, Dawson was dragged for only twenty-five seconds?" asked Gino.

"Yes. We talked to Doctor Morgan about that" replied Richards. "Being dragged in the sand for twenty-five seconds at 45 mph is an eternity. The sand erased Dawson's face and the twisting and turning, from being tied by his wrists to the mechanical hare, can cause immeasurable damage, as it did."

They looked over the control panel and the rod with the black sock—a new one—and the control panel that starts and stops the mechanism. They then walked around the facility and saw where greyhounds are kept prior to the race. In cages, he saw, barely large enough for the dog to turn around it. No dogs were present at this time.

"Were there any caged dogs here on the night of the attack?" asked Gino.

"Yes," the official replied. "At least twelve. That's primarily why we had nightwatchman here. But now we see that it isn't very difficult to disable him. We are going to make changes to ensure that the dogs are protected."

"Hard to see how they are protected by being in those cages," Gino said, and he walked away.

Chapter Twenty-Six

Back at the MIT office, after a quick stop at a local pub for a sandwich, Gino and DI Richards first went to DCI Lawrence's office and them the three of them moved to a nearby conference room. Black-covered portfolios were on a rectangular table, one set for each of them.

"Before we start looking at these activist groups," Lawrence began, "we uncovered information from Dawson's computer. He was in debt and owed money to several bookmakers. Looks like he was an avid gambler and from the various bookmaking websites he frequented, he may have owed around £50,000. A financial check revealed that in no way he could have repaid these debts from his normal revenue. This is what the tech guys found so far. It could be worse."

"I know bookmaking is legal here, but it always had a kind-of unsavory image. You know, smoke-filled back rooms, and all that. What about in the UK?" Gino asked.

"A world of difference," said Lawrence. Here, they are major sophisticated operations that cover all sports—in all countries—as well as casino games, video games, dealing with all major currencies. They use the most up to date technology you can imagine. What Dawson was involved in is small potatoes to what these bookmakers handle. There are hundreds of them, big and small, and not all are in the UK, doing business here, but all are licensed by the government. Horseracing is probably where this business started out, but today you can probably bet on how fast it takes for a chicken to cross the road."

"And we know who Dawson owed money to?"

"Yes. Bookerboys, Spreadsheets and Universal Betting, all based in the UK. Most of Dawson's gambling was on horse races, but he also placed bets on football matches—your soccer—and occasionally he played slot machines. Go to one of their websites and you can see the plethora of things to bet on, and in any currency, including bitcoin.

"God," remarked Gino, "this opens up a totally new avenue to investigate. There was nothing like this in the other countries, and no victim had serious financial issues. Would it not be past he bookmakers to take revenge against someone in debt to them?"

"Hard to say. Most of these enterprises are quite legitimate, with very lucrative business operations. Some are held in higher regard than others and most require a deposit to bet. This could be as little as £5 or £10, but that does nothing to cover losses. There are a fair number of bookmakers that are—using your words—unsavory, and there are many appeals by bettors to the on-line United Kingdom Gaming Commission and their UKGC-backed Resolve system. Appeals can also be made directly to bookmakers via the ABB—Association of British Bookmakers—a loose coalition of the UK's most prestigious bookies, but the one's Dawson owed money to are not part of this group. But of course, bookmakers have their own systems and can lock-out a bettor. In some cases, they can let their lock-out be known, alerting others of a risky gambler.

"But getting back to your question, there are also smaller bookmaking shops, store-front betting parlors that number in the thousands, which do not do an on-line business, and I cannot attest to the character of such operations. However, from what we have seen, Dawson's gambling seemed to have been all on-line."

"Well, DCI Lawrence, this opens up another person's-of-interest group, but is the money owed by Dawson enough for one of these organizations to murder him and eat the losses?" asked Gino. "You know, setting an example for others?"

"I doubt it," replied Lawrence. "Not the licensed, on-line bookmakers. They just make too much money. Some of the smaller betting shops, maybe, as a £20,000 to £30,000 debt would be more important to them. But to your question, would they be willing to eat the debt and kill the guy? Not likely, but not out of the question. Nevertheless, with this situation, we have another avenue to pursue in addition to the anti-greyhound racing activists."

* * *

Returning to the issue of the anti-greyhound racing groups, Gino had a suggestion. "In the other countries, we profiled both the larger, international, and European animal rights groups, separately from the local organizations, where we felt there was a greater propensity to more aggressive and violent activism. I think we should eliminate— no not eliminate, but put off to the side, these larger European and international groups. They tend to focus more on lobbying and public education. Let's focus, at least initially, on those local groups, possibly more suspect."

"I agree," said Lawrence. Let's go through the information we have in front of us, make notes on who might have a greater propensity toward violence."

Gino asked that a whiteboard be set up in the room, with colored marking pens to start listing groups of interest. Both the Interpol and

MIT/Crime Division analysts gave them a good head-start on where to start looking. After more than an hour of study, Gino rose and started the discussion.

"As agreed, we have put off to the side. PETA, the European Association of Dog and Animal Welfare, National Animal Welfare Trust, Humane Society International, RSPCA—Royal Society for the Prevention of Cruelty to Animals, Grey 2K USA-Worldwide as well as the UK's Hound for Heroes." Moving to the whiteboard, Gino started writing. "Now let's review which groups we want to look into further as a start. Call out any others you want to add.

- Retired Greyhound Trust
- CAGED – Campaign Against Greyhound Exploitation and Death
- ALIC – A Lifetime in Cages: End Greyhound Racing
- AFG - Action For Greyhounds
- Greys – Cruel and Unusual Punishment
- God's Gift- The Greyhound
- League Against Cruel Sports

"Not listed, and not part of our suspect list, are all the government agencies charged with animal welfare, like the Greyhound Board of Great Britain, the Greyhound Racing Association and other county regulatory groups that are totally ineffective. This has nothing to do with the murder of Dawson, but I had to get that off my chest."

"I couldn't agree with you more," said Lawrence, "but add 'Bookmakers" to the list, out to protect their betting pool."

"Okay, good point. As to the activist groups, all of them have a very legitimate mission and in some ways, are well respected, but they are also the most vocal groups. Further, as we have seen elsewhere, splinter groups of cells can split from very legitimate organizations, to take more aggressive action, without taking responsibility."

"Anonymous," said Richards.

"Yes, anonymous, which is why we have to go deeper into each group. Who are the leaders? Who are their members? We need to profile the individuals. Let's see how far we can go with the data we have and then begin a round of informal contacts as a first step in getting deeper. Anything intrigue you so far?"

"Yes," offered Richards. "The issue of caging these animals, I believe, is a very emotional one. In fact, there is one of the groups with that name; ALIC—A Lifetime In Cages. I'd start there, as well as CAGED—Coalition Against Greyhound Exploitation and Death. Very passionate animal rights groups, but the issue is so emotional, radical confrontation is not out of the question."

"God's Gift - The Greyhound, also intrigues me. When you bring religion into the issue, it could foster extreme counter measures, in the name of God," offered Lawrence.

"Okay," said Gino, "we get your guys and gals to do a deep dive into all of these groups; backgrounds on all the leaders and key players in each organization, and then we go to Phase Two."

"Why don't we call it a day guys," said DCI Lawrence. It has been a long day especially for you Detective Chief Superintendent."

"That's fine. It has been a long day and a fresh start tomorrow makes sense, but no more Detective Chief Superintendent. I'm Gino."

Laughing, DCI Lawrence said, "And I'm Liz and he's Graham."

DI Richards suddenly jumped to his feet. "Gosh, I forgot. I still have your luggage in my car. I never asked if you had a place to stay for the night."

Gino laughed. Yes, I'm fine. They booked me at the Holiday Inn Express. Not the most elegant of accommodations, but my administrator said it is right in town. She thought it would be convenient."

"Oh, it is alright. You could almost walk to it. By the way, are you free for dinner?"

"Sure Graham, I look forward to it."

* * *

Dinner, at a local pub, was pleasant and friendly and after a satisfying, complimentary English breakfast at the Holiday Inn, Gino was able to walk to MIT headquarters. Convenience indeed, topped elegance.

"The staff worked overnight and got us a bit deeper, as you requested, Gino," said Liz." I got in early so I took the liberty to add our list, citing leadership in these organizations. That same information is printed and on the table."

The list now was revised to;

- ALIC - A Lifetime in Cages: End Greyhound Racing, Maidstock, Kent
  - Jeremy Ainsworth- leader, IT Manager, Barkly Bank, Ashford
  - Edwin Bolton – nuclear scientist at Dungeness Power Plant
  - Terry Sinclair – tour guide, Leeds, and Canterbury Cathedral. Sister Alice married to Bolton
  - Alice Bolton – runs greyhound adoption center, Maidstock, HQ for ALIC.
- God's Gift – The Greyhound. Gloucester, UK
  - Paul Westlake – former missionary, Lutheran church, Uganda. Professor Agriculture, Hartpury College

- o Brian Winchell – Asst Prof, Veterinary Medicine, Hartpury
- o David Tennison – Prof Vet Med, Hartpury
- Greys – Cruel and Unusual Punishment, Manchester
  - o Elspeth Graham – Real estate agent, office HQ for Greys
  - o Fern Cranston – ticket agent, Brit Air, Manchester
  - o Peggy Frost – set designer, Manchester opera
- CAGED – Campaign Against Greyhound Exploitation and Death
  - o Disguises location, suspect London. Disguises names due to attacks against them. Funded from national donations
  - o Rita, founder
  - o Mike, co-founder, director promotion
  - o Sandi, project coordinator/data research
- AFG - Action For Greyhounds, Norwich, Norfolk, UK
  - o Leaders anonymous
  - o Promotes hounds as pets – foster and forever homes (adoptions)
  - o Campaigns to abolish greyhound racing

"After further study, Retired Greyhound Trust and League Against Cruel Sports were removed from the priority list as the analysts thought the organizations listed here," pointing to the whiteboard, "offered the most promise, or we still have more digging to do."

Gino looked over the list, then walked to a table at the side of the room that had some pasties and tea. "Hey, guys, I love your tea, but any chance of getting some coffee in here?"

"Bloody Yanks," said Richards while laughing, "I'll get you some," and he left the conference room.

Focusing again on the whiteboard, Gino remarked, "By more

digging to do, I assume you are referring to CAGED and AFG. Seems we are missing some pieces with them."

"That's true," replied Lawrence. "CAGED and AFG are well known in terms of what they do, but they try to keep their leaders and membership obfuscated. Donations go to P.O. boxes, registered to lawyers. Leadership and membership lists are held by these legal firms and not published. Look at CAGED, Rita, Mike and Sandi appear on their web side, but we doubt that is their real names. Apparently, some years ago, there were attacks on members, retaliation for their efforts to ban greyhound racing. Thereafter, both groups went kind-of underground. Even tax records don't help because we don't really know the names of leadership and they probably take no compensation from the non-profit entity, so nothing to track down there. Further, no one seems to care that these people are anonymous. The only ones who want to dig into this are those groups that want to curb their activism. The press doesn't care and neither does anyone in government. They publish pamphlets, send reports to regulatory agencies, and organize any protests or picketing via E-mail to membership, citing time and place of activity and a strict protocol for actions. Can we really unmask leadership? Probably, but for now, I'd rather concentrate on the others, which have shown some aggressiveness in the past."

"Sounds reasonable," said Gino, suddenly distracted as Graham returned, toting pump dispenser with coffee. "Good man, thank you," Gino said, moving to the table for his dose of caffeine.

"Unfortunately, these others are spread out in different jurisdictions with their own police forces and investigative teams," continued Lawrence.

"Can we bring them in on this?" asked Gino.

"Theoretically, yes, but it would be a bureaucratic nightmare and slow things down considerably."

"So, what do you propose?"

"I think that your approach to keep initial contacts informal, not as official interrogations, might work. The MIT is just seeking to learn more about the organizations we've identified, to better understand the importance of the anti-greyhound racing mission and objectives in England. How they work? How are they funded? How successful are they? What could be done better, especially at the national level? Because they have not been identified as suspects, there will be no need to caution them—a bit slippery, I admit—as we are just seeking greater understanding. With this approach, we may be able to steer clear of involving other jurisdictions. This will have to be cleared by Commissioner Cox, and possibly, Chief Constable Hamilton of the Essex Police. Assuming it's a go, we'll organize teams of detectives to make first contacts. We'll divide up the list and provide each with a discussion protocol, as you did in the other countries."

"Two comments," added Gino. "First, I would include a couple of the 'above reproach' organizations, like the RSPCA, Greys 2K USA-Worldwide, or even PETA, if they have an office here in England. That would make the cover of just information gathering more credible. Second, any plans to dig further into the anonymous groups?"

"My initial thought is to approach the Greyhound Board of Great Britain," responded Lawrence. "Because all these activist groups have to be registered, it could be that in the past, there were names associated with these organization— before they went underground. Older tax records may also have included names. It's just a digging exercise and I'll let our analysts get out and handle this."

"I'd certainly like to sit in on some of these meetings," said Gino.

"I would too," said Lawrence, "but for the first contacts, I'd leave it to our detectives. After we get their feedback and impressions, we can determine which groups need a closer look and a more formal interview."

"Fine, that's how we handled it in the other countries. In the meantime, I'll return to Madrid and also get Lyon to dig deeper into the list we generated. Their world-wide database might reveal something we have not uncovered yet. It will take a few days, or more, to make those initial contacts, assuming the people we want to reach are around. Thereafter, I will return and perhaps you and I," looking at Liz, "or Graham and I can participate in round two."

"As Fox said yesterday, 'that's a plan,' but we have to get him to sign off on this first," concluded Lawrence.

Chapter Twenty-Seven

Returning to the hotel to collect his luggage and check out, Gino placed a call to Klaus Schickhaus. Giving him the names of the activist groups, they identified as *of interest,* and MIT's preliminary contact plan, Gino said, "Klaus, the analysts did an outstanding job. This was a most comprehensive list of the anti-greyhound racing groups in the UK, but I need them to go deeper in the five I just gave you. Absolutely everything they can find about those individuals associated with them, and whatever profiles they can come up with. The MIT group will also pursue this, including any police encounters with members or supporters, but Lyon's computers may be able to go faster and deeper.

"And while you're at it, we came up with a few bookmakers that Dawson owed money to: Bookerboys, Spreadsheet and Universal Betting. Find out who runs these organizations, any nefarious connections, and their finances. See if there is any history of legal issues, police encounters and violence. You know the scope of things we'd be interested in. They are based in the UK but do business globally."

"We'd likely be duplicating the efforts of the Essex MIT group," offered Schickhaus.

"I don't doubt that" commented Gino, "but I don't want to leave anything to chance. And speaking about leaving anything to chance, I should add that Fox and Chief Constable Hamilton have to sign off on our contact plan because it involves other jurisdictions outside of Essex,"

"Involving other jurisdictions may prompt them to consult with the National Crime Agency before giving any green light. It now rates as a national issue not just a county one. The crime was in Essex County, but the activist groups you identified are in other parts of the country"

"So, the National Crime Agency would get involved?" asked Gino.

"Likely," replied Schickhaus. "It's a relatively new agency, consolidating responsibilities from other crime units. Terrorism is their primary focus, but the NCA is charged to investigate all crimes it deems to be warranted. And the NCA is also a point of liaison for Interpol. We have had contact with the NCA's director general over the last few years regarding human trafficking investigations as well as exploitation of children and two instances of serial killers. This investigation would easily fall into the serial killer category, and we probably should be talking with them."

"Let's leave this to the MIT and Essex Police to bring up," said Gino.

"Well, one way or another, however, the NCA should be brought into this, and if truth be told, their Serious Crime Analysis section could be equal to ours. My only concern is that with the constant reorganizations going on in the UK's criminal investigation units, the right hand may not know what the left hand is doing."

"I can understand," remarked Gino. "After 9/11, multitudes of intelligence units were created and that did cause some confusion regarding who was responsible for what. Things were not always done in a timely and efficient manner."

"I think that is what the UK is trying to avoid with these ongoing consolidations and the creation of uniquely, specialized units, but they too haven't achieved a real level of efficiency yet. Plus, you know how each unit wants to protect its turf, so they are still working things out," commented Schickhaus.

"Well, as I said, I'd prefer for the Essex police to take the lead in bringing in any national agency. You are probably right that Hamilton will bring in the NCA at some point but I don't want that to be initiated by Interpol. Lawrence is setting up these informal, informational contacts now, and I'd prefer for her to sell it to her bosses. I don't want us to add bureaucracy to this phase of her investigation," said Gino. "If they want to bring in the NCA, let them initiate it."

"Okay, I'll go with your recommendation for now, but be prepared for the NCA to become a collaborator in this, if not taking over the investigation entirely. You may also find yourself in London someday soon, meeting with them," concluded Schickhaus.

* * *

Before catching his flight from Stansted to Madrid, Gino called Mercedes and told her he would be home for dinner, but first wanted to go to his Interpol office and update his team on the developments in England. He made it back to his office before the normal close of business that afternoon, but typical of Interpol investigations, the close of business was a shadowy figure of speech. Theirs was not a nine-to-five operation.

Entering the office, he first stopped at the coffee machine for a double cup of *café solo*, Spain's espresso coffee. With cup in hand, he proceeded to give Juanes, Gonzalez, and Elia Castilla an update of the situation is the UK.

"Apart from the activist groups, the wrinkle in England is the role of bookmakers in the sport of greyhound racing—in all sports for that matter—and the fact that Benny Dawson owed money to three of them. Almost £50,000, with no visible means to repay these debts. This could easily be a motive for the killing of Dawson, and DCI Lawrence and DI Richards were investigating this angle. But of course, there was another white feather, so the link to animal rights groups remains a key direction of the focus there."

He also alerted them to the possibility of the UK's National Crime Agency getting involved, and perhaps even becoming Interpol's primary contact on this crime. "Time will tell." Gino added.

For dinner that evening, Mercedes had prepared a *tortilla Español*—potato, onion, and egg omelet—and a green salad, and crusty bread. Something artisanal, complimented by a nice Rioja wine.

"I've been thinking," Mercedes said in between bites of the tasty omelet and sips of wine, "that it would be worthwhile to set up a teleconference with all of the lead investigators in this string of murders. Myself, Capitaine Cousteau, Inspector Arden or Chief Inspector Aaldenberg in Amsterdam and DCI Lawrence. You said Lawrence seemed to be quite capable. It may be worthwhile to have each of us to provide insights on the incident in each of our countries. I know you shared with them our reports, but sometimes conversations can be more revealing than reading the crime reports."

"That's a great idea Mercedes, but it would be best to wait until DCI Lawrence completes both phases of our contact plan. First the informal meetings and then the more formal interviews with the leaders of each group, like we did in the other countries. After phase II—and I'll be participating in some of the follow-up interrogations—it would be more meaningful for all of the lead investigators to share their thoughts, suspicions and frustrations with each other. You'd all be working with more or less the same experiences by that time. When we get to that point, I can get one of the techies from Interpol to set the whole thing up. I'd like to participate in that session, not formally, but to be a silent ears dropper if that's all right with you."

"That might prove to be embarrassing. Someone might say what an a-hole that Interpol guy is, Gino."

Gino almost spit out the wine he was drinking after Mercedes made that remark. "Well, thanks a lot. I guess it could happen, but I'll let you think about it."

"I guess it would be okay to bring up *La Pluma Blanca*. From what I understand all the investigations have kept that issue out of the press, but the white feather has appeared in all of the crime scenes," said Mercedes.

"We definitely have to, knowing that will put Victoria Valenzuela in the cross-hairs. But if we are going to share, there is no way you can keep this from them, but that issue must stay with just the four of you. Valenzuela's name should not find its way into any of the other investigator's files," Gino stated.

"Got it, and I agree. Of course, Valenzuela was the first of your perfect alibis, followed by the same dead-end in the other countries, regarding suspects or persons of interest. It both intrigues me because we still may not be looking in the right places. Besides intriguing me, it also bothers me—a lot. I really look forward to having the other investigators open-up and discuss this and challenge each other. From what you told me, and from what you know of the investigation here, none of us have a viable fallback. We are stuck in neutral. After all these weeks—albeit the UK's investigation is just starting—we have found no other primary suspects beyond the few we have some suspicions about, and all of them have been essentially cleared. Such violent attacks, with such notoriety and publicity, and we are all failing. We are not getting pressure from the public, but the press continues to hound us, and in Madrid, the pressure from my superiors and from a few branches of the government, is constant. They really are losing patience. I'm sure it is the same in Paris and Amsterdam, and eventually in the UK. We have to find a way to break through this wall of, what? —fog?"

"I know," said Gino. "On the other cases you and I have been involved with, we have always been able to find a way forward, no matter how impossible the situation may have seemed. We brought an end to a plot to convert Spain into an Islamic monarchy, when such a conspiracy was unimaginable. We found and returned abducted women from desert kingdoms in the Middle East, avoiding a diplomatic nightmare in the process. The killings we are dealing with now are tame in comparison, quite creative and daring, but nowhere near the potential level of global impact that we dealt with before. These are serial killings, and while we haven't found that way forward yet, we will."

* * *

DCI Lawrence called Gino the next afternoon and confirmed the suspicions he and Schickhaus had discussed. "Chief Constable Hamilton is supporting our plan," she began," but felt compelled to alert the National Crime Agency of the situation. Hamilton is friends with the NCA's director general, as he was promoted to this position from being Chief Constable in Oxfordshire, the same position Hamilton has in Essex County. The director general is allowing us to carry out our phase I of informational contacts but has assigned a liaison officer—a Lionel Churchill out of the Directorate of Intelligence—to work with us. The NCA wants to use their Violent Crime Linkage Analysis System—ViCLAS—to do the deep analysis we talked about. Their initial reaction to probing the anti-greyhound racing groups was suspect, as these groups are generally regarded as the good guys, trying to stop the abuse of these animals. However, they recognized the possibility of more radical forms of activism flowing out of a benevolent mission. Plus, as greyhound racetracks are spread throughout the country, with protests occurring in each of these locales, they felt that their system would be better able to identify behaviors that warrant further investigation. That works for us, Gino, so we have relinquished that aspect of our investigation—behavioral analytics—to NCA.

"You know, we get to see the same police dramas on USA television, here in the UK. We see how the FBI is not always regarded as a constructive, collaborating partner by local police agencies. Well, the NCA has often been referred to as the 'British FBI,' so barriers to collaboration have popped up. Each agency wants to run the show, but so far, what the NCA is offering to us makes sense, We probably have Chief Constable Hamilton to thank for getting support from the NCA without them taking over.

"So, the MIT will continue with our plan and I'll let you know when phase II is set to begin. Oh, I've been told that you will get a call from Lyon, advising you of this collaboration, that now includes Essex, Interpol and the NCA. That will require your meeting with Lionel Churchill, to apprise him of the Interpol investigations in the other countries."

"Well, Liz, I think we have dodged a bullet. Good luck and keep me informed. By the way, have you contacted the bookmakers yet?" asked Gino.

"Meetings are being set up now and Graham and I will start interviews tomorrow."

Chapter Twenty-Eight

Discussions with the managers of Universal Betting and Spreadsheets were set up for the following day, with Bookerboys scheduled for the day after. Universal Betting's operation was in the North of London, in a modern-looking glass and steel cube-like building with many antennas and satellite dishes visible from the street. Its managing director, Aben Choudhary, London born of Indian descent, was a graduate of the London School of Economics. An elegant-looking man, about fifty, with a light brown complexion and thick gray-black hair, combed back. He was dressed in a bespoke gray, double-breasted, pin-striped suit, with a white starched shirt and a blue and gray tie—all undoubtedly from Saville Row tailors. His baritone voice was typical London-British.

After introductions, Choudhary said, "Please call me Abbie, everyone does." Not surprisingly, he knew nothing of Benny Dawson.

"You have to understand that our everyday betting operation includes many thousands of individuals, betting on every sporting event imaginable as well as casino games. There is no way that I would have any knowledge of an individual bettor, unless they were regular high-rollers or owned their own Arab Emirate," he laughed. "What did you say his debt to Universal Betting was?"

"I didn't, but records we uncovered indicated it was £19,000," said DI Richards.

"I would not say that is an insignificant amount, but to be honest, such a debt would never be brought to my attention. Further, our system is so sophisticated, people are rarely involved. Off-track betting is totally computerized and is based on algorithms profiling the bettor, The system automatically shuts off the individual at a certain debt level and alerts are sent to him or her. I can get one of our analysts to find his profile and see what actions the system took. His history of betting, —racing, sports, casino games, whatever— payments, late-payments, failed payments are all part of his individual algorithm, and the software manages the process."

"Can you get that information for us, Abbie? We need to see the kind of profile you have on Benny Dawson," asked Lawrence.

"That information is confidential, Detective Chief Inspector."

"Mr. Dawson is deceased, Abbie, so confidentiality is not an issue here."

"In that case, give me a minute," and he pulled out a cell phone— the latest I-phone by its looks—and pushed one button to make a call. He spoke for not more than ten seconds and ended the call. "This will only take a few minutes. Can I offer you any refreshments, tea, coffee, water, anything?"

Both Lawrence and Richards politely declined the offer and Choudhary pointed out the array of sporting events being broadcasted on the dozen or more large-screen televisions around the large, open area of the facility. In five minutes, a young woman—also very nicely dressed—descended a chrome and black marble staircase from a balcony that overlooked the open area below and handed Abbie a file folder

"Our servers and a group of analysts work up there," pointing to the upper lever which was surrounded by a chrome-railed barrier. "The fact that poor Mr. Dawson is deceased," Choudhary said as he flipped through the pages in the file folder, "is a cause of some concern as we might be out £19,000," he laughed.

"It says here that Dawson is—or was—a frequent gambler, not wagering substantial sums and his record of payments is spotty and you are right, he owes us £19,000, from bets made over the last sixty days. His shut-off would come at £20,000, but a letter was sent to him last week alerting him to the deficit."

"And what happens if he doesn't pay the debt," asked Richards.

"First, an alert would be sent out to the bookmaking industry advising all other operations to proceed with caution with the individual, stating he has been cut-off from any further wagering with us. Second, the system triggers an alert to our legal department which could take action with his employer, seeking to garnish his wages because of the debt. That could be tricky and the issue is likely to end up in court."

"So basically, you would sue him directly, as there is no employer to go through. He is self-employed," added Richards.

"Absolutely," replied Abbie.

"You don't send out debt collectors, to visit him?" asked Lawrence.

"No, not in this case, but we have sent lawyers to visit clients, prior to taking legal action. Usually this would take place at the employer's place of business as a follow-up to written advisories. We have too big an operation, a well-respected operation, and we are registered with the government, so all our actions are legitimate, transparent and in accordance with the law and the UK betting authorities. But again, I must emphasize that much of these actions are generated by our software system and only at the very end of the chain, will actual people be involved."

"But as managing director, you do get reports of unpaid debts," Lawrence pressed.

"I get a report everyday identifying income and indebtedness, but Dawson's debt will likely not appear. It would fall into the 'all others' category until it reaches £20,000. What happens sometimes, is that if a better knows he is approaching a cut-off level, he starts betting with another bookmaker, building indebtedness there."

If Universal Betting was one of the earliest bookies he owed money to, this could have occurred with Dawson, sending him elsewhere to continue his wagering, thought Lawrence.

"Well, thank you Abbie, you have been very helpful and we appreciate your time. It has been enlightening and I wish you luck in getting back your £19,000," said DCI Lawrence.

Next up was Spreadsheets, also based in the Greater London area. The managing director wasn't in—being unexpectedly called away for an issue in the European continent—and Richards and Lawrence met with Operations Director, Clyde McFadden. The Spreadsheets operation was in a stand-alone, concrete, and tinted-glass structure, three stories tall. Whatever tint they used on the glass made it totally reflective and impossible to see inside. Once inside, like Universal Betting, flat-screen televisions were located throughout the first floor, beyond the reception area, televising events from all over the world. A second level was enclosed with floor to ceiling glass overlooking the open, circular area below.

McFadden was in shirtsleeves, open collar at the neck, with crisp, pleated black trousers and high-end athletic shoes, bearing the Nike logo, that probably cost north of £300. He was young, not yet forty, with long, blond hair, flowing over his collar, and with a healthy tan. He would look at home at the helm of a sailboat. McFadden had read about Dawson's demise in the newspaper.

It was much the same story. An operation totally run by computer software with detailed algorithms managing the process. Dawson's £14,000 debt had not triggered a hold on accepting further bets yet, but a computer-generated alert was issued, with no threat of legal action, just advising Dawson he was nearing his betting ceiling.

"Sometimes, this kind of an alert drives a gambler to another bookmaker, even if no hold is placed on the account," explained McFadden. "Then the guy starts over again."

Lawrence had indeed determined that Universal Betting was the earliest wagering cycle. The betting dates placed Spreadsheets, second, *which probably then drove Dawson to Bookerboys,* thought Lawrence. But once again, no suspicions arose from this visit.

Bookerboys was the seediest of the bookmakers visited. Based almost on the border with Buckinghamshire, at the West of London, in an industrial sector of the city. Their brick and timber building looked old, but not shoddy. It may have been a residence back in the day and bore a pub-like placard hanging above the front double, wooden doors, with the name Bookerboys above a pair of white dice. Inside there was a small reception office and once through, a large open area again, with TV monitors all around, mounted on dark, wood-paneled walls, broadcasting mostly casino games—roulette, overhead views of blackjack tables and rotating slot-machine dials. Two monitors were showing what could have been video games, with car chases and explosions. The floor was worn linoleum. Nothing like the bright, airy operations of Universal Betting and Spreadsheets. The Floor Manager—they change floor managers every six hours and operate 24/7—Reggie Lightfoot, was of short stature, overweight, almost bald and was in a short-sleeved shirt, with the shirt having trouble staying in his trousers. He *looked* like a bookie—the old stereotype—not a businessman. He had an unlit, half-cigar in his mouth.

After introductions, Lightfoot said, in a very Liverpool accent, "No smoking allowed in here, but I am permitted to chomp on a cigar, as long as I don't light it," he laughed.

Richards and Lawrence explained the situation with the deceased Dawson, which drew no reaction from Lightfoot. As to Bookerboys operation, Lightfoot's description mirrored what Lawrence and Richards heard from the bookmakers visited the day before. However, each bookmaker, Lightfoot explained, build their own system of algorithms for each bettor, based on their wagering history, managed by the criteria they build into the profile,

Advised of Dawson's debt to Bookerboys, Lightfoot asked for Dawson's file to be brought to him. He had no problem discussing Dawson's betting history, certainly not evoking the cloak of confidentiality.

"Yes, we see that his current debt to us is £13,000. That wouldn't have triggered any alert. If the debt exceeded forty-five days, or if it rose to £15,000—the ceiling set for him by the software program— computer-generated letters and E-mails would have been issued." Flipping through the pages in the file he was holding, he remarked, "He has had a couple of advisory letters in the past but was never in serious arears. Doesn't look like any alerts were issued lately, but unless his check is in the mail, that £13,000 goes up in smoke, unless we can get it from his estate."

"Not likely Mr. Lightfoot. I don't believe Dawson had much of an estate at the time of his death," said Richards.

"Bloody hell, but I'll alert the legal department anyway," Lightfoot murmured, pulling the cigar out of his mouth, and wiping his lips with a rumpled handkerchief.

"Just one more thing," DCI Lawrence asked. "How does your system work when advisory letters are issued and no payment is received? What is your collection process?"

"The legal department gets involved and explores all avenues of debt collection."

"Do you ever use debt collectors?"

"Sometimes, depending on the amount involved and progress from the legal department's efforts. We have one-dozen field operatives located throughout the country, as betting comes from all over the UK. All very up-and-up," he explained, "as all are licensed solicitors. No strong-arm stuff that you see in the movies. Our guys may visit employers—which bettors usually want to avoid at all costs—creating a debt collection plan with them."

"I'd like a list of all your collection solicitors, Mr. Lightfoot," Lawrence asked.

"We can do that," replied Lightfoot. "Give me your E-mail address and I'll send it over this afternoon."

DCI Lawrence handed Lightfoot her card. "Before I forget, what is the process with out-of-town bettors?" she asked.

"We have stronger protections built in the system, requiring deposits before bets are accepted."

"Well, you seem to have a tight management system, Mr. Lightfoot. We appreciate your time. We won't keep you any longer. Have a good day," added Lawrence, and the two inspectors departed the Bookerboys' facility. Outside they talked.

"Not exactly the classiest of guys," remarked Richards.

"No, and the soggy cigar he clenched in his teeth was starting to make me nauseous," added Lawrence.

"But his operation seemed efficient and effective, although Bookerboys was the only bookie that admitted to using debt collectors. He said they were all licensed solicitors, but I'd like to confirm that. Lightfoot said no strong-arm stuff, but who knows?" commented Richards.

"Let's get Churchill from the NCA to get his ViCLAS group to dig into that and see if there have been any incidents associated with this group of solicitors. Complaints to any of the regulatory agencies or any legal action against them. I think they are clean, but let's put them on the person-of-interest list anyway," said Lawrence.

"We should also ask them to check into the financing of all three," added Richards. "Self-financed, investor-backed, whatever. They are all privately owned, but it would be good to know who is on their boards and if there are any nefarious connections."

"Good thought. Who pulls their strings?" concluded Lawrence.

Chapter Twenty-Nine

By the end of the week, initial contacts with all targeted animal rights groups had been made. Despite their cloak of secrecy, CAGED—Campaign Against Greyhound Exploitation and Death—and AFG—Action For Greyhounds—were regarded as very legitimate operations, heavily focused on raising awareness of the plights of greyhounds, educating the public with comprehensive reports and booklets outlining the cruelty of the sport. Both were also involved in fostering adoptions and having greyhounds regarded as worthy of family pets. No incidents of unruly demonstrations or protests requiring police action have been recorded. With such violence hidden in the sport, the activities of these groups were benign.

The other groups, ALIC—A Lifetime In Cages, God's Gift-The Greyhound and Greys-Cruel and Unusual Punishment were also recognized as having legitimate, praiseworthy missions, but the detectives reported back to MIT that further probing is warranted. Preliminary analyses noted a few disorderly conduct arrests in some instances and police action to quell out-of-control protests. No real violence against breeders, trainers, promoters nor racetrack officials, but someone—unknown—had destroyed cages intended for use with greyhounds, at a warehouse near Dover.

The information and observations by the MIT detectives, supplemented by data generated by the ViCLAS unit of the NCA, expanded the profiles and this information was posted on the whiteboard in the conference room of Harlow MIT headquarters. DCI Lawrence, who remained the SIO on this case, called Gino in Madrid and updated him.

"We are ready to proceed to phase II, with three of the targeted groups," she began. "We are going to leave it to the NCA and their intelligence unit to dig further into the bookmakers we interviewed, but for us, we focus on these three animal rights groups."

"That's excellent, Liz. When do we start?"

"We are striving to set up our follow-ups with the leaders of each group. We want them all to be there and we can use the authority of the NCA if we need to play that card."

"And the NCA liaison, Chief Inspector Churchill, how is that working out?" asked Gino.

'Totally supportive. He dropped by and met with Fox and Hamilton, while Graham and I were out meeting with the bookmakers Dawson owed money to, but I'm meeting with him later today, going over our phase II interview plan. He is looking forward to meeting with you as soon as possible."

"Give me his contact information. I'll give him a call and we'll work out the best time to meet, and where? In the meantime, how are you dividing up who will interview who in this next round Liz?"

"I thought it would be best for you and me to pay a visit to the ALIC—A Lifetime in Cages— group. They are just south of here in Maidstock. Graham will take the lead with the God's Gift group in Glenchester, in the West of the country. The Cruel and Unusual

Punishment organization is up North, in Manchester, and we are still working on getting the key players together."

* * *

Gino made arrangements to meet with Lionel Churchill at NCA Headquarters and flew to London the next day. Churchill looked like a parliament minister; tall, slim, in a three-piece, blue, pin-striped suit with matching tie and breast-pocket handkerchief and a lightly patterned, pale blue shirt. He was relatively young, in his late thirties with prematurely gray hair, slightly long and elegantly coifed. Good looking except for his teeth, which could benefit from an orthodontist. He probably shouldn't smile very much.

Churchill's speech pattern was very British, with a slow, strained cadence and he had the habit of raising his eyebrows and opening his eyes wider, several times in the same sentence. Nevertheless, the meeting was cordial and Churchill took the time to show Gino around his intelligence operation, which included a large bank of computers, with all levels of diversity analysts behind each monitor.

He was very interested in the killings in Madrid, Paris and Amsterdam and the progress being made. Gino was somewhat embarrassed by the fact that local and national police detectives, supported by Interpol, had so few concrete leads. Suspicions, persons-of-interest, but not much more than that.

"Perhaps we can alter that scenario in the UK," said Churchill. "With the NCA and our intelligence systems, we expect to make a bit more headway than you have made in the other cities."

"I am very optimistic that we can, Chief Inspector. Tomorrow I will join DCI Lawrence in our first follow-up interviews and we hope we can narrow down our suspicions and come up with some solid evidence," Gino said.

"We are here to support the efforts of the Essex MIT unit and with the NCA and Interpol, I too am optimistic."

The two said their good-byes, promising to remain in-touch.

* * *

Gino got to Harlow that afternoon and with DCI Lawrence and DI Richards, reviewed their plans.

"Before we get on with our visits," said Lawrence, "I wanted to mention that the CCTV cameras on Harlow Road, Royden Road and Elizabeth Way—all adjacent to the stadium—gave us nothing. At that time in the morning, there were virtually no cars on the roads, and those that we could identify have been checked out. We are speculating that the perpetrators concealed themselves somewhere and then were picked up by a collaborator later, out of camera range, when morning traffic began. It was a foggy morning and no way to check out the hundreds of vehicles on the road after 6:00 AM. They could have swiftly been on the A414 or the A1019 and gone anywhere from there."

"Too bad," said Gino.

"As to our visits, this time we will press the leaders on their whereabouts the night of the Dawson murder. Maidstock is close to Harlow and ALIC's proximity to the crime scene is noteworthy," began Lawrence. "Our first contact with them did not include meeting with Jeremy Ainsworth, who is the leader of ALIC, although without any official title. This time, we will meet with all key players, all four of them."

It was less than an hour from Harlow to Maidstock, where they would be meeting with Jeremy Ainsworth, Edwin Bolton, and Terri Sinclair, at the greyhound adoption facility run by Terri's sister, Alice Bolton, wife of Edwin.

The adoption center was out on a country road, a totally enclosed structure with chain link fencing surrounding it, primarily for the rescued greyhounds to get out and about, generally one or two at a time. Adjoining the structure was a cottage where Alice Bolton lived with Edwin, and a back room served as the headquarters for ALIC.

When they arrived, Alice was already outside and insisted that they tour the rescue center, which currently housed fourteen greyhounds, some being rehabilitated from injuries and/ or abuse. A local veterinarian—Clive Harris—came every day to manage recoveries, getting the animals ready for adoption.

Inside the center there was space for twenty greyhounds, and each one had its own four meter by four-meter habitat. Alice said that they hated using the term 'cage' and preferred the word 'habitat' for their rescued animals. Each habitat had a back door that opened to the outside for walks and exercise. The building also had a large examination and treatment room as well as a fully equipped surgical theater where Alice Bolton assisted Dr. Harris, when necessary. There were two recovery habitats adjoining the surgery theater.

Completing the tour, Alice led Lawrence and Cerone through a covered walkway to the side of the cottage. "This leads to our office, where the rest of the group is waiting for you. I primarily run the Rescue and Adoption Center. We don't have any signs outside, for obvious reasons. The others manage the activities of our organization. We have a membership of only forty and much of their work is generating donations for our center, promulgating adoptions, and educating the public on greyhound abuse.

As they walked, Gino asked, "How did you get into this mission to save greyhounds, Ms. Bolton?"

"Our father—Terri's and mine—was a local veterinarian, small animals, horses, not farm animals, so we were always around animals, caring for them. I am a licensed Veterinary Technician, as is Terri, and we always worked closely with our father. Dr. Harris, the veterinarian who volunteers here, worked with our father until he passed away about eight years ago. Dr. Harris took over the practice at that time. Our father was always passionate that greyhound racing should be banned and their plight disturbed him greatly. I think his heart eventually gave out with sadness. Anyway, from that point we became involved and built this rescue and adoption center. We met Jeremy, who you will meet in a minute, at a CAGED presentation, He became a benefactor in our project and helped us create the ALIC. His organization skills have helped us create our life's mission, in honor of our father."

"Very, very commendable, Ms. Bolton," Gino added.

Opening the side door to the cottage, Alice led them to a fairly, large room, undoubtedly once a spare bedroom. Inside were the other members of the group who were busy with one thing or another. There were three desks, two with visible laptops and another with a large screen monitor and a sizeable server and wi-fi unit alongside that desk. Shelves lined two sides of the room, with booklets, reports, and stacks of flyers. Two photocopy/printer machines were tucked in beneath one of the shelves.

Ainsworth, Sinclair, and Edwin Bolton rose from their desks and introduced themselves to Lawrence and Cerone, who introduced themselves and showed credentials.

"I believe our investigators met with you and Ms. Sinclair a couple of weeks ago" said DCI Lawrence, looking first at Edwin Bolton and then Terri Sinclair.

"Yes," replied Bolton. "We actually met at the library in town as Jeremy was away and my sister was very busy with the rescue center. She was completing two adoptions and that takes priority over everything."

"I can imagine," said Lawrence. "Well, you all are here now and I thank you for your cooperation. We may be going over some issues you discussed with our colleagues, but we are investigating a serious crime and need to get as much information as we can, both on your operation and the whole anti-greyhound racing movement, which is a very emotional issue—cruelty to these animals—that is."

"We'll help you anyway we can inspectors," said Ainsworth. "You are right, this is a very emotional issue, with passion on both sides. You know that greyhounds spend 80% of their lifetime in cages, released to race and then back in a cage. Horrible, We have to outlaw this barbaric sport."

"Yes, I know. We are greatly saddened at what we have learned. You work at Barclay's Bank in Ashford, is that correct Mr. Ainsworth?" asked Gino, looking to move from the propaganda to the purpose of this visit.

"Yes, I am the head of information systems for all the banks in Essex County."

"Is that your computer?" Gino asked, pointing to the large desktop monitor.

"Yes. I commute to Ashford for the bank but can work from here coordinating all the activities of our group; meetings with regulatory agencies, managing donations and our finances, coordinating with affiliated groups, both inside and outside the UK and assisting Alice with adoption inquiries and outreach. This is the epicenter of our work."

"Impressive, Mr. Ainsworth. You live in Maidstock, commute to Ashford for Barclay in a job with significant responsibility yet find the time to do all this work for ALIC. How do you manage it?" asked Gino.

"I manage it. We all have jobs with responsibilities, but we are very dedicated." Then Ainsworth laughed, "And sophisticated software systems make the work here easier to manage. Some of the programs I developed myself."

"And where were you on the evening in May when Mr. Benny Dawson was murdered in Harlow? I have to ask that question," said Gino, "so we can eliminate people and organizations, and focus our attention where needed."

"I understand, Inspector. Terri and I were in Copenhagen, Denmark, meeting with one of our sister groups. Denmark also has greyhound racing and while the anti-greyhound racing groups there are not as numerous and active as in the UK, we discussed tactics and strategies toward getting the racing of greyhounds banned in that country. We were there for two days and if necessary, I can provide flights and hotel receipts as well as who we met with."

"Great, and that will be necessary, I'm afraid, just to tidy up our elimination process," said Gino.

"Of course. Give me your contact information and I can scan our receipts and E-mail them to you."

"And the people and the organization you met with?

"That too, Inspector," added Ainsworth.

"And Ms. Sinclair," began Lawrence, "your sister Alice said that you are a licensed veterinary technician, but our information has it that you work in the tourist industry?"

"That is correct. It brings income and it gives me flexibility for our work. I conduct tours of Leeds Castle and Canterbury Cathedral during the tourist season. I earn enough to live comfortably—minimal, but comfortable—and it give me time to work on our mission. Plus, I can help out Alice and Dr. Harris if needed."

"And Mr. Bolton," Gino said, now turning to Edwin, "I note that you work at the Dungeness nuclear power plant."

Yes, I am a nuclear physicist and keeping the Dungeness facility operating safely and with full efficiency is my contribution to clean energy."

"That's an admirable responsibility, Mr. Bolton, but I imagine it take a significant amount of dedication and effort," said Gino.

"Less than you would think, Inspector. Computer systems manage the process and has been doing so for many years, so I am more of a watchdog, making sure there are no anomalies of surprises."

God, more computer systems running everything, thought Lawrence.

"And where were you on the night in question, Mr. Bolton? Gino asked.

"I was here. Alice and I live in this cottage and I commute to Dungeness every day. It isn't that far. That evening, after returning from the plant, I was here with Alice, who rarely gets to go anywhere, being dedicated to this rescue and adoption center 24/7."

"Last question. What is your impression of the killing of Benny Dawson?" Gino asked.

"An absolutely horrible incident Inspectors, but Benny Dawson was not a very likeable guy, I am told. We hate what he does, or did, but he tried to screw all those he worked with, squeezing trainers, racetrack officials and clearly not caring a bit about the care of these beautiful animals. Promoters are supposed to maintain the integrity of the sport, but from what I hear, and what I have read, integrity and Benny Dawson do not belong in the same sentence. Come back with me to the rescue center," continued Alice Bolton, "Let me show you the abuse these animals suffer. God's creatures housed in cages their whole life. I hate Benny Dawson and his whole profession but killing him goes way beyond our mission."

"Well said, sister," added, Terri while Jeremy and Edwin nodded their agreement.

Giving thanks for their time, Gino and Liz took their leave and walked out to their car. "This is more of the same, Liz. Another perfect alibi, although Bolton and his wife, technically have no alibi and Harlow is very close-by. But I just don't see how the two of them could pull this off."

"I agree, Gino. We have no evidence to take this further. We'll go over and double check the receipts Ainsworth sends to us, and look into their finances, but I don't expect much. Ainsworth seems to have the whole operation expertly managed with his computer systems,"

"Rather a large server, though," remarked Gino. "Seems like overkill, but who knows?"

"No way we'd get a warrant to see what's on that computer, but that could prove interesting." added Lawrence.

"Indeed. We keep them on the radar, but I'm not optimistic it is going to lead anywhere. On the other hand, the work they are doing with that rescue center is phenomenal."

* * *

Gino and Liz returned to Harlow and later that afternoon, DI Richards returned from his visit to the God's Gift group, which turned out to be equally inconclusive.

"The principals in the God's Gift group are all professors at Hartpury College, all involved in veterinary medicine in one way or another. The three—Paul Westlake, Brian Mitchell, and David Tennisson—seem up and up, but come off a little weird. They invoked the name of God—they actually said The Lord—throughout or conversation, sometimes bordering on a little fanatical. The top guy, Paul Westlake, was a Lutheran missionary in Africa—Uganda of all places—helping locals with agricultural farming and the raising of goats, for milk and for food. Hard to believe that he, as well as his God-fearing associates would be involved in murder, but you know that religious fanatics do strange things. Just think of the Taliban, for instance. None of them have water-tight alibis for that night. All were at the collage that day, and two, Winchell and Tennisson, had dinner together that evening at a local Italian restaurant. They split the bill and VISA and Mastercard have a record of that expense. Where they were at two in the morning is unknown, but it's a long haul to get from Gloucestershire to Harlow, do the deed and get back for classes the next day. Westlake was at a church dinner that night until nine o'clock. They all seem very tame, devoted to getting greyhound racing banned, but seemingly, good men. I'd cross them off our list."

"Between travel and your meeting with these candidates for sainthood," raising her eyebrows and smiling, "are you up to flying to Manchester with me tomorrow?" asked Liz.

"Definitely. I enjoy doing The Lord's work," replied Richards, with a mocked deadpan expression.

* * *

The flight to Manchester the next day was uneventful and both Lawrence and Richards looked forward to meeting with the ladies—Elsbeth Graham, Fern Cranston, and Peggy Frost— running Greys – Cruel and Unusual Punishment. Two of the three were working the day of the incident, Cranston at the British Airways ticket counter at Manchester Airport and Graham, with a full day of real-estate showings. Each ended their day at around 6 PM. Both ladies were petite young women, in their late thirties. Frost, a set designer at the Manchester Opera House in her mid-forties, worked well into the evening on the sets for Don Giovanni, an opera scheduled to open next month. It would be impossible for any of the three, much less all of them, to travel from Manchester to Harlow and carry out the complex killing of Benny Dawson. Lawrence and Richards flew back from Manchester late that afternoon, feeling a bit defeated.

At the MIT office in Harlow, Gino, Liz, and Graham debriefed each other.

"Two highly unlikely, close to impossible, scenarios involving God's Gift – The Greyhound and Greys – Cruel and Unusual Punishment and almost perfect alibis with the leaders of ALIC," said Lawrence.

"I'm getting to hate that expression, 'perfect alibis," said Gino. "It's getting to be too perfect."

"I know," lamented Liz, "but if the persons of interest are somewhere else, hard to retain them as suspects."

"Churchill is going to love this. With the full force of Interpol, the NCA and the Harlow MIT unit, we are nowhere near solving this crime," said Richards.

"Just like everywhere else," said Gino," Just like everywhere else."

Chapter Thirty

Gino called Klaus Schickhaus from the airport before getting on the flight to Madrid, updating him on the investigation in the UK.

"You are keeping one of the bookmakers and the A Lifetime In Cages animal rights group on your list of possibilities?" asked Schickhaus.

"Yes, Klaus, but without a lot of optimism," replied Gino.

"Okay, Detective Chief Superintendent, what's next? We have four governments breathing down the neck of local law enforcement and us. We need a breakthrough and soon. You have always demonstrated that you can find a way," said Schickhaus.

"Well, I'm going back to Madrid and getting my better half to provide some stimulus."

"But Gino, she's stuck in the mud also."

"She is, but she wants to set up a teleconference with each of the lead investigators in the four countries to pick each other's brains and challenge each other's investigation. I think that's a good opportunity to generate something—anything."

"Go for it Gino, and sorry for the Detective Chief Superintendent remark. A failed attempt at some levity."

"No offence taken, Mr. Chief of Criminal Investigation," replied Gino, and closed the call.

* * *

"Time to set up your show, Mercedes," said Gino after returning to Madrid and his apartment on Apolonia Morales. "You should organize a ZOOM hook-up with each of the investigators—Cousteau in Paris, Arden in Amsterdam and now, DCI Lawrence in England. We are at a dead end, so hopefully you can shake something loose from your experiences."

"*Estupendo.* They don't know me, so we should alert each of them that I will contact them and we'll set up a ZOOM teleconference as soon as possible."

"Agreed. I'll E-mail each of them now and you can take over from there.

"*Bueno.* This is coming at a good time. The surveillance we placed on Victoria, led nowhere. She just continues to work with *Salvan Los Toros* and she has given us nothing. Your *La Pluma Blanca* seems above reproach."

"She's not *my, La Pluma Blanca,* Mercedes, but we can't ignore white feathers at each crime scene, like the perpetrators were leaving a calling card, so we have to stay with that. There can't be a dove flying around Europe, dropping feathers at each of the murder scenes. I really like her, and don't think she is behind this—not here in Madrid—but you know how I feel about coincidences."

"I know. No such thing as coincidences, at least not in our work."

"No. We know that those feathers, those tail feathers, came from the same dove. DNA testing has confirmed that. Maybe we have to look for anyone who keeps a dove in a birdcage in their home," Gino said, laughing. "Can you imagine asking a judge for a search warrant to check for a bird in a cage?"

"I'm certainly not going to ask for that. You can, but not me. I'm still young enough to have a career."

"Are you implying that I am old?"

"Would I say that my dear? You are just a mature cop. How many agencies have you worked for? The US Secret Service, Spain's National Police Force, an investigator for Spain's Minister of the Economy, the US State Department and now, Interpol. You just can't keep a job."

"Okay, okay. Since I got involved with you, I have been assigned to, or associated with, each of those agencies on the cases we have handled together. You're the one that keeps me bouncing from service to service."

Moving closer to Gino and kissing him on the cheek, Mercedes said, "That's because you are so good at what you do, that everyone wants you. Now, are we eating at home or going out for dinner?"

"Let's go out. Call *El Bodégon*, where de Portillo ate before his demise. Returning to the scene of the crime. I'll put it on my expense account."

* * *

In two days, Mercedes set up a Zoom conference with the investigators in Paris, Amsterdam and in Harlow, England. Each set up the teleconference from their individual offices where they could draw on support from colleagues, if necessary.

"Welcome, everyone." Mercedes began. "I am pleased to meet you, face to face, even if it is via a computer screen. As each of you don't know one another, I thought it would be helpful to give a brief introduction including your position and the service you work for, and a brief summary of the killing that took place in your city. We have all had access to the crime reports from your agency but hearing it from you can be helpful. Let's start with myself, as Madrid was the first killing. Then we will proceed chronologically based on the date of the assassination you are investigating. Later, we will go over your chief suspects and where you are in your investigation."

Mercedes started, giving her rank as Detective Chief Inspector in the National Police Force—CNP. She then discussed the killing of Alejandro de Portillo, renowned bullfighting promoter in Spain, the date and nature of his murder—attacked by a fighting bull in *Las Ventas* bullring. The only evidence at the scene was a white feather, *una pluma blanca*, and the nature of the drugs that were used to incapacitate the victim and the guards at the arena. "*Las Ventas* is the largest and most prestigious bullfighting arena in all of Spain," she concluded, "and somehow a bull was released in the middle of the night, with a drugged and defenseless de Portillo in the ring."

Capitaine Vivienne Cousteau of the Paris Police Prefecture followed, describing the incident at the Saint-Cloud Racecourse, outside of Paris, and the victim, Claude Le Clerc, a successful trainer of thoroughbred racehorses, with a somewhat tarnished reputation. She described the nature of his death—trampled by Desert Prince, one of the horses he trained to be entered in a forthcoming prestigious race and the drugs used in subduing guards and Le Clerc himself. And the presence of a white feather at the scene of the crime.

Inspector Guus Arden of the Dutch National Police came next, describing the atmosphere in the Netherlands regarding the use of animals in medical research, the nature of the horrific assault on Dr. Arnold von Beek—by chimpanzees—in a primate research facility operated by Orion. He described the drugs used to incapacitate von

Beek, both at his home, where he was abducted, and the guards at the satellite research center, and the white feather found at the scene.

"Last, but not least," said DCI Elizabeth Lawrence of the Essex County MIT unit, and she began her summary of the killing of Benny Dawson, a promoter of greyhound races, with somewhat of an unsavory reputation. Dawson was tied to the apparatus that moves a mechanical hare around the track for greyhounds to chase, dragging Dawson to his death. She described the drugs used on the victim and the guard at the stadium in Harlow, not unlike the drugs used in the other cases. The plight of greyhounds and the abuses they suffer was a very emotional and sensitive issue in the UK, but bookmakers play a large part in sustaining the sport, and the gambling money generated. No leads, no evidence at the scene, only a white feather.

Mercedes thanked the investigators and then gave a summary of what was disclosed.

"Horrific murders against individuals who are involved in the cruel treatment of animals, be that in sports, or in the case of Amsterdam, in the use of animals for medical and pharmaceutical research. Magnificent fighting bulls in Spain, slaughtered in front of passionate spectators, horses abused by trainers who stop at nothing—using performance enhancing drugs or other drugs to mask injuries—to win races bolstered by huge betting pools.

"In England, and in other parts of the world, where trainers abetted by promoters, keep animals in abhorrent conditions, and as in horseracing, use drugs to enhance performance and mask injuries. Spending 80% of their time in cages may make this the cruelest of sports, but again, like in France, a huge betting pool needs to be protected, despite the public outcry against the sport.

"Then, the use of animals—all kinds of animals—in medical research, but especially monkeys and chimpanzees, which are the closest species to humans. The Netherlands has taken many measures to curtail the use of animals in research, but it still goes on, supposedly for the benefit of mankind.

"And each of you have reported the discovery of a pristine white feather at each crime scene, which we have to conclude links all of these murders together." All the investigators nodded in agreement.

"Now, I'd like to open discussion on where we all are in identifying perpetrators. We are all leaning toward animal rights groups as being the most logical persons of interest in these killings. The anti-bullfighting movement in Spain, the anti-greyhound racing furor in England and anywhere these animals are raced, the outcries against the use of animals in research and those groups fighting against the abuses horse suffer in racing. All of these passions have generated hundreds and hundreds of local, national, European and International animal rights groups which use all measures of leverage to curtail abuses. We have all focused our attention here, but without success, even though these groups are the most motivated to take action. Many live and breathe the cause. From your reports I have seen many groups or individuals have been determined to have motive, but we cannot tie that to opportunity, as all suspects have perfect alibis.

"Before we take this discussion further, I most reveal part of our investigation in Madrid that we have withheld in all our reports, at least in those that we have shared outside of the CNP."

Mercedes then revealed the primary person of interest in the Madrid slaying, Victoria Valenzuela, daughter of a famous bullfighter, brought up on her family's fighting bull breeding ranch and yet, totally opposed to bullfighting and the killing of these creatures, directing the actions of *Salvan Los Toros,* a rights group of her creation. She then gave the background of Valenzuela's upbringing on the breeding ranch in the South of Spain. She loved the *corrida,* the fighting of the bull, but never the moment of truth—the killing of the animal. As a girl and young women, she trained as a *matadora,* fighting the young bulls at the family's training center. Her fearlessness and passion to combat the animal astounded all that watched her, but she never entered the ring with a sword. She also never wore the traditional cap of the bullfighter, preferring to go bare headed in her battles. Her distinct lock of pure white hair above her forehead, framed against her raven hair earned her the nickname of *La Pluma Blanca,* the White Feather.

Each of the participant's eyes opened wide with the revelation of *La Pluma Blanca.*

"There has to be a connection to Victoria Valenzuela to the crimes in each of our cities," exclaimed Capitaine Cousteau. The white feather at our crime scenes, looks like a calling card, don't you think?"

"Absolutely," replied Mercedes, "but she was somewhere else, hundreds of miles away from Madrid at the time of the murder. Perfect alibi. No way to connect her to the crime. She is a unique woman with a Japanese mother and Eurasian features. Beautiful, charismatic, intelligent, confident and without fear. She openly told us of her background, even the death of her father—in the bullring—where she holds promoters responsible for his loss of prestige and ultimately his death, although it was thirty years ago. She gave us a motive, but we cannot connect her to the crime."

"We too in Paris have potential suspects, one individual with an apparent motive, but the members of this group were out of town at the time of Le Clerc's killing. Perfect alibi."

"And in Amsterdam," added Guus Arden, "one of our suspects is a hospital pharmacist with access to the types of drugs used to disable guards and our victim, but he too, was confirmed to be out-of-town, nowhere near the attack on Dr. von Beek. Another perfect alibi."

"No different in England," said DCI Lawrence. "Our most likely suspects, or at least the group we cannot eliminate as persons of interest, despite the wonderful work they are doing in rescuing greyhounds, all had perfect alibis. None were near the crime scene at the time of the killing."

"Can there be a connection here between all our persons of interest?" asked Mercedes. "Some kind of innovative collaboration amongst these animal rights groups?" Do they know each other? We need to do some digging here with regards to associations they may belong to, somewhere they have had the opportunity to meet."

"Interesting," chimed in Guus Arden. The alibi of lone of our suspect groups—End Animal Research-Now—involved just such a group. Two of these activists said they were in a board meeting of the International Animal Rights Group, in Luxembourg at the time of the killing. We indeed confirmed that and were planning to have one of our officers attend their next conference to check it out."

"This is good. It's an opening. We need to identify other organizations that these animal rights groups belong to, conferences they might attend that support the animal rights movements. Anywhere that they may go to hone their efforts, where they may have crossed paths and build a cabal to take revenge against those who perpetrate cruelty to animals, be they bulls, horses, greyhounds, or monkeys," said Mercedes. "We never really pursued such a direction. Let's put Interpol on this. What are the associations in Europe that support and foster collaboration amongst animal rights groups? What conferences are being offered for training and experience exchanges? Who are their members, who are registered to attend these conferences? If we can find organizations, but especially conferences, where each of suspect groups participated, that could be the link.

"DCI Lawrence, this is also something that your National Crime Agency can look into. I don't care if there is a duplication of effort with Interpol. Let's get all of our analytical units involved. Then, we can follow-up to see if the groups we are interested in were at the same place at the same time. I'd go at least five years back in checking this out. I think we have something here. For the first time in months, I'm excited. As soon as we get something, we'll meet again and lay out next steps and responsibilities, Thank you all, this was great," concluded Mercedes.

After the teleconference, Gino called Mercedes. "Thanks for letting me listen-in. That was a very insightful discussion," said Gino, who participated in the Zoom call, but as a listener only, not on any of the screens. "It got me thinking. I'll tell you about it tonight."

Chapter Thirty-One

That evening, during dinner, Mercedes asked, "You said the teleconference got you thinking. Do you have something to share with me?"

"Yes, but it may sound a little crazy. There's a television station in the States that shows classic films from sixty, seventy years ago. Most are black and white, featuring all the big stars from the 1940's and 1950's. Anyway, I remember seeing this movie—I'm pretty sure it was on this station—Strangers on a Train. It starred Farley Granger—a well-known actor at that time—and Robert Walker, who was also the lead in one of my favorite movies, One Touch of Venus, with Ava Gardner."

"God, you and Ava Gardner," Mercedes commented.

"What? I loved her. Okay, not really *loved*, but loved her as a movie star, especially in that film."

"You are showing your age, and she's probably old enough to be your mother—or grandmother."

"Ignoring her barbs, he continued. "Anyway, Strangers on a Train, directed by Alfred Hitchcock. You know of Alfred Hitchcock?"

"Psycho."

"Yes, Psycho and many others, usually with some kind of twist. In this movie, two guys meet on a commuter train—Granger and

Walker—total strangers, and they get to talking, you know, as commuters might when they continue to see each other. During one of their commutes, one guy—the Farley Granger character, who I think was a tennis player—reveals that he wants a divorce from his promiscuous wife, so he can marry someone he really loves, but his wife will not consider it. The other man—the Walker character—whose name I think was Bruno, confesses that he really hates his father and wishes him dead.

"Eventually, Bruno—who is a psychopath—proposes a solution. Each would murder the other's nemesis. Bruno would kill the tennis player's wife and in turn, the Farley Granger character—can't remember his name in the movie—would kill Bruno's father. Bruno conceives this as a perfect plan, as each would murder a total stranger, having no motive, so neither would become a suspect. When Granger's wife was killed, he would be somewhere else, with a perfect alibi and likewise with Bruno. He would be nowhere near the killing of his father, also with a perfect alibi. How many times did I hear you guys on the Zoom call mention perfect alibis?"

"Okay, they swap murders and set up alibis so they would not be considered as a suspect," said Mercedes.

"Exactly."

"So, what happens?"

"Bruno—the psychopath—does kill the other guy's wife while her husband is away somewhere. While the police initially suspect the husband, he is cleared because of his perfect alibi."

"And then, the tennis player kills Bruno's father," added Mercedes.

"Well, Bruno prepares the other man to carry it out. Gets him a gun, gives him the floor plan for the house, but here my memory gets hazy. The Farley Granger character gets cold feet, which enrages Bruno. In some kind of confrontation—the details escape me—Bruno is killed. In the end, the police find evidence that Bruno killed the tennis player's wife, so he did not get away with the murder, but ironically, the tennis player did. As there was no evidence that he got Bruno to commit the murder, he was free to marry again. End of story."

"Fascinating plot, Gino. I can see why our teleconference got you thinking."

"Yes. Just suppose that somehow different groups of activists come together and create a plan, like Strangers on a Train. The group in France, for example, carries out the attack on the researcher in Holland, but the probable Dutch suspects all have perfect alibis. And the Dutch group organizes the attack on de Portillo in Madrid, with all of the Spanish suspects having perfect alibis for the crime."

"*Dios mio,*" exclaimed Mercedes. "That does sound a little crazy, incredibly crazy, but this did come up in our discussion. We talked about finding opportunities where these groups—the key persons of interest in Madrid, Paris, Amsterdam, and Harlow—could meet one another. But four murders, swapped between groups with the greatest motives, that's quite a leap. Such a scheme would take an enormous amount of planning and tutoring of each group on logistics and critical organizing issues relating to the assigned targets."

"Like Bruno did in providing a weapon and floor plan for the tennis player," added Gino.

"Yes, each team of perpetrators would have to have a detailed plan and materials—like the drugs that were used—to execute their part of the bargain. We wouldn't have thought of this if it weren't for our Zoom call. We were going nowhere and this opens a new approach for the investigations. Those rock-solid alibis may not be so perfect after all," said Mercedes.

"Well, you have properly set up the next steps by wanting

Interpol and the UK's National Crime Agency to start digging into organizations that each of the groups belong to and conferences where they may have met and had the opportunity to plan their assassinations. I'll handle the Interpol analysis of this. Between Interpol and the NCA we will have a good list of places to go looking. Thereafter, we might need the strength of Interpol into getting to look at memberships and particularly conferences, where these individuals may have registered. Lyon will also have to determine where and how court orders may be required." Then Gino added, "And let's not forget how these groups would have to communicate with one another. That big server at the ALIC office and Jeremy Ainsworth's skill at computer programming may be the critical link with all of them. He no doubt has the skill to set up a secure network for communications. At some point we will have to get into their computers before they suspect what we are doing as well as checking into traceable travel for all the individuals on the dates of each crime" Then he laughed, "And let's hope that my uncanny memory of old films is leading us down the right path. We cannot afford any more dead ends. Last point Mercedes, we need to keep this a stealth as possible. Please caution the others."

Chapter Thirty-Two

Five years earlier

Victoria Valenzuela and Max de Groot had met several times at various conferences in Europe tailored to the support of animal rights groups. Victoria's looks always commanded attention which she politely and adroitly rebuffed. In Max's case however, the two hit it off and for a brief period they were more than just friends, but the relationship reverted back to an amicable 'colleague' status, as both were totally committed to their work—banning bullfighting in Spain and outlawing the use of animals for research in Holland and beyond. Both had witnessed some progress in their missions, but not enough to fully achieve their goals,

They appreciated these kinds of conferences and belonged to several support organizations as there was always something new to be learned, be it exposure to new research and investigations by activists, demonstration tactics, lobbying strategies, fund raising efforts, new literature and reports as well as lectures by activists in the field from all over the world. This included conferences organized by PETA—probably the most prolific in support programs, the European Society of Dog and Animal Welfare—ESDAW, and the International Animal Rights Group, which always hold their annual conference in Luxembourg in the fall. One of the interesting things about some of these conferences is the occasional inclusion of a seminar by the Animal Liberation Front, a leaderless, decentralized political and social resistance movement advocating direct action in protests against animal abuse. Operating in forty country, clandestine cells undertake a sliding scale of activism, including violent protests, destruction of facilities, liberating animals from laboratories, bordering on terrorism in the eyes of some. It is a fuzzy area and its decentralization make it impossible to authorities to monitor.

One evening, after both Victoria and Max attended a seminar on creating a legal team within animal rights organizations, the two went out to dinner at a restaurant near the Hilton DoubleTree Hotel, where the International Animal Rights Group held its conference in Luxembourg.

"We need to do more, Victoria," Max began. "We have made good progress in strengthening public awareness for our causes, but it is like walking through *crema Catalan,*"—a Spanish custard pudding.

"I know Max. I have often thought of doing something spectacular, something that would appear on the front pages of newspapers, instead of a small article in the back pages, or saying nothing at all of one of our actions."

"Something spectacular? Anything in mind?" asked Max.

"Hard to say. I have often thought of taking revenge on those promoting bullfighting, the men—and they are always men—who relegated my father to obscurity, and who continue to enhance their wealth by the slaughtering of Spanish bulls, as well as squeezing all who participate in the sport, from *matadors* to all the others involved in putting on the show, the *corrida*, in front of thousands of spectators."

"I know what you mean, Victoria. The use of animals in medical and cosmetic research continues in my country. We have saved the chimpanzees, but other primates are still sacrificed in the name of research. It is a very slow process and more and more, the public supports us, but the large research organizations and pharmaceutical companies—and the money behind them—prevent any breakthroughs. I too, have tried to think of how we can make our issue a front-page story, as you alluded to."

"You know, Max, that doing something spectacular will likely put us outside the law. In your case, freeing rabbits and monkeys from a research facility would ultimately be viewed as amusing and forgotten the next day. It has to be bigger than that."

There was silence between Max and Victoria for several minutes. They picked at their food and sipped their wine, lost in thought.

"Okay. Now don't spit out your wine Max but let me tell you of a vision I have had for many years. It involves a bullfighting promoter—they are the evilest ones—lying dead, trampled to death by the running of the bulls in Pamplona, or gored and pummeled to death by a fighting bull in a bullring. All alone, just the promoter and the bull, in the dead of night," said Victoria, her green eyes shining as she spoke.

"Ha," laughed Max. "Not that your vision is funny, it is really diabolical. I laughed because I have often thought of one of these primate researchers, one of the top men, not a laboratory assistant, being ravaged by marauding chimpanzees, tearing him apart.

"The key, Victoria, is can we get away with something like that? Your organization and mine would be immediate suspects and I don't want this to be a suicide mission, no matter how passionate we are."

"Well Max, I don't have a plan—yet—but suicide is not part of my vision. Languishing in some Spanish prison cannot be how it ends. Maybe we need to find others who feel as we do, feel the need for the kind of front-page story that will both send a very clear message that can galvanize the masses. Americans like to use polling that identifies approval ratings—of their president, a governor, mayor, whomever. The men behind their cruelty to animals that we refer to have very low approval ratings. They do their business, but nobody likes them, yet they are tolerated. Their demise would be tragic on one hand, but almost immediately the public will gravitate to the cruelty they foster, not toward the person himself."

"So, what are you thinking about?"

"There are others who think about this. I know for a fact that a member of a French activist group blames an unscrupulous horse trainer for ending her father's career. This trainer was found to have used performance enhancing drugs on one of his horses, which was eventually disqualified from a race. He put the blame on her father, an innocent stable attendant, who eventually lost his job and was banned from horse racing. The group she belongs to is Not The Sport of Kings, and the woman—and the leaders of this group—would have no qualms of exacting revenge and putting the whole abuse of racehorses on the front page of *Le Monde*."

"How do you know this woman?" asked Max.

"We met at a PETA seminar a couple of years ago. Nice girl, but don't get her on the subject of horseracing. Her father is now a janitor or something. She grew up around horses, because of her father's job and the hurt has never left her. The trainer who implicated her father had to move to Australia to continue racing horses, but so many others just get their hands slapped and constantly flout the rules, abusing these beautiful animals. She is now part of a group seeking better control of this sport."

"You know, Victoria, that the cruelest of sports is probably greyhound racing. I sat in on a seminar about the abuse of these animals and could not believe how they are treated. Kept in cages for most of their lives, except when they raced. I met a member of a rescue and adoption group in England at that seminar. Sat next to him. Jeremy Ainsworth, if I recall correctly. I was lamenting about the use of animals in research programs and he then told me about his group's efforts to ban greyhound racing in the UK. I remember how red his face got when he was discussing the atrocities of that sport. One thing that he mentioned was that gambling on the races was an important part of the sport, with lots of money involved. It would be the same in France with horseracing, and the need for big players to protect that pool of money—no matter what."

"Well, maybe we have some allies in this. Why don't you feel out this Ainsworth fellow and I can do the same with Camille Beaumont, the woman I mentioned in the French group. We can see how interested they might be in generating some kind of spectacular event—maybe events. I think both of our colleagues might be here this week. I know that Camille's group always attends the conferences of the International Animal Rights Group," concluded Victoria.

* * *

It took months for the four activist groups to come together on a very dangerous mission. Victoria met with Max's friend from England and the others in the A Lifetime in Cages group. Max went to France, meeting with Camille Beaumont and her colleagues in Not the Sport of Kings. Their discussions were over the phone initially, then Ainsworth set up a secure communication system, which each group put on a single laptop, totally separate from the systems they used to manage their business and activities. They also used pre-paid, so-called burner phones to communicate, discarding them every three months.

Things eventually came together. To keep each group's actions above suspicion in their own cities, they swapped responsibilities. The team from Not the Sport of Kings would be responsible for the action against the bullfighting promoter, which Victoria decided should be at the *Las Ventas* bullring in Madrid. The French team was felt to be the most athletic and better able to handle the logistics at that venue. The *Salvan Los Toros* group—Victoria, Martina, and Luz—would take responsibility for the action against a prominent horse trainer in Paris. Victoria's upbringing on a ranch and familiarity with horses made her the best choice for the action there. The ALIC group, with their veterinary experience, would focus on the animal researcher in Amsterdam, leaving Max's team responsible for the action in the UK against a greyhound race promoter.

Each group was responsible for victim selection and they distributed a profile of the man, his residence, his day-to-day activities and where the attack might take place—and how? Subduing the victim and any guards at the designated facility became the responsibility of Niels Beekhof, from de Groot's organization. As a hospital pharmacist, he would devise what incapacitating agents would be used, on whom and method of delivery.

Then, months and months of training by one group to the other, which also involved benign visits to the venue and testing of the pharmaceutical agents, which Beekoff tried out on the homeless in Amsterdam.

The planning and the logistics of each operation tightened and all felt comfortable in their assignments. Victoria then had the idea of planting a white feather at each crime scene. Because of her unique lock of white hair, Victoria knew suspicion would likely fall to her, certainly in Madrid. She had no fear, knowing she would have a perfect alibi, but also thought it could serve as a diversion. Let the authorities look at her, not elsewhere, protecting her colleagues.

Chapter Thirty-Three

Gino went back to the first reports compiled on animal rights groups, but this time focusing on the larger, international, and European organizations. They were excluded—really put off to the side—from the first deep analysis while they focused on local activist groups. He had the analysts in Lyon combine this first screening, updating it with their current re-investigation into groups that local organizations might belong to for support.

One of the surprising developments from this second look was that PETA—People for The Ethical Treatment of Animals—long considered the gold standard amongst legitimate and respected animal rights groups, was the largest organization of this kind in the world, yet it was also, one of the most aggressive in protest and demonstration tactics. It was enormous in its scope of activities, from birds to fish to mammals of all species. Further, some of these sub-groups could be very aggressive, including throwing red paint at women wearing fur coats, speedboats harassing fishing trawlers using nets to catch tuna, chasing down Japanese whaling vessels to abort their hunts—all very dangerous tactics. Plus, of a more benign nature, organizing a myriad of events, conferences, seminars, and symposia—in person and virtual—to support the work of animal protection groups all over the world. Their educational efforts also included internships within their various disciplines including law internships. It appeared that no international agency was as organized and prolific as PETA.

So, PETA headquartered in Norfolk, Virginia, in the USA, is at the top of Interpol's list, successfully securing membership from a wide array of interested parties—organizations and individuals—estimated at more than nine million, all interested in the protection of all species of animals. In one way or another, this included birds, chickens, geese, primates, sharks, whales, dolphins, horses, donkeys, fighting bulls, farm animals, animals in zoos, and on and on. All are part of PETA's mission to save and protect.

With dozens of sub-groups, Gino now believed that some —if not many—could go off rails with violent forms of activities. He thought, *Did we miss something here?* Nevertheless, PETA was not the only organization that the activist groups of interest in this investigation could belong to and provide opportunities for them to meet.

Gino asked Mercedes to join him his office in Madrid to go over the analyses from Lyon.

As usual, Gino was standing by his whiteboard and was starting to list the organizations that the Interpol analysts had identified.

"As you can see, Mercedes, I have PETA at the top of our list, but with nine million members, their legal team may give us a hard time in getting their membership details. They, like the others, have strict privacy policies, but with court orders it is possible, although we would have to do that in the state of Virginia. Besides PETA, there are other organizations that are geared toward, not only specific, and direct animal rights activities, but also to the support of smaller groups who share in their mission."

He then continued to write on the whiteboard.

- PETA – Norfolk, Virginia, USA
  o Huge and well organized
  o World-wide
  o Multiple disciplines
- Animal Liberation Front (ALF) -? UK origin
  o Leaderless
  o World-wide, 40 countries
  o Extremely decentralized with underground components
  o Clandestine, independent cells
  o Supposedly, non-violent. SUPPOSEDLY.
- International Animal Rights Group - Luxembourg
  o Primarily education and support to members mission
  o Annual Conference in Luxembourg
- ARKANGEL - UK
  o Activist support magazine
  o Association with ALF
- International Fund for Animal Welfare (IFAW) – Washington, DC
  o Very hands on activities
  o Action versus education
  o Heavy rescue focus
  o Partnership with Nestle and Interpol
- World Animal Protection – Toronto, Canada
  o Formerly, World Society for Protection of Animals (WSPA)
  o News, reports, updates of efforts
  o Education programs for members
  o Hands-on disaster relief. Hurricanes, earthquakes, floods
- Humane Society International – Washington, DC
  o Use of animals in research

- o Fur trade and fur farms
- o Dog abuse
- European Society of Dog and Animal Welfare (ESDAW) – Brussels
  - o Education
  - o Focus on companion animals
  - o Policy and analysis to support members

"Two things stand out, Mercedes. One, it will be challenging to get into the membership files of these organizations. Take PETA, for example. Nine million members and strict privacy policies, and undoubtedly a huge cadre of lawyers to protect them. But Interpol believes that with court orders, we should be able to manage that. On the other hand, the Animal Liberation Front is a totally decentralized political and social resistance movement that purports to be non-violent, but there has been widespread criticism that they fail to condemn acts of violence, or themselves have been a part of it. In the UK, ALF actions are regarded as domestic extremism and they have been investigated by the UK's National Extremism Tactical Coordination Unit. As there is no central entity, investigation is limited to group or cell activity that authorities have been able to identify. It is regarded as an organization that cannot be infiltrated and cannot be stopped."

"Jesucristo," exclaimed Mercedes. "Any one of those cells could be a suspect in each of the murders."

"Yes. I don't want to think about it. It could take us back to square one and I don't want to go there until, and if, we cannot tie the groups we are looking at to those attacks.

"The second point I want to make, is that the groups we are investigating are likely members of one or more of these organizations, taking part in their conferences and meetings, aimed at increasing their effectiveness. We know that two members of the Dutch group are on the Board of the International Animal Rights Group, the one with its annual conference in Luxembourg. Ultimately, it is important that we find out who has registered for these events.

"We have to strive to get the court orders to include that information—if it is retained in their files. Another option is to get those details from conference centers or hotels where events like these are held, We can also check out all hotels in the area where the conference is held and determine who has registered for a hotel room. A lot more work, but if we become blocked by the conference venue, we can investigate that option," said Gino.

"Those options, I expect, are doable," replied Mercedes, "but you at least have a list of the conferences or meetings that these various organizations have held, say over the last three to five years?"

"Lyon has put together that information. That was relatively easy to do by scouring their web sites. Plus, back issues of Arkangel include advertisements for such events. All is included in a dossier I have for you. Each organization's list of conferences, seminars, and other events they have organized by subject—if there is one— agendas, where and when. Lyon did go back five years but focused only on European events."

"Okay, that's where we will start, but how?" asked Mercedes.

"Schickhaus has sent the same dossier I have for you to Churchill at the NCA. Between Interpol and the NCA, they will divide up the organizations and each will fine-tune the events identified. Once done, then we must find out who have been the participants. As I said, the major organizing entity should have that, but I don't know how far back their records go. Alternatively, we approach the conference centers or hotels where such meetings were held. Usually, the conference organizer maintains a registry of participants but as I said, we don't know how far back they maintain that information.

"The third point is—as you can see—several organizations have headquarters in the USA, Canada, as well as Europe, so that will be a time-consuming effort. We will need to tap into the resources there to get access to those files. Probably, Interpol will request intervention from the FBI and Canada's CBI. We'll be looking for events where two or or more of the individuals in our suspect groups were registered."

"What about the lead investigators I have been coordinating with?" asked Mercedes.

"I want you to continue to take the lead with them. Send each of them a copy of the dossier I have given to you. I think the French law enforcement group can approach the ESDAW in Brussels and the Dutch National Police will have responsibility for the International Animal Rights Group in Luxembourg. England's NCA can approach Arkangel for their membership details, and whatever they can do with the ALF—if anything. The other agencies, like your CNP, will approach conference centers or hotels where events were held in those countries. Outside of the four countries where the crimes were committed, Interpol agents will make the inquiries. But all will have to wait until Interpol and the NCA fine-tune what we have."

"*Bueno,* Gino. We wait until the analysts finish their work and then we start to dig."

"Yes, we wait, but as we say, there is a light at the end of the tunnel—I hope."

Chapter Thirty-Four

Obtaining membership lists from the animal rights organizations identified, proved challenging. These organizations had strict privacy policies and regarded their membership lists as confidential, and they were always suspicious of government and big corporation inquiries. Wouldn't whaling or tuna fishing companies like to know who—actual names—were behind the harassing and demonstration tactics affecting their labors. However, the law enforcement agencies were successful in getting the necessary court orders for their investigation, but in some cases, the animal rights groups acquiesced only to search for the entities or individuals they were interested in. At the same time, tax records in the crime scene countries, allowed for forensic accountants to identify outlays by the suspect groups to the identified support organizations—membership dues, outlays claimed as business expenses—to identify memberships.

Eventually, membership of the suspect entities, and members, were able to be identified. The hard part was determining which meetings, conferences, seminars, etc., suspect individuals attended. Some of the key organizations retained such records, others did not. Again, tax records supplemented the effort, where expenses were recorded in tax declarations. Travel and hotel expenses were recorded in association with the event, keeping the finance and tax ministries in France, Spain, Holland, and the UK, very busy. Still, inquiries with conference centers and hotels were required to build a complete profile. Hotel registrations were quite complete as most hotels maintained files of their patrons, especially for loyalty programs.

When obstacles arose, the law enforcement agencies utilized tactics of their own. Mercedes mentioned to one of the Melia Castilla general managers that police cars would have to be positioned at the hotel, while waiting for management to acquiesce to CNP's request. In short order, CNP accountants were at work in the hotel's finance department, extracting the information they required. European conference venues and hotels were besieged by local law enforcement or Interpol agents over several weeks.

Gino then headed a Zoom meeting with Mercedes and the lead investigators in Paris, Amsterdam and Harlow, England.

"Good morning, all. It is good to see you again. I want to thank you and your agencies for the work we have completed. Interpol has put together a report that includes the results of your own investigations as well as those completed by Interpol agents, the American FBI and Canada's CBI. It was a massive project and we also have to acknowledge the work by the forensic accountants in each of these organizations. They don't generally get out in the field but they were instrumental in bringing together what we believe is very promising information.

"First of all, the animal rights groups we have been investigating— *Salvan Los Toros* in Spain, Not the Sport of kings in France, End Animal Research-Now in the Netherlands and A Lifetime in Cages in the UK are all long-term members of the following groups," projecting a slide on the participant's screens.

- PETA
- International Fund for Animal Welfare (IFAW)
- International Animal Rights Group
- World Animal Protection
- Arkangel (subscription)

"We also found one or two of our suspect groups belong to;

- European Society of Dog and Animal Welfare (ESDAW)
- Humane Society International

"No records could be found regarding membership in the Animal Liberation Front, but that is not surprising, given the clandestine nature of that organization. All subscribed to Arkangel, the magazine that is supposedly affiliated with the ALF, but of interest is the fact that they regularly advertise conferences and seminars being held throughout the world. Getting into back-issues of Arkangel helped in getting details of such events.

"Most important is that each of our suspect organizations regularly sent participants to conferences throughout Europe. But all four organizations had members—virtually all the leaders we talked with—present at the annual International Animal Rights Group's conference in October, for the last five years. Before that, we found only Max de Groot and Victoria Valenzuela participated. Important is the fact that this was the only conference where all four of our suspect groups were present. Max de Groot, Jeremy Ainsworth, and Terri Sinclair participated in several PETA conferences, one featuring cruelty to greyhound dogs. All leaders of the UK's A Lifetime in Cages attended ESDAW meetings and twice, Victoria Valenzuela and members of Not the Sport of Kings, also were present at an ESDAW meeting, overlapping with the ALC group. Sporadically, each group participated in IFAW meetings, as their hands-on approach was always of interest, particularly to the End Animal Research – Now group, who was at several of their meeting each year. Again, however, I want to emphasize that only the International Animal Rights Group had all four of our suspect groups there at the same time, for many years.

"The Double Tree by Hilton in Luxembourg was always the venue for their annual conference and their records indicate that either Max de Groot or Victoria Valenzuela booked a separate meeting room during this conference, presumably for all of them to meet and plan together. This hotel has twenty-two meeting rooms, besides their large conference room, and there never was a time that a separate meeting room wasn't booked, alternating between de Groot and Valenzuela."

Gino let that information set in for a minute or two.

"What's next, Gino," asked Liz Lawrence.

"Now, we tread carefully. One of the first things we need to determine is where these people were at the time of the incident in each country? We know that the Dutch were not around at the time of the attack in Amsterdam, but where were the others? The Spaniards were not around at the time of the killing in Madrid, but again, where were the others? Lyon believes that all of your agencies can be successful in getting warrants for each of the groups—for their offices and homes—particularly for access to their computers and telephone records. We now need to document connections between them and the content of their communications."

* * *

While the FBI was accessing the records at PETA's headquarters, one of the agents called out to his colleague, "Hey Pete, one of the groups we are looking into is Save the Bulls, right? I don't see it here."

"It's *Salvan Los Toros*, dummy. The name is in Spanish," the other agent called out to his partner. One of the clerks who organized the files for the FBI, heard the comment. She was an intern at PETA from Spain and was well aware of the work of *Salvan Los Toros*. It was early in the morning, so she looked up the animal rights group's contact information and placed a call.

Upon learning that the American FBI was investigating her group, Victoria Valenzuela immediately sent a text to Jeremy Ainsworth, Alain Chapelle, and Max de Groot, using her secure burner phone. There was only one pre-arranged word, "HOT." The meaning of the word was simple. Destroy and dispose of the phones they had been using to communicate. There would be no further contact between them. Also, destroy and dispose of the hard drive in each of the laptops that had been used in planning and executing their assaults. Either replace the hard drive with another—a clean one—or dispose of the laptop entirely. That evidence must end up in a canal, a river, or the ocean, never to be seen again and impossible to retrieve.

All members of the groups had been prepared for this day, and immediately phone and laptops were destroyed and disposed of, hard drives removed from the computer itself. In one hour, any evidence of communication amongst the four groups was permanently disposed of. In addition, Victoria released the white dove she held in a birdcage in her Paseo de la Castellano apartment, replacing it with a gray, African parrot. The dove's cage was disassembled and disposed of and a new one acquired for the parrot. The enclosed terrace where she kept *Bianca,* was steam-cleaned, destroying any evidence of the white bird. At the same time, Niels Beekhof disposed of any evidence relating to the drugs and apparatuses used in the attacks. They found their way to the bottom of an Amsterdam canal.

Satisfied that there would be no way to associate any of the members of the four groups with the killings, Victoria then thought of putting in motion another event, aimed to confuse investigators even more.

Chapter Thirty-Five

Not without some difficulty, search warrants were secured in each of the four countries and the jurisdictions in the cities involved, with the lead investigators orchestrating the effort. Once in hand, on the same day and at the same time, detectives and forensic teams confronted the suspect groups in their offices; San Agustín de Guadalix for *Salvan Los Toros,* Gentilly, outside of Paris, for NOT The Sport of Kings, Amstelveen, for End Animal Research Now, and Maidstock, Kent in the UK for A Lifetime in Cages, as well as for their residences. In the cases of the French, Dutch, and British groups, two warrants were presented, as Alain Chapelle, Max de Groot and Edwin and Alice Bolton's residences also housed their activist office.

Separate teams hit the residences of Victoria Valenzuela and Martina Muñoz in Madrid and Luz Sánchez in Alcobendas, covering the targets for *Salvan Los Toros.* Camille Beaumont and Juliette Jordain, of NOT The Sport of Kings, both lived in Paris and Niels Beekhof and Jan Hendricks lived in small apartments in Amsterdam. Lastly, Jeremy Ainsworth, the leader of A Lifetime in Cages, lived in the eastern side of Maidstock and Terri Sinclair resided in Canterbury. All residential warrants were served at 7:30 AM, as previous surveillance indicated that all targets would still be home. Conchita Verdura of the CNP waited outside the office of *Salvan*

Los Toros along with Paloma Retuerta and José Maria Duarte of the CNP forensic team, but Miguel Alonso wound up having the choicest assignment, as his team went to Victoria Valenzuela's apartment in Madrid. She opened her door wearing a black negligée, with a sheer black cover-up, earning smiles from all the men and hard stares for the two women in the unit.

Computers were removed, files searched, all cell phones confiscated and telephone records expunged from the offices and residences of thirteen individuals being investigated. After three days, the lead investigators reported back to Gino that there was nothing to be found.

"Shit," said Gino to Mercedes, "Nothing?"

"So far, nothing," she replied. "You know how thorough Paloma is. Her teams scoured everything in residences and the office—including all computers—and there is absolutely no evidence relating to the attack on de Portillo."

"And what about the three women's whereabout during the incidents in the other countries. Do they have alibis?"

"Well, nothing as perfect as their whereabouts for the de Portillo attack, but presumably, good enough. After all this time, memories have faded, but we have no evidence placing any of them at the scene of the other murders."

"And what have you heard from the other investigators/" Gino asked.

"I have been in touch with all of them, and it is the same story. Nothing in their offices nor in their homes turned up any evidence of, neither the murders, nor communication with each other. Oh, there was some E-mails between de Groot and Victoria, but only asking if one or the other was going to an upcoming conference. They did arrange to have dinner together at a PETA Legal Work For Animals meeting, in Brussels, but that's it. Nothing nefarious there."

"So, de Groot and Valenzuela know each other. Any other relationships between them?"

"There is some familiarity, but I couldn't call it a relationship. Paths crossed at various conferences and Victoria has met and communicated with Camille Beaumont in France, but again, nothing relating to our investigation. The records we went over from Lyon has indicated that some of our targets were together at several European meetings, but beyond that, there is no indication that they had contact with each other, and as you know, the only place where all four groups were at the same meeting is the annual conference of the International Animal Rights Group, in Luxembourg.

"What we all have seen is a tremendous amount of communication throughout the whole animal rights network, particularly between groups with similar interests. For instance, Victoria Valenzuela's phone shows multiple contacts with the *Partido Animalista* in Bilbao, most notably, Joseba Aguirre and Gorka Mendoza. Also, multiple contacts by phone and E-mail to people in the International Movement Against Bullfighting, League Against Cruel Sports, *Derechos para los Animales,* and on and on. It's the same in France, England and Amsterdam, these people are in constant communication with each other. Victoria's contact list goes on forever—Spain, Europe, the States, and that's not including people in government and the press. Interestingly, our Victoria did have a bird in her apartment, but it is a gray parrot."

"And I suppose the investigators got nowhere in determining where these individuals were at the time of the other attack?"

"All of them said the same thing, Gino. For the most part, they can't remember where they were, although a few did have some specifics placing them elsewhere at the time of the killing, but it is hard to challenge them because they have no recollection of where they were so long ago. Checking credit cards for travel also got us nowhere. If they did travel to these other cities, they certainly covered their tacks well. I hate to say it, but we are all at a dead end."

Gino organized another Zoom call with the lead investigators, and all reiterated the report by Mercedes. In all instances, each mentioned that their superiors were more than disappointed and started to question whether they were on the right track. However, Liz Lawrence, Vivienne Cousteau and Guus Arden were all convinced they were right. They were sure the targets planned these swapped assassinations, but they had no evidence to support their theories.

"Gino," said Liz Lawrence, "this has been the most comprehensive and expensive investigation we have ever done. The NCA has pointed out that we have spent countless man-hours, coordinated with law enforcement across four countries, with follow-up in the USA, Canada, Belgium and Luxembourg, and have nothing to show for it."

"Could there have been a leak in any of your agencies, tipping them off. Or a leak out of PETA or any of the other groups where we investigated membership and conference attendance?" asked Gino.

"That is certainly possible," replied Capitaine Cousteau. We were cautioned, and tried to keep a tight rein on this, but considering the number of detectives and analysts involved, checking into the files of the major animal rights organizations, then conference centers and hotels, some sympathizers could have revealed what we were doing and who we were investigating."

Feeling defeated, Gino shook his head. "That could very well be what happened, Vivienne. So many inquiries, to so many people and organizations, something was bound to slip. As these activists are so passionate about what they do, it wouldn't be out of the question that someone would want to protect on of their colleagues, and considering the ingenious planning involved with these attacks, I don't doubt that they would have a comprehensive plan in place to destroy any evidence, including communication with each other. But I have to raise the question, could we have been wrong?

"I would like to say no, but now, we seem to have a *collective*, perfect alibi. I have the feeling that it may be too perfect, too clean, I just don't believe it," lamented Gino.

"Neither do I," added Liz Lawrence, with all the other Zoom participants nodding agreement.

"Well, I am pleased that we all concur, but to keep all of our bosses happy, I am going to direct Lyon to do direct a deeper dive into the Animal Liberation Front. The ALF is the most stealth, most clandestine organization out there, and I suggest that we try to identify as many as their cells as we can in each city. Find out what activists may be responsible for, or suspected of, violent actions of any kind. Any kind. I don't care if they are protesting the force feeding of geese, the use of antibiotics in chickens, the abuse of donkeys, whatever. Your files may already have data of this type. Dig it out, go over it again.

"And Liz, your group was going to investigate further some of the bookmaking operations in the UK. The debt collectors working for Bookerboys were a question mark and you were going to look into who finances these operations.? It's not likely they would have anything to do with the killings outside of the UK, but I want them eliminated from the attack on Benny Dawson or retained as a viable suspect. I don't want to box us in on our collaborative planning theory in case the racetrack incident was a one-off operation."

"Despite the white feather?" asked Capitaine Cousteau.

"Yeah, we still have that, don't we?" murmured Gino

"Look, my opinion is that these efforts—into the ALF and the UK's bookmakers—will not be productive, so we must expand our investigation. As I said, I'll have Lyon dig further into the ALF, but you don't have to wait for Interpol. You all have enough to get the ball rolling. For now, however, we have to close the books on our four suspect animal rights groups. So sorry."

* * *

Months passed with nothing surfacing, nothing related to who killed Alejandro de Portillo, Claude Le Clerc, Dr. Arnold von Beek nor Benny Dawson. However, intensive investigation into the operating cells of the ALF did produce some results. Authorities were able to arrest seven individuals in the Netherlands for destruction of property in the release of animals from a research laboratory, the arrest and conviction of four persons for releasing minks from a breeding farm in Denmark, and the closing of a meat-packing operation in the north of France for accepting abused horses for butchering and sale. Small victories in the scheme of things as the European summer began to blossom.

Chapter Thirty-Six

Rafael Martínez Naranjo is groggy as he is led into the morning light by someone. He cannot remember anything other than he came to Pamplona for the *Feria de San Fermin*. As an event promoter, he has organized this event, the famous running of the bulls and the subsequent bullfights at the renowned Plaza de Toros Pamplona for many years but today, he does not remember such details. His senses begin to emerge from the cloud he is in, but he remains disoriented. He does realize he is being helped along by someone. He sees that this good samaritan is dressed in white, with a red sash around his waist, a red bandana covering his face below the dark, aviator sunglasses covering his eyes. He is also wearing a white, Panama hat. Naranjo notices that people all around him are also dressed in white with red sashes. Looking down, he sees that he too is also dressed in white. This seems strange to him. As some memories start to return, he thinks that he belongs in his box at the Plaza de Toros and pictures himself, resplendent in a blue, double-breasted suit, white shirt, and red tie.

His legs feel leaden as he shuffles along, giving the impression that he is one of the revelers all around him, who have been up all night, partying before the spectacle about to take place. He senses excitement in the crowd as the runners, similarly, bedecked in white and red, start pushing toward the barricaded street where they will run in front of charging bulls. Then, something stings his neck and he suddenly feels a jolt of energy, while he is pushed to the forefront of the surging crowd who will try to avoid the horns and hooves of a phalanx of charging, muscled bulls, each weighing more than five hundred kilos. Now, into the street, he no longer senses his companion, and sees that he is well behind the younger, faster runners as the bulls are released and close ranks on the frenzied people in front of them. He finds the energy to run, to escape, but is suddenly struck by the bull leading the pack. He is gored and then trampled, as the bulls make their way down the street toward the bullring, eight hundred meters away.

* * *

The *Feria de San Fermin* takes place in early July in Pamplona, Navarra, in the north of Spain, south of San Sebastian. The bulls have been running in this spectacle since 1591 but the event was formally organized in 1922 by the *Casa de Misericordia*—The House of Mercy—charity that benefits from the week-long event, made famous by the novel of Ernest Hemingway, The Sun Also Rises.

People come from all over the world to run in this iconic festival where fighting bulls, along with six to ten steers, are released from the *Coral de Gas* and the *Corales de Santa Domingo* to run 830 meters down the barricaded Mercaderes Street, to the *Plaza de Toros*. For seven days, the running is repeated at 8:00 AM each day, followed by spectacular *corridas* in the afternoon. News reports are written, televised, and filmed detailing the running of the bulls and the bullfights thereafter. The reports particularly capture the dangers of the event, citing the injured and often killed, runners who could not make it to the safety of the barricades, nor the spacious bullring.

* * *

Detective Chief Inspector Mercedes Garcia Rico was in her office at CNP headquarters in Madrid, when Rosa, her administrative assistant, entered with a fresh cup of *café solo*.

"Four idiots have been taken to the hospital this morning at the Running of the Bulls. Someone was also killed," she said, while placing the coffee on Mercedes' desk.

"*Dios mio,*" Mercedes remarked. "Another American or Brit?" knowing that Americans and British nationals often comprise a large contingent at the event, trying to outrun the marauding bulls.

"I don't know *Jefe*. A news flash popped up on my computer but gave no details. Only four injured and one killed."

"Will they ever learn?" commented Mercedes. "This is only the first day and one fatality already. God knows how many more will be injured and killed by the end of the week."

A little while later, Miguel Alonso, the primary inspector in her unit, knocked at the open door and entered her office.

"Would you believe it *Jefe?* Rafael Martínez Naranjo, one of Spain's most prominent bullfight promoters, was killed this morning in Pamplona. Apparently, he was trampled during the Running of the Bulls. Early reports say this is something he has never done before. He had no identification on him and was dressed like the runners in white, but someone at the hospital thought they knew him, and it checked out."

Putting down her coffee, which by now was cold, she said, "I don't know the man but he couldn't have been very young. *Qué demonios*—what-the-devil—was he doing, running with the bulls?"

"He was fifty-nine years old, *Jefe,* and I doubt he was in shape to try to outrun the bulls. Crazy, no?"

A sudden flutter in the pit of her stomach, made Mercedes pause. 'Miguel, get on the phone to CNP headquarters in Bilbao and have them liaise with the local police. I want to know everything about this. Get a team down there and find out everything—everything— about what went down this morning. Why on earth was this man out there? Have the local police get to the hospital, or the morgue, and make sure they do a full toxicology screen, immediately. I have a bad feeling about this." She then called Gino with the news.

* * *

That afternoon, Dr. Agustín Cebrían, the medical examiner for the city at the *Hospital de Navarra,* gave his report to the CNP investigators and detectives from the *Policia Foral de Navarrra.*

"Rafael Martínez Naranjo, age fifty-nine was killed as a result of blunt force trauma and exsanguination. He was gored by a bull, tearing his femoral artery, and bled to death, in addition to being trampled by, I don't know how many bulls. His toxicology screen showed the presence of scopolamine as well as an amphetamine. The scopolamine turned him into a zombie, totally lacking any free will. He could have been led into this situation, unaware of what was going on. I found a needle mark on his neck, probably where the amphetamine was administered, which could have given him a spark of energy as he was led to what became his death. With the presence of these drugs, I have ruled that this is no accident. This was a murder," Dr. Cebrían concluded.

Reviewing the news from the medical examiner, Mercedes called Alonso and Conchita Verdura to her office. It was close to 1:00 PM.

"We are going to Pamplona," she said. "Go home and pack an overnight bag and Rosa will book us on the next flight to Pamplona."

She then called Gino with the news from the medical examiner.

"Scopolamine, again?" he said. "We need to immediately find out where Victoria Valenzuela was this morning—immediately."

Mercedes thought for a few seconds and then made a change in plans. "Rosa, quickly find Miguel and Conchita. I need to get them to San Agustín de Guadalix."

Catching them before they left the building Mercedes gave them the new directive. "Miguel and Conchita, I need for you to get to the *Salvan Los Toros* office and find out where Victoria Valenzuela was this morning. Confirm the whereabouts of her two assistants also. I'm going to Pamplona with Gino, but you need to find out who was where this morning." She then called Gino again and told him to pack a bag for each of them as they would be going to Pamplona.

While Rosa was booking their flight, which would be late that afternoon, Mercedes called Elizabeth Lawrence, Vivienne Cousteau, and Gus Arden, directing them to find out where each of their persons-of-interest were between 7:00 and 9:00 AM this morning.

Chapter Thirty-Seven

Victoria Valenzuela was in her office that afternoon, after doing some shopping at *El Corte Inglés* in the morning.

But Victoria's activities actually began just after midnight when she arrived at the San Agustín de Guadalix office, meeting Martina Muñoz there. The two switched cars, Martina taking Victoria's BMW and Victoria taking Martina's Toyota Camry. Inside, Martina pinned up her hair and put on a wig; short, full black hair with a prominent cluster of white hair at her forehead, above her left eyebrow. Victoria had purchased the wig some time ago during one of her travels to Italy, at one of the foremost wig makers in Milan, just in case a need arose. This day, it did.

Victoria, dressed in jeans and a white shirt and wearing white athletic shoes and a generic baseball cap, tossed a duffle back in the back seat of the Toyota and set out for the almost four-hundred-kilometer trip to Pamplona. Martina, basically of the same height and build as Victoria, returned to Madrid and to Victoria's apartment on Paseo de la Castellano in Madrid. The apartment had no doorman at this time of night, and Martina was able to enter the apartment without incident. In the morning, around 9:30 AM, she donned the black wig with the white splotch of hair, descended to the parking garage and drove to *El Corte Inglés* to start shopping. Dressed in jeans and a white, man-tailored shirt and large, dark, white framed sunglasses. No one would be able to notice that she did not have Asian eyes.

Just after midday, Victoria was back at *Salvan Los Toros'* office, reuniting with Martina there, who no longer wore the wig she had on all morning. Inside, they exchanged car keys once again. Victoria had changed into a white outfit with red sash and red bandana, in the car at a deserted section of a gas station just outside of Pamplona on the way there. Returning to Madrid, she changed again at the same gas station, removing the white and red outfit, Panama hat and the thick, padded vest that disguised her feminine, hourglass figure, all going back into the black duffle bag in the back seat. She was now in the jeans and white shirt again, with the gray baseball cap. On the return to Madrid, each of the items she changed out of were placed in a brown plastic bag and were disposed of at various rest stops along the way, careful to elude any security cameras that may have been there.

The scenario Victoria had concocted was that she spent the morning shopping in the heart of Madrid, being observed by a multitude of other shoppers, salespeople—with Martina using Victoria's charge card—and several CCTV cameras in the parking garage. Returning to the *Salvan Los Toros* office, the BMW was parked outside with her clothing purchases in the trunk. Luz took the wig Martina had used and, in the bathroom, cut all the hair off and flushed it down the toilet. All that was left was fibrous skull cap. She then drove about a kilometer away, to a McDonalds, where she bought three quarter-pounders with cheese, three cokes and before she departed, placed what remained of the wig in a brown plastic bag, depositing it in a dumpster behind the building. In short order, the three ladies were in their office eating lunch, Victoria (really Martina) after a morning of shopping and Martina (after posing as Victoria) getting to the office late, having endured an upset stomach in the morning and Luz, at her desk until the others arrived. Perfect alibis, and to ensure that, Victoria took the clothes Martina had purchased into the office and tried them on, not for size, but to get her DNA on the garments.

By pre-arranged and secure communication, Victoria had instructed all her partners in crime at Not the Sport of Kings, A Lifetime in Cages and End Animal Research-Now, to be visible, somewhere, that morning. It was relatively simple, with all the French team at their jobs or in a meeting (Chapelle), Jeremy Ainsworth behind his desk at the Barclay Bank, Edwin Bolton at work at the Dungeness power plant, Terri Sinclair conducting a tour of Leeds Castle. Her Dutch colleagues were equally occupied with de Groot and Hendricks at their jobs at Phillips, and Niels Beekhof at his apartment after working at the hospital all night, clocking an hour of overtime, and leaving Slotervaartziekenhaus at 5:00 AM. If they would need alibis, they had them—perfect ones.

Later that afternoon, when Miguel Alonso and Conchita Verdura arrived at the *Salvan Los Toros* office, Victoria—their primary person of interest—Martina and Luz were busy working. Victoria, after a morning of shopping—with the evidence in the trunk of her car—could not have been anywhere near Pamplona that morning. As with de Portillo, Victoria would shed no tears for Naranjo. Martina, after being ill that morning, supposedly arrived at the office late, but the investigators could do nothing to discredit that and Luz, being in contact with several supporters, was at the office all morning, and telephone records would support that.

* * *

"So," Gino began, addressing Mercedes the following morning at the Hospital de Navarra, "you are telling me that all of the *Salvan Los Toros* staff and Victoria were in Madrid at the time Rafael Martinez Naranjo was killed. Have you heard back from Liz, Vivienne or Guus?"

"Just DCI Lawrence, so far. All the Lifetime In Cages group were accounted for. They all were working at their jobs and Alice Bolton was with her dogs."

"Of course, why would I think any of them was at the Running of the Bulls in Pamplona? Out of the question," he said sarcastically.

"While we wait for Vivienne and Guus to get back to me, I have instructed the local CNP detectives to work with their counterparts and search everywhere for CCTV cameras, as well as pressing local and national news outlets for pictures or videos of this morning's event. This is the most photographed spectacle in the world, so once in hand, we'll be able to search the crowds for Naranjo and anyone he may have been with."

Gino and Mercedes then met with Dr. Cebrían early the next morning, who once again gave his findings. Nothing changed. Naranjo was trampled, gored, and bled to death before any medical help could reach him.

"Naturally, we removed his clothes Inspectors, and they are in two bags over there," pointing to two, white plastic bags with a string tie. "Also found this," picking up a small, zip-lock bag. "A feather, probably a pigeon feather by the look of it. It was tucked in his pants pocket, and I'm afraid it took a bit of a beating," pointing to the bent and broken feather, although still in one piece.

Mercedes took the bag from Cebrían, and held it up, examining it on all sides before passing it to Gino. They then looked at each other.

"No *pluma blanca*," said Gino.

"No, *una pluma gris*"—a gray feather—remarked Mercedes, "and it doesn't appear to be cut. Maybe the white dove flew away?"

"It certainly may have," replied Gino. "If anyone of our suspects were housing a white dove, the source of all those white feathers, it could have been released, not destroyed—although that could have happened."

"Not likely, considering that protecting animals is their main mission," said Mercedes.

"It could be that they used whatever feather they could find in this incident. The white dove is gone, hopefully flying fine without several tail feathers, and they used this pigeon feather to taunt us, letting us know they are still in business. Can we get a DNA check with your office in Bilbao?" Gino asked.

"We can do it here in Pamplona," offered Dr. Cebrían, "at the *Clinica Universidad de Navarra*. Might have it here by tomorrow."

"The job is yours, Doctor. Once you have the data, call me," handing Cebrían on of her cards. "I'll arrange for the feather and your report to be picked up by one of our detectives," said Mercedes. "They will also pick up the clothing and get it to our forensic team."

Rafael Martinez Naranjo's body was then slid back into a narrow wall containing six stainless-steel drawers.

Walking out of the basement morgue to an elevator, Gino said, "Let's have your people check out where Naranjo was staying. I understand he lives in Bilbao and undoubtedly had a hotel here for the week. He is the impresario of this event and would likely be involved in all aspects of the feria, and certainly, not dressed in the clothes in those bags."

Laughing, Mercedes said, "For sure. He was undoubtedly put into that outfit by someone, or several perpetrators, at his hotel. We'll find out where he was registered and get a forensic team over there before somebody cleans the room. I'm sure our CNP guys and local police are on this already. Let me make a call," and they entered the elevator to go up.

* * *

Mercedes and Gino were staying overnight in Pamplona at the Hotel Pamplona Plaza in Old Town, a short walk from where the Running of the Bulls starts. The two CNP Bilbao detectives that traveled to Pamplona were also staying over, at a lesser, but nearby hotel.

Arrangements were made for the two CNP Bilbao detectives and representatives from the *Policia Foral de Navarra,* the autonomous police agency for the community of Navarra, which includes Pamplona, to meet later that morning. *Policia Foral de Navarra's* autonomy from the CNP—Spain's National Police Force—initially created some tensions as some of the CNP's responsibilities were transferred to this Basque unit. However, in instances of national implications, the two worked together as they would be doing now.

They came together for a late breakfast at the Hotel Pamplona Plaza. Representing the Navarra police was Mikel Montoya and Nikola Ibaiguren. Mikel was tall, slim, in his thirties with a thick black hair and a full black beard. Nikola, about the same age, was a petite woman with black hair pulled back into a tight ponytail and with hard, dark eyes below thick black eyebrows. The CNP Bilbao detectives were Xavier Vegara and Marko Ibarra, both in their late thirties. Both men were clean shaven with Vegara sporting a bushy moustache and neatly trimmed black hair and Ibarra, chestnut brown hair, long, covering his ears and flowing over his shirt collar. The four detectives were drinking coffee and eating some kinds of croissants when Mercedes and Gino joined them. Introductions were made and

Gino and Mercedes pored themselves coffee from a carafe on the table.

Mercedes began, explaining that the incident in Pamplona could be related to a killing in Madrid and others in Paris, Amsterdam and outside of London—equally harsh and violent. The four detectives exchanged looks with each other. "When I heard about the killing of this bullfighting promoter, I immediately asked the CNP in Bilbao to coordinate with local police and collect everything that they could about the victim and the circumstances of his death. I understand that they immediately alerted your unit in Navarra."

"Si," said Nikola," who appeared to be the senior agent. "We obviously heard about the incident and it was only when CNP contacted us did we understand that this was no accident, but a planned murder. May I relate to you what we have learned in the last twenty-four hours?"

"Yes, please."

Nikola opened a notebook and began to read. "Rafael Martinez Naranjo, age fifty-nine, lives in Bilbao with his wife Estrella. Married thirty-four years with two children. The son is twenty-eight years old and his daughter, twenty-five. Neither lives at home. The son resides in San Sebastian and is an importer, and the girl is studying in the *Universidad de Salamanca.*

"Naranjo has been organizing and promoting the *Feria de San Fermin* for twelve years as well as promoting other bullfighting events in the north of Spain. He is quite successful and very well known. He has been in Pamplona two days, staying in a suite at the Gran Hotel d'Oro"

"We had a forensic team in there late last night, dusting for prints and checking everything for any signs of evidence," added

Mikel Montoya. His dress clothes were still in the closet. Nothing of interest yet."

"Does the hotel have electronic keys," asked Gino. "Can we determine if anyone entered the room, other than housekeeping, when Naranjo wasn't there?"

'Unfortunately, no," replied Nikola. "They still use those clunky, heavy metal keys, that you leave at the reception desk when you leave the hotel."

"So, someone may have accessed his key when he was out."

"Possible, but the hotel says there is someone on duty at the reception desk twenty-four hours a day," replied Nikola.

"Okay, sorry to interrupt detective Montoya," said Gino.

Montoya continued. "Naranjo had dinner last night at Kartuzarra, one of the finest restaurants in the city. He ate with an administrator of the *Casa de Misericordia*—Terese Gamiz— the charity that supports and benefits from the *Feria de San Fermin*. Gamiz and her staff work closely with Naranjo throughout the year, planning the feria and the events surrounding it. They finished dinner after 11:00 PM and then went their own way. The restaurant is in walking distance from his hotel, and staff at Kartuzarra remember him walking in that direction. He returned to the hotel, asked the receptionist for his key and the man remembers seeing him walk to the elevators."

"Was he alone?" asked Mercedes.

"He can't remember. The lobby was very crowded with people already celebrating the event, and they were quite noisy. He saw him walking through some of the crowd toward the elevator and nothing more," replied Montoya.

"And that is where we are so far," added Xavier Vegara of the CNP. "We have contacted all news and public relations groups to obtain copies of videos taken of the crowd before the bulls being released. There are CCTV cameras around the plazas, at Mercaderes Street and near the bullring. We are in the process of getting that footage but have not secured anything yet. There will be no issues. We will get everything later today."

"What about visitors to Naranjo while at the hotel?" asked Mercedes

"No one that we know of, but again, the lobby has been quite crowded the last few days with people checking in and spill-over from the bar and dining room, which are just off the lobby," said Vegara.

"Any cameras in the hotel?" asked Gino.

"Yes," said Nikola, pausing and then adding, "but they are not working."

"Wonderful," said Gino, softly. "Did anyone see Naranjo leave the hotel yesterday morning? He was dressed like most of the runners, but he is a bit overweight and given his age, he should have stood out."

"No one from the hotel staff can remember him, but the lobby was extremely crowed with tourists, as most were preparing to head toward the start of the event or line up behind the barricade to view the running. Some of my officers showed Naranjo's picture to hotel guests that afternoon, but again, no recollection of the man."

"Then we have to wait for CCTV and other videos taken that morning," said Mercedes.

Despite the incident from the day before, the Running of the Bulls took place as scheduled the following day. After Gino and Mercedes' meeting with the detectives, much of the crowd had dissipated, and the two of them walked to the barricaded street. There were a few injuries that morning—two Americans, a Brit, and a young man from Sweden—but none seriously, and Gino and Mercedes decided to walk the eight hundred and thirty meters to the bullring.

"These runners keep the hospital quite busy during the feria," said Mercedes. Dr. Cebrían told me that they bring in additional orthopedists as broken bones are the main injury of the runners. Turning to Gino she asked, "Would you ever consider running with the bulls?"

"I read The Sun Also Rises by Hemingway when I was in college, and there was a movie made with many big stars of the day, Tyrone Power, Errol Flynn—and I don't want to hear you moaning—Ava Gardner."

"Oh, God. Here we go again," Mercedes lamented.

Ignoring her, Gino continued. "I read the book and saw the movie, and there is no question, it was terribly exciting, especially to a young man. But no, I would not have tried it if I had the opportunity. You have to be a little mad, or a little drunk, to try to outrun a charging bull—many charging bulls."

The two continued walking down the now-deserted street, except for those cleaning up the area, to the bullring, where tourists continued to mull about the arena. All peaceful until later that afternoon when the *corridas* take place.

* * *

By early evening, several sources of videos and film footage was in the *Policia Foral de Navarra's* headquarters in the city. The agency, aided by two CNP computer technicians, created a digital image of Naranjo, using his face and body type, adding the clothes he would have been wearing that morning. Along with three analysts from the forensic team, an 8 x 10 created picture of the man, dressed as a runner, was propped up beside each's monitor as they reviewed footage from the cameras and the news teams. It was tedious work, looking through the crowds, freezing images, and continuing again.

"I think I have something," one of the analysts cried out. Immediately, she was surrounded by members of the detective squad, as well as Gino and Mercedes.

"Look, look, that could be him," she exclaimed, freezing the image she had isolated.

"You may be right," Mercedes said, "It could be Naranjo. Keep running the film—slowly—and keep tracking him."

Playing with her controls, the young woman focused on the image they believed could be Naranjo, as he negotiated through the crowd. "He is with someone. Freeze it there," said Mercedes, and magnify the image."

The crowd was intense, shoulder to shoulder, shuffling toward the starting point. "There," Mercedes said, pointing to the image on the screen. "Is that someone with him, holding him?"

It was extremely hard to make out the images in a sea of people— mostly young men—all blending together, but it looked like a man, dressed in white with a white hat, was next to Naranjo, and stayed with him as the crowd moved. "White hat, red bandana and sunglasses," said Mercedes. "Can you make him out?"

All could see the image they had isolated, and they continued to track the men, frame by frame, but nothing better emerged. Naranjo looked to be guided by a man in a white hat, red bandana covering his face and dark, aviator sunglasses. Then, they lost them in the crowd. They could not make out the Naranjo entering Mercaderes street in front of bulls, but other videos could see Naranjo entering the street and then being struck and trampled, but his companion was never seen again. Over and over, they reviewed the films, but in only one could Naranjo and his companion be detected.

"Well," said Gino, we almost got to see the crime in progress," turning to address the others. "That's more than we ever had."

"Yes, it is extraordinary," added Mercedes, "but there is really not enough here to identify this other person. We barely could see them, bobbing heads amongst hundreds, but yes, it is more than we have ever had."

Backing away, she pulled out her phone from her purse. "Just got a text from Cebrían. The feather is from a plain, old European pigeon, *Columba palumbus.* The plazas throughout Spain are full of such feathers. They probably just picked one up. It tells us nothing."

They then began again at square one, as they did with the de Portillo case. Possible enemies, threats to Naranjo, complaints, and petitions against him to various regulatory agencies, meeting with the Casa de Misericordia staff, anything, and everything to come up with a lead. And, since they were in the area, Gino and Mercedes would pay a visit to the Partido Animalista in Bilbao.

Chapter Thirty-Eight

Following the running of the bulls the next morning, Mercedes met with the two CNP Bilbao detectives and laid out two tasks for herself and Gino.

"Before we return to Madrid, I want to meet with Señora Gamiz of the *Casa de Misericordia* and thereafter, travel up to Bilbao to meet with the leaders of the *Partido Animalista de Bilbao.*" Turning to Xavier, she asked, "If you are returning to Bilbao sometime today, maybe we can ride with you, after we meet with Señora Gamiz."

"No need to make the trip, *Inspector Jefe*. They are here in Pamplona. I saw that they had a registration tent set up near the car-park on the far side of the bullring."

"We never walked that far yesterday," said Gino, looking toward Mercedes.

"No, we stopped and turned around at the point where the running bulls enter the ring. To Xavier, she asked, "Do you know who was at that tent?"

"I didn't look that closely, but I know that the *Partido* will be here all week, as they usually are during the *Feria de San Fermin*. Beside protesting the Running of the Bulls as well as the bullfights—passing out all kinds of literature and making a nuisance of themselves—they try to register as many Spaniards as they can for their political party.

They are close to securing official status, which would allow them to field candidates for political office in this autonomy."

"That's great. Hopefully, the people we want to talk with are here. Gino and I will go there now and save our visit to the *Casa de Misericordia* for later."

* * *

The *Partido de Animalista de Bilbao* was set up in a tent, about four meters by four meters square. There was a high counter in the back with three stools in form of it and two small tables with three chairs to the left and right of the entrance to the tent. Another table had stacks of literature and registration forms. A large sign bearing the name *Partido de Animalista de Bilbao* hung over the entrance portal.

Remembering Miguel Alonso's description of Gorka Mendoza, leader of the activist group, Mercedes entered the tent—with Gino following—striding directly to the small, slender man with a full, black beard, near the counter. His image, as described by Alonso, was hard to forget. As he was bald on top, with long, flowing hair over his ears and down the back of his neck, obscuring his shirt collar. Miguel said he looked like a cross between an orchestra conductor and a member of the Taliban, so the image stuck in her mind, suppressing a smile as she neared the man.

"*Señor* Gorka Mendoza?" she asked, stopping directly in front of the man.

"*Si,*" the man responded with a look of mild curiosity at the attractive woman before him.

Mercedes showed her credentials and introduced herself and then Gino, using their official titles.

"Interpol and the CNP," Mendoza responded, "And what have I done to warrant a visit from such prestigious authorities?"

"Nothing—I hope," answered Mercedes. "You have, of course, heard about the incident involving Rafael Martinez Naranjo."

"Yes. I would like to say, 'how terrible,' but we shed no tears for this man. Besides, what was he doing running with the bulls? He had to be drunk."

"Not drunk, *Señor* Mendoza, but you soon will read that he had been drugged and this was not a thoughtless act of a man testing his virility. This was murder."

Pausing for a moment, Mendoza remarked, "Well now. This sounds like the incident involving Alejandro de Portillo over a year ago. Some of your people visited me and my colleagues then. Are you aware of that, *Inspector Jefe?*"

"I sent them, *Señor* Mendoza. Considering your history, the *Partido Animalista* becomes a subject of interest when such violence occurs, none more than now, with Naranjo murdered in your back yard, and you right here at the scene of the crime."

Now joined by two other individuals that were in the tent, Mendoza said, "We are always here during the *Feria de San Fermin*, Inspector. It is our most active event during the year, especially for securing new registrations for the *Partido*. Despite so many people coming for the Running of the Bulls, you would be surprised that so many, many, are sympathetic to our cause. Maybe their lust for blood and violence against these animals makes them feel a little guilty, so they come to our tent after the running and before the *corridas* in the afternoon. They enjoy a little Rioja—which we will be offering soon—talk with us, and many from this autonomy register for our party. Oddly," looking toward Gino, "many Americans want to register with us. You are American, are you not?"

"Yes, I am," replied Gino.

"Well, we thank the Americans for their interest, give them some literature, but unfortunately, we cannot register them with our political party. Spaniards only, *si*?" Pausing, he then added, "Forgive my bad manners. Joseba Aguirre and Esteba Zubin"—pointing left and then right to the two men that had gathered around him—"are my trusted colleagues and are very committed to our cause." Aguirre and Zubin nodding with Mendoza's introduction.

"Since each of you are so committed to your cause," Mercedes asked, "would you be so kind to tell me where each of you were, two nights ago and the following morning, between 7:00 and 8:00 AM?

Smiling, Gorka Mendoza replied, "We were right here. We set up the tent the night before the running and were here early that morning to set up our literature and registration forms. I think the local police will attest to that."

"All of you? "asked Gino.

"All, plus Nikola Ibarra. We ate dinner together at the Bar La Comedia on *Calle Comedias* at around 10 o'clock. Then returned to the Hostal Arriazu, where we stay every year during the *feria*. Very close to everything."

"And the *hostal* can attest to your being there?" asked Mercedes.

Joseba Aguirre laughed. "Well, this isn't a five-star hotel, Inspector. Sometimes there is someone at the front desk, sometimes there isn't, but I do believe that someone was there the night you are asking about. We are still registered there, so you can check with them. It's right off the Plaza del Castillo."

"We will, *caballero's*—gentlemen. I thank you for your time, You may hear from us again," added Mercedes and she and Gino turned and left the tent.

"Oh, by the way, where is this Nikola Ibarra?" asked Gino.

"At the printer," replied Mendoza. "We ran short of registration forms."

Back at their hotel, Mercedes tracked down Xavier and Marko. "Xavier, advise Montoya and Ibaiguren that we spoke with the key players of the *Partido Animalista de Bilbao*—Señores Mendoza, Aguirre and Zubin. Check that they were at the Bar La Comedia the night before the incident and then with the Hostal Arriazu, where they are staying. See if they remember them returning to the hostal sometime after 10:00 PM and if anyone left during the night. A Nikola Ibarra as well. We need to confirm their alibis. Gino and I are going to visit with Terese Gamiz, so it will be up to you and your colleagues from the *Policia Foral de Navarra* to investigate threats or any complaints about Naranjo with local and regional authorities. Someone from the *Policia Foral* has contacted *Señora* Naranjo in Bilbao, but I want you to visit her and see if she can add anything regarding possible enemies. Get authorization to investigate his office files in Bilbao as well."

Chapter Thirty-Nine

La Casa de Misericordia—The House of Mercy—dates to 1706, when the charity was founded to support the elderly and poor of the municipality. Essentially it is a nursing home that today houses almost six hundred people, with three hundred medical and nursing professionals caring for them. This private charity is both the beneficiary and organizing body for all the events of the Feria de San Fermin. *La Comisión Taurina de la Junta de la Casa de Misericordia*—The Bullfighting Commission Board of the House of Mercy—owns and operates the bullring in Pamplona, selecting the ranches from which bulls will be drawn to run and fight in the ring. The charity runs the whole thing.

Originally founded by the Pamplona City Council—under the invocation of Our Lady of Mercy—in order to control the beggars and homeless of the community, it soon took on a more benevolent mission to support them in line with Christian doctrine. Originally their mission included the care of impoverished children, but evolved to primarily, care of the elderly.

Its current building was inaugurated in 1932, but it's very first home for the elderly and the poor was at the time of its founding, located within the then-walled area of the city. Over the years, the Provincial Council continued to support the charity, improving its facilities, and including donations of land. These land acquisitions were used to create fairgrounds as well as improvements to town infrastructure, and most importantly, ownership of the *Plaza de Toros de Pamplona*, the third largest bullring in Spain.

Terese Gamiz is a member of the Board of Directors that plan and operate the events associated with the feria and all things relating to the bulls, the marquis feature of the Feria de San Fermin. In her early sixties, she was a tall, stately woman with short—almost blue—gray hair, coiffed in soft waves. Her eyes were piecing blue, ice blue, rare in this region of the country. A quick check before confirming this appointment, Mercedes discovered that Gamiz had been a mid-level member of the Pamplona Provincial Administration, breaking through a glass ceiling in her middle age, at the time, the only woman achieving such a position, eventually leading to her joining the administrative staff of the nursing home. Her husband was a physician, also employed by the *Casa de Misericordia* until his death four years ago. The Gamiz name was well established and respected within the charity as well as with ongoing donors.

"I understand you want to speak with me about Rafael Martinez Naranjo," began Gamiz after introductions. "You know we had dinner together the night before he died."

"Yes, we are aware of that Señora. We would like to know the nature of your conversation that night, particularly if he mentioned any concerns or threats, he might have received. You know his death has been classified as a murder, so any light that you can shed about his demeanor that night might be helpful," said Mercedes.

"Well, first of all, you should know that I disliked the man. I have been a senior administrator of the nursing operation—and still am—but I have been on the *Comisión Taurina* for the last five years, where I have had the displeasure of working with Señor Naranjo."

"Why did you dislike the man," asked Gino, in moderately good Spanish.

"Gamiz smiled. "We can converse in English Inspector Cerone or is it Superintendent Cerone?" glancing down at the card he had given to her.

"That would be most helpful, Señora, and either is fine," replied Gino.

"*Bueno. Entonces*—Then—why did I dislike him? It was about money. It is always about money, no? About 30% of the revenue from the operation of the festival and all associated events, go to the cost of running this facility. We have almost six hundred residents here, many under continuous medical care. We employ three hundred doctors and nurses and another one hundred and fifty for orderlies, kitchen and dining staff and janitorial service. Then there is the cost of maintaining this almost one hundred-year-old building. So, it is always about money, and I'm sure Naranjo was taking bribes.

"Taking money that he was not entitled to?" asked Mercedes.

"Yes. The most important activity that goes into this week of spectacles is the selection of the ranches we work with to procure the bulls for the *corridas*, and the running, of course. These are largely decisions by our Board, but Naranjo actively participates, based on his knowledge of all the breeding ranches and the quality of their bulls. The same occurs with the selection of the *matadors* and their *corrida* teams. That process starts right after we complete the current year's event and we begin evaluations and planning for next year's *feria*," Gamiz explained.

"We also strive to be fair, paying the breeders and the *toreros* what they deserve. I thought, and I must say that I was the only one, who believed Naranjo was extracting payments from the breeders—some, anyway—and the *torero* teams that were selected." She thought for a second. "Under the table?"

"Was that what you discussed at dinner, accepting bribes?" Mercedes asked.

"It was. It had come to my attention—quite unofficially— that payments were being extracted by Naranjo from those that had been selected, but I had no proof and no one wanted to come forward to confirm what was going on. The man was arrogant, rude, disrespectful, but nevertheless, a very successful promotor who, over the years, had developed an allegiance with many of the Board members. Traditions are hard to break, you see. As I was the only one on the Board with these suspicions, my concerns were not taken seriously, and Naranjo knew that. The *feria*, year after year, continued to be the most successful bullfighting spectacle in the country. The whole world knows of the Running of the Bulls," pausing, "while virtually no one know who Saint Fermin was."

"The patron saint of Pamplona." Gino added.

"Yes, of course, although he remains somewhat of a mystery. May I share with you some background?" Gamiz asked.

"Please," said Mercedes.

"Fermin was a holy man and martyr, sometime in the third century. Ordained in France, he returned to Pamplona as its first bishop, but was persecuted for his belief in Christianity. More legend that historical fact, Fermin was supposedly martyred by being tied to a bull by his feet and dragged to his death. Hence, the connection of San Fermin and the fighting bull, and the feria that celebrates him."

"That explains something," added Gino. "I thought it was odd that a Christian charity and the benevolent mission of the *Casa de Misericordia*, could be tied to such violence against Spain's magnificent fighting bull, but I guess that how Fermin was martyred, explains some of that."

"Yes, but never forget tradition. It is quite hard to break in my country. The Running of the Bulls goes back hundreds of years. Despite the outcries from animal rights groups—and we hear this all the time—the work we do in this community, the lives we save, are due to the revenue generated by the *Feria de San Fermin,* so we give thanks for the sacrifice of these bulls. In many ways, they are our patron saints."

Thinking that they were getting more information than they needed, Mercedes sought to bring Terese Gamiz back to the demise of Naranjo. "So, Señora, your evening with Naranjo seemed to have been somewhat confrontational."

"He wanted to make peace and urged me to stop raising issues of his integrity and devotion to the success of the *feria* and —as he reminded me—the massive contribution the event makes to the *Casa de Misericordia.* It would be a mistake to tarnish this spectacle with rumors that could only damage its image to the world. In the end, we enjoyed an excellent dinner and went our own way."

"Last question, Señora Gamiz. Could you think of anyone that would want to murder this man in such a symbolic way," asked Gino.

"No one, I'm afraid, although I regard this as a stain on the *feria* as well as the *Casa de Misericordia.* I did not like him, but would not wish him harm, and I must say that our Board thought very highly of him."

Thanking Terese Gamiz for her time and insights, Gino and Mercedes wished her well, and departed.

Chapter Forty

Reluctantly leaving the ongoing investigation in the hands of the *Policia Foral de Navarra* and the CNP detectives from Bilbao, Gino and Mercedes booked a late afternoon flight to Madrid. At the airport, Gino called Klaus Schickhaus and brought him up to date.

"So again, you're saying you have nothing," Schickhaus commented.

"We still have suspicions about the *Partido Animalista de Bilbao*, but their alibis seem to be holding up. Mercedes and I met with them, but they have witnesses that confirmed their whereabouts at the time of the killing."

"Ha, what else is new?" Schickhaus added. "We have crimes—murders—five murders and all suspects have perfect alibis. This is just unacceptable, Gino. Unacceptable and embarrassing. Four national police forces, armed with an incredible amount of information and profiles, supported by all the resources of European Interpol, and we have no evidence whatsoever."

"No hard evidence, Klaus, but we know we are being duped. Who can create and execute such a conspiracy across four nations, and leave us in the dark? What kind of mastermind are we dealing with?" said Gino, almost to himself

"In terms of achieving their mission—to save and protect

animals—these perpetrators have succeeded enormously," added Schickhaus. "Never has the furor against greyhound racing, the use of animals in research, manipulating thoroughbred horse racing and the slaying of bulls in arenas before cheering spectators, have ever been so great. Donations to animal rights groups have tripled in the last year. PETA has never seen such levels of contributions to their causes and the pressure on governments is unrelenting. These people—whoever they are—have done more in one year than has been accomplished over the last five years. That is what we are hearing."

"There is no doubt that they have achieved a lot of good, but at the expense of five lives. Five, not so innocent lives, but five human beings have been murdered. It is like a Jack The Ripper scenario. Bodies, mutilated bodies all over the place, but no killer. Only a legend persists in England and we may be on our way to creating another one with these attacks," lamented Gino.

"I make no apologies for saying this Gino, but this has to fall back to you and Mercedes. You have unraveled such conspiracies before, involving some really bad guys. The difference here is that we seem to have some really *good* guys doing incredibly bad things. That is the twist that must be unraveled. Get back to it, Gino. Unravel, think unravel. Do it," concluded Schickhaus.

* * *

On the plane, Gino and Mercedes said very little after Gino apprised her of his conversation with Schickhaus. It was an exhausting two days and they needed the short flight to decompress…and think.

Back at their apartment, Gino said, "Unravel, Mercedes. Schickhaus fully expects us to unravel this conundrum."

"And where do we start, Gino? Start again, really. We have been down this road again and again for almost a year and a half."

"We go back, Mercedes. We start again at the beginning, with *Salvan Los Toros.*"

"With Victoria Valenzuela, you mean."

"Yes, we start again with Victoria Valenzuela, and I will take the lead on this," Gino asserted.

"We interview her again?"

"*I* will interview her again. She talked very freely with me and I want another crack at her."

* * *

This time, Gino made arrangements to meet with Valenzuela at her apartment. He prepared by going over everything they had developed before; notes from Mercedes' visit with her, notes from his own conversation, information garnered from their visit with Kim Watanabe, Victoria's mother, and details from Miguel Alonso and Conchita Verdura's meeting with her only a few days ago, and then challenging Interpol for an updated psychological profile of the woman.

"*Buenas tardes*, Chief Superintendent Cerone," Victoria said, opening the door to her apartment and inviting Gino in.

"*Buenas tardes, Señorita*" Gino replied, walking into her foyer, and following her to the living room. "Thank you for seeing me."

There was no question that the beauty of this woman was disarming and her Asian features just added to the mystery about her.

"I was told that you still had an active warrant for my office and residence, so I had no choice but to comply," Victoria said. She was wearing a one-piece, black, short-sleeved, form-fitting jumpsuit opened at the neck and with trousers, slightly belled at the bottom.

She wore black silk slippers with a low heel, with what appeared to be Japanese characters embroidered in bright green on the top. Emerald studs embellished her ear lobes, a compliment to her jade-green eyes.

"Please sit," she said. "Can I get you a glass of wine?"

"If you will join me, yes. That would be very nice."

A Rioja?" she asked as she moved to a small bar at the side of the room.

"Of course," Gino answered as he sat in a white leather armchair.

All the furniture in the room was white leather. A sofa, loveseat and two armchairs. A glass top table was centered with the furniture, all on a blue, green, red, and gold oriental carpet. Off to the right was a large birdcage, with a quiet, immobile, gray bird, perched on a crafted tree branch. It was light gray with white circles around its eyes and with bright red-orange tail feathers. It was about thirty centimeters tall, including the tail feathers and the cage was more than a meter high.

As Victoria returned with the two glasses of wine, Gino remarked, "What a lovely bird. A parrot, no?"

"Rafa is an African Gray Parrot. Its species is generally found in North Africa. Rafa's lineage, however, is from the Ivory Coast."

"Beautiful bird. Is it confined to its cage or do you let it out sometimes?" Gino asked.

"Oh, yes, I do let Rafa out most of the time when I am at home. It often perches on my shoulder when I am reading or watching television. He flies back to the cage when he wants to eat or to relieve himself."

"Quite well trained."

"Yes, he is. I would love a dog, but keeping it cooped up in the apartment wouldn't be fair, so Rafa is an excellent companion and very easy to care for. He knows sixteen words and a few sentences.

He says '*Mommy mierda*—poop—when he flies back to his cage to defecate. Funny, no?" Then raising her glass of wine, she said "*Saludos*—to your health—and they both sipped the Rioja.

"Very nice," Gino commented.

"It is a 2010 vintage. Quite an excellent year, but now, how can I help you?"

"First a question. How is it that you keep an animal—a bird, Rafa—in a cage? Isn't that a form of abuse? Shouldn't Rafa be free?"

"You are quite right, Chief Superintendent. Rafa was amongst almost one hundred Gray Parrots smuggled into the country, destined for pet shops. The police, perhaps your wife's CNP, discovered the illegal activity and arrested the smugglers, confiscating the birds. Many were in poor condition, and the ornithologists at the Madrid Zoo took over their care and rehabilitation. There was no way to send them back to Africa and free them. The zoo set up an exhibition with many of them and me and many friends, adopted the others, caring for them and giving them a safe home, albeit, in a cage. This was the best outcome of a disturbing situation."

"Commendable Señorita. But now, to the purpose of my visit. I must advise you, that you are under no obligation to talk to me. With two bullfighting promoters killed by bulls in Spain, you and other anti-bullfighting groups are, of course, subjects of interest, but if you would feel more comfortable to have a lawyer present, we could do this another day."

"No, this is quite comfortable. I enjoyed our conversation before, so no need to bring in lawyers."

"Good," Gino replied. "The notoriety of these killings—including the one in Bilbao earlier this week—has, I have read, generated a tremendous number of new contributions to *Salvan Los Toros* and other similar groups."

"Yes, that is very true. Donations have been spectacular and the press has been very helpful in reporting about the savagery these animals endure in the bullring."

"So, these deaths have benefitted your cause?"

"Yes, as never before, so while the deaths are quite tragic, they have brought more attention to the plight of these magnificent animals. I said to you and your colleague—Mercedes, your wife —that I shed no tears for Alejandro de Portillo, nor for Rafael Martinez Naranjo, who died in Pamplona. These men propagate the cruelest of sports and we won't rest until bullfighting is banned in this country. But of course, you know that the activist groups against greyhound racing, the doping of racehorses and the use of animals in medical research have also benefited by these tragic circumstances. Throughout Europe there is an uproar against our horrible treatment of innocent animals.

"You have contact with these other groups?" asked Gino.

Laughing and throwing her head back, she replied, "You know I do Chief Superintendent. We are an aligned community. I am a friend of Max de Groot, so I am familiar with the work of his group in the Netherlands against the use of animals in research."

"And Camille Beaumont. You also are friends with her and are aware of her group's efforts to clean up horse racing in France," remarked Gino.

"In France and all over the world. Camille and I have met at a few European conferences and I do consider her a friend, although we don't see much of each other. But I have many friends amongst the animal rights community."

"Do you also have friends in the anti-greyhound racing movement?" Gino asked.

"I can't say that I do, but greyhound racing is probably the cruelest of organized sports in the world. I know about the killing of a promoter in England some time ago, and again—sorry—no tears."

"I find it strange that you are friends with people from groups that have been investigated about these killings, don't you?"

"Strange? No. Any one of these groups will have friends throughout the animal rights movement. These groups have allegiances with each other. We pray for each of them to be successful in their missions. Our paths cross from time to time, at conferences and meetings throughout Europe and we often call or E-mail each other. Nothing strange nor coincidental about that."

Victoria then paused, sipped some more wine, and continued to lock eyes with Gino, as he also sipped his Rioja.

Turning and looking toward Rafa, Gino asked, "Have you ever kept a dove here, *Señorita*, a white dove?"

"Smiling and slowly moving her head from side to side, Victoria said, "Oh Chief Superintendent, you are looking for *una pluma blanca*, a white ..." stopping in mid-sentence.

"What about a white feather, *Señorita* Valenzuela, *una pluma blanca*?" Gino quickly asked.

Stammering, Victoria blurted, "Nothing. Nothing at all. You mentioned a white dove and feathers came to mind. No reason, and no, I have not kept a white dove here, only my Rafa."

"I am not sure I believe you, *Señorita.*" Gino said very slowly, intently looking into her green eyes.

Quickly recovering, she said, "I am *La Pluma Blanca,* Chief superintendent. I know you heard that from my family, from the days I trained at the ranch." Pointing to her shock of white hair, she continued, "That somehow popped into my head. *Una paloma blanca* is Spanish for white dove and it sounds just like *una pluma blanca*—a white feather. I mixed them up."

There was silence between them now. No movements, no sipping of wine, with Victoria dipping her head ever so slightly, starring at Gino. The air stood still in the apartment. Not a sound, not even Rafa moving.

"Are you trying *aiki* on me, *Señorita* Valenzuela?"

"*Aiki?*" she laughed. "You had to have gotten that from my mother. She believes that using the Japanese martial art of *aiki*, I can subdue a fighting bull—just by staring into its eyes. Oh, if that were true, I could have been the greatest *matadora* of all time, the greatest bullfighter of all time, not to mention being able to convince authorities to ban bullfighting altogether."

"Well, just in case, take no offence that I will avoid starring into those green eyes. I'll just focus on your…white feather."

That is a shame," Victoria commented. "We should be able to converse by looking into each other's eyes, but I will look away from time to time," laughing again, and totally recovered from her potential blunder earlier.

"I'd like to be straight with you *Señorita,*" Gino said.

"Oh, stop with the *señorita*. I am Victoria. You must call me Victoria, and you are Gino. We have spent enough time together, as you have with my family, so can't we dispense with the formalities.?"

"Unfortunately, not, Victoria. As an investigating police officer, you shouldn't be using my name. Chief Superintendent will have to do, but there is no problem with me calling you Victoria. But what I was about to say is that I do believe that you are involved with these events, perhaps even planning, and coordinating with your animal rights friends. If you weren't in *Las Ventas* with *Señor* de Portillo, then you know who was. Likewise, if you weren't in Pamplona last week, again you know who was. That's right, isn't it?"

"Gino, Gino. Oh, I'm sorry, Chief Superintendent. You have

investigated me time and again, I was at my family's ranch when de Portillo was killed and shopping in *El Corte Inglés* when Naranjo was killed. That you know. Perfect alibi. As to my friends, you will have to ask them, but I am sure that they too have perfect alibis for the events in the other countries. We can't be in two places at the same time and you have absolutely no evidence to the contrary."

"You are starring again, Victoria."

"*Dios mio*—my God—you are locked into this *aiki* thing."

Now was Gino's turn to laugh. "I'm sorry. Just a precaution. Perhaps this is something you could teach me to do. It would come in handy in interrogations."

"I don't think we have the time for that. I studied *aiki* and other Japanese martial arts for many summers in Japan, but it is discomforting to know that you think so poorly of me. We just want to save and protect God's creatures and you think I am leading a conspiracy to kill animal abusers. Maybe I should try *aiki* on such men. I would be able to will them to change their ways. My mission would be much simpler."

"That's something you should think about, Victoria. Maybe with Spanish regulators as well. One last thing. We danced around the issue of *una pluma blanca*—the white feather. This is something that could be important to our case—our cases, actually—and as soon as I leave here, I will be instructing Chief Inspector Garcia to have a forensic team up here immediately. We are going to look for the presence of DNA evidence relating to a white dove in this apartment."

* * *

"I got your message Gino," said Mercedes after he returned to their apartment. "Paloma and José Maria are on their way over there now. You think she had a white dove, caged in her apartment that was the source of those white feathers?"

"A long shot, but why not check it out?"

"I agree, and who knows? It could be a piece of evidence in a case that has no evidence at all. What else did you learn while there?"

"I laid all my cards on the table. She knows that I regard her as complicit in all these crimes, possibly the ringleader."

"And how did she react to that, Gino?"

"Very little reaction at all, but she did slip up on the white feather. We kept that out of the press—in all the murders—but she definitely knew about it. She recovered quickly, but she slipped, nevertheless. She made a mistake, so we must keep pressure on her. Let's put surveillance on her again and keep monitoring her communications. And, of course, let's see what Paloma turns up at her apartment."

"Gino, what I fear is that she simply closes up operations and from this day forward she's a saint, running *Salvan Los Toros* as a legitimate, respected animal rights group. She and her colleagues have accomplished so much already. Maybe it is enough for her and she returns to business as she did before all this began."

"Maybe," said Gino, quietly.

Chapter Forty-One

Not surprisingly, the forensic team found no DNA evidence of a white dove in Victoria Valenzuela's apartment. There was considerable evidence relating to a Gray African parrot, but considering Rafa's circulation within the apartment, which was expected.

"So, no *una pluma blanca*," said Gino after Mercedes related the report to him.

"No. If she did have a dove in there at one time, we should have been able to detect something, but after all this time, and countless cleanings, nothing to be found.," replied Mercedes. "My superiors were a little upset at the cost of this forensic analysis, scouring the apartment, the carpets—everywhere—and then doing DNA analyses on dust."

"I said it was a long shot, but if we could have found evidence matching the DNA from the feathers at the crime scenes, it would have taken this investigation to a whole new level."

"But it didn't," lamented Mercedes. She paused in thought. "Gino, I've been thinking. We have five crime scenes, but Pamplona is the only one where we actually see someone with the victim. We see the commission of the crime. I know that the CCTV footage is not good enough for an identification, but our investigators in Pamplona have collected additional videos and images from tourists using their cell

264

phones. Xavier and Marko, working with the Navarra police, made a tremendous effort to go back amongst the crowds and ask to see the photos and videos they took the day of the incident. They eventually, with the help of the CNP's computer technicians, were able to put together a collection of images where Naranjo and the man with the Panama hat appear. They isolated them and put them together with the videos we extrapolated from the CCTV cameras. Nothing great, but several additional images from different angles to scrutinize. Still not enough to make an ID, but with some help, we may be able to make something out of it."

"What kind of help, Mercedes?"

"Well, last year, I contacted someone from your FBI. You may remember that."

Gino nodded, remembering.

"I worked with Kimberly del Rio from the FACE Services Unit. We had a body, found at a construction site. It was mostly skeletal, but we wanted to establish identification. Del Rio's family emigrated to the US from Cuba and she spoke Spanish, and we hit if off fairly well. With the FBI's facial recognition and reconstruction technology, she was able to construct a face and from there, we were able to identify the person. Dental comparisons confirmed those findings and we finally put a name to the body."

"Yes. Now I remember it well," said Gino. "You were quite impressed with what they did."

"Well, they—your FBI—does offer such services to law enforcement agencies worldwide, so it made sense to ask if they could help, and they did."

"So, what are you thinking about with our case? We really have nothing that they can work with."

"Maybe we do, Gino. We have the CCTV images and now, a

collection of additional images of Naranjo and the man in the Panama hat. Maybe they can study what we have and give us some insights. We really don't have anywhere else to go."

"So, what is your plan?"

"I'd like to send all of those images to del Rio. What kind of facial characteristics can be obtained from the bandana worn on the face of the man with Naranjo? The sunglasses totally obscure his eyes, but del Rio's unit has all kinds of facial recognition software. I'd like to see what they might come up with. Besides the face, what else? Height, weight, anything that could help us put together a physical profile of that individual. My idea is to send the FBI photos of all our persons of interest and see which one of them—if any—approximate the person behind the bandana. If the FBI can come up with some facial characteristics, then they can compare them to the photos we send them."

"I think that is a great idea. I'll call Shane Guiness, the FBI director we worked with on the case with the kidnapped girls. I'm sure he'll be able to get some priority for this."

"Good. You call Guiness and I will contact Kimberly del Rio. Then we'll see what exactly they require to get this in motion."

* * *

Gino's call to Shane Guiness allowed the two to catch up with each other and re-live the success they had in returning kidnapped women to their families, and dismantle the *Saqr*—Falcon—group, who were likely wasting away in some dungeon prison in Dubai—or worse.

"Charlie Deevers heads up the Facial Recognition and Construction Unit within the Science and Technology Group. Kimberly del Rio reports to him, and I am aware that she is quite an asset. It will be quite a challenge to do any kind of facial recognition with someone wearing sunglasses and a bandana, but—what-the-hell—sounds interesting and they are really good at what they do. I'll alert Charlie and ask him to make this a priority. What did you say? So far, five murders?"

"Yes Shane, five people killed in rather horrific ways and the murder in Pamplona is the only one where we have any kind of lead."

"Well, good luck Gino. This sounds like a real challenge, even to our team, but maybe it is something we can help with."

* * *

Via E-mail, Mercedes sent all the CCTV images they put together, plus the additional images and videos from the tourist cell phones. With the driver's license photos of the persons of interest—from Spain, France, the Netherlands, and the UK— and other photos taken from the activist's web sites, del Rio said she had plenty to work with. She cautioned Mercedes that this was quite a challenge and not to have high hopes that they would generate anything definitive. She was, however, excited about the challenge, especially when her bosses gave the green light to put a priority behind the project and to access any additional resources she might require. After one week, she called Mercedes in Madrid.

"Mercedes, this has proven to be quite an interesting project. We have never attempted to put a face on someone wearing aviator sunglasses and a bandana covering most of their face."

"I can imagine," said Mercedes, but were you able to make any headway?"

"Some, but let me explain our most interesting finding.. We had to get some help from our anthropology group, but the person with *Señor* Naranjo is most likely a woman, about 5'6" tall. Naranjo, from the information you provided, is 5'8" tall and the other person is about the same height, with the hat. Remove the hat, and that person is about 5'6" tall"

"Okay, someone 5'6" tall, but how could you determine it is a woman?" asked Mercedes.

"Some of the images from the tourist cell phone's gave us a bit more than the CCTV videos. In two instances, we could see almost the full bodies of both individuals. Magnifying the images and putting them through our software analysis, revealed that this person was wearing some kind of vest, a padded vest. Our anthropologists concluded that #1, the vest could conceal and flatten a woman's breasts, and #2, would fill in the natural waistline curves of a woman. We could make out a line beneath the shirt where the vest ends, just at the curvature of the hip, making the torso appear completely straight. No natural female waistline. The curves are completely shrouded. And #3, from the buttocks of the person, we can deduce it is a woman. Her buttocks are lower and fuller than a man's would be."

"So, no mistake. It is a woman," Mercedes said, somewhat incredulously.

"Without question, Mercedes. The person in the Panama hat is a woman."

"*Dios mio*—My God—that is an incredible revelation."

"Yes, that was a very significant find, as it helped us with the facial construction, although our findings here are more subjective that definitive. You sent photos of thirteen individuals—your persons of interest. The Spaniards; all three, are women. Two of the French individuals are women, as are two from the UK. That gives us seven faces we can compare to, albeit our suspect's facial characteristics are completely masked."

"Not much to go on," added Mercedes.

"Not much, but at least, a little. The tautness of the bandana allows us to make out some facial characteristics. For instance, the nose is not large; somewhat petite you might say. And while the eyes are covered, we can detect that the person has high cheekbones. We could not make any conclusions regarding the lips behind the mask, but in some on the images we can make out some of the jawline, but not enough to draw any conclusions.

"So, between the nose and the cheekbones, three of the women could fit the pattern, Victoria Valenzuela, Camille Beaumont and Juliette Jordain. A Spaniard and two French women. But Juliette Jordain is a lot taller than the other two and does not match the stature of the person with Naranjo. Only the Spaniard and the other French woman—Beaumont—meet those criteria."

"That's incredible. From seven women, you narrowed down our persons of interest to two."

"I'm glad this helps, but as I said, some of this is speculative and nothing I have presented could serve as evidence, but as you said, we went from seven to two. Last point. It looks like the person's hair is pushed up under the hat. There are a few strands showing below the hat line, and they appear to be black. Beaumont is a blond. I hope this is helpful."

"It is more than helpful, Kimberly, and your last observation may take our list from two to one. You and your team have done a fantastic job. I can't thank you enough."

"My pleasure. Send a note to my boss, Charlie Deevers, expressing your satisfaction with our work. I'll send you the full report with all our conclusions, observations, and speculations via E-mail. I wish you good luck with this. *Adios amiga.*"

"*Adios* Kimberly, *y otra vez, muchas gracias.*

* * *

Mercedes called Gino at his office and gave him the gist of del Rio's analysis.

"That's fantastic, Mercedes. That was a brilliant idea to bring in the FBI on this. We've advanced light years in this investigation, at least as far as the Pamplona incident is concerned. It sounds like we are down to Victoria Valenzuela as our one and only suspect, but we know, of course, that Victoria was shopping in Madrid at the time of Naranjo's murder."

"Yes, as we probably have to discount Beaumont, because of the black hair at the hat line."

"God, black hair, white feathers, this is ridiculous," commented Gino.

Laughing, Mercedes said, "For a guy that likes to use multiple colors in his work—recalling his Technicolor white boards—having to deal with just black and white must drive you crazy."

"This whole thing is driving me crazy, but we must go over it again, tooth and nail, and see if we can break Victoria's alibi.

"Agreed, but remember Gino, what we have learned will not serve as evidence. It takes us closer—so much closer—but a judge will throw most of this out. Maybe not identifying the killer as a woman, but everything else is speculation, good scientific speculation, but speculation nevertheless."

"I know," sighed Gino, "but we are closer than we have ever been."

Chapter Forty-Two

"Well, what do you think?" Mercedes asked, handing Gino an 8x10 photograph.

Gino took the photo, looked at it and gasped, 'What-the-hell. Where did you get this? How did you get this?" while starring with wide eyes at the image of Victoria Valenzuela, dressed in white trousers and shirt, with a red sash around her waist, amongst the throng of revelers at the Running of the Bulls in Pamplona. "Seriously, where did you get this?"

Following a full-throated laugh, Mercedes caught her breathe and said, "It is something I asked Kimberly del Rio to create for me. She used one of the images from the tourist cell phones, and with the photos of Victoria I had sent to her, created this photo-shopped picture. Took away the hat and there she is, black hair and white streak totally visible. This is our killer in Pamplona, no?"

"It is certainly what we believe. Good touch in getting rid of the Panama hat and we almost have a full view of her face, *la pluma blanca* in full view. Very, very well done, but what did you think we could do with this?," holding the photo out to Mercedes.

"We should talk about this," said Mercedes, taking the photo back from Gino. "We have unmasked Victoria—perhaps in more ways than one—and I thought we might be able to use this," holding the picture up, "in a confrontation with her."

"And how do we do that? That composition you and Kimberly cooked up is amazing, but this is no evidence," said Gino.

"I know that, but look," gesturing to the glossy 8x10, "something like this could shake her. I thought I," pausing, "maybe better you, since you are so buddy-buddy with her and…"

"Whoa. Where does this buddy-buddy come from, and who is teaching you these English phrases?"

"Well, you have gotten close to her, meeting with her in her apartment."

Gino rolled his eyes.

"But just listen to me and stop making those faces. You set up another meeting with her. It could be at her apartment or at her office. No, at her apartment is better where you can be one-on-one. At some point, you show her the picture. We have to get the words right, but you say nothing until she reacts. She'll say something like, 'What is this? Where did you get this? What games are you playing?' Then you say, 'We've been working with the American FBI's Facial Recognition and Construction Unit, using CCTV videos and images we obtained from the crime scene the morning of the incident,' something like that. That is no lie. It is the truth."

"I see you are trying to skirt the issue of lying to the suspect," said Gino.

"Absolutely. We say—you say—that the FBI has amazing technology that has proven that the person with Rafael Martínez Naranjo is a woman and that they are also able to generate facial characteristics even though the person is wearing a full, facial bandana and sunglasses. Again, no lie. That is what they did."

"Mercedes, the FBI did not generate Victoria's face—as in this picture—from their facial recognition technology."

"No, but she wouldn't know that, and you didn't say that," Mercedes said with excitement in her voice.

"You are certainly walking an ethics tight-rope here. She has not been lied to and I would have said nothing about this picture, but okay, then what?"

'Maybe she relents and confesses. Maybe the photo of herself, *la pluma blanca*, shocks her into confessing her involvement in the killing of Naranjo."

"A lot of maybes, but I must say, I like it. I think we should discuss this with your lead prosecutor, just to see if a confession, obtained under this scenario, could hold up," Gino added.

"Likely that would be José Luis Donadeo or possibly Maria Elena Mercade. Before we get that far, however, I have to take this to Superintendent Balmaseda, take him through the whole thing. He and I went over the FBI's report and he was shocked to learn we have a woman suspect, but he also knows that up to now, we have no evidence to take to a prosecutor. We could be seen as implying that the FBI was able to extract this image from the material we sent them. It would be—how do you say—a stretch to think otherwise, no?"

"A stretch, yes. I want to take this whole scenario past Schickhaus as well," replied Gino. "We are very close and I don't want to destroy our case—as much of a case as we have, anyway. You approach Balmaseda. Scan a copy of that photo and E-mail it to me. Then I'll go over the plan with Klaus."

* * *

It took a few days for all the legal and ethical angles to be explored, with both the CNP and Interpol working with a bevy of legal experts to assess the level of deception to be employed. In the end, Mercedes and Gino got a greenlight to approach Victoria Valenzuela again.

"I had another thought, Gino," Mercedes said after getting the go-ahead to proceed. "I checked and the warrant for Victoria's apartment has expired. I want to renew it so we can collect the items of clothing Victoria bought—or someone bought—that morning of the incident at El Corte Inglés. If she really was in Pamplona, as we believe, then someone disguised as her bought the clothing and presumably, tried them on. We need to check the DNA on those items and confirm who tried on those blouses."

"Good idea. I can use this as an excuse to go to her apartment with Paloma to collect those garments and take them to the lab for analysis. I'll stay there after Paloma leaves, then show Victoria the photo and see what transpires."

"Okay," said Mercedes. "We have a plan and you will confront your buddy," laughing, while Gino rolled his eyes again, "And watch out for her *aiki* tricks," she added, continuing to laugh.

* * *

Paloma Retuerta and Gino made an appointment to meet with Victoria at her apartment, Paloma took a DNA swab from Victoria, and José Maria Duarte did the same with Martina Muñoz and Luz Sánchez at SLA office in San Agustín de Guadalix.

Gino remained in the living room while Paloma and Victoria went into the bedroom to retrieve the garments as well as the receipts from the purchases at El Corte Inglés. Paloma then left and Gino remained.

"A glass of wine Chief Superintendent?" Victoria asked.

"Not this time. I have something to show you," Gino said, pulling

out the 8x10 photo from an envelope he was carrying. He presented the photo to Victoria and said nothing.

Victoria took the photo, looked at it, starring as the seconds ticked away. She said nothing at first, just holding the picture, continuing to stare at the image of her, presumably in Pamplona.

"You know this isn't me," she eventually said. "I was in Madrid, buying those items your colleague just left with."

Gino then went through the work of the FBI, not only identifying the person with Naranjo as a woman but being able to develop facial characteristics from the images obtained that fateful morning, despite the person being masked.

Again, Victoria was silent, still holding the photo and starring at it, studying it.

"I am sorry Victoria, truly sorry, but we now know it was you behind the sunglasses and red bandana," said Gino, breaking the silence.

"Well, you think it was me. The technology used to create this photo is remarkable, but that same technology could have put Antonio Banderas's face on that body, no? I think, however, that I must now decline to speak any further with you and bring a lawyer into any subsequent conversations, or is it now interrogations? I have nothing further to say."

"As you wish, *Señorita*," Gino said, rising and leaving the apartment.

* * *

"She did not take the bait?" Mercedes said when Gino called her after he exited the apartment building.

"No, she wisely shut down any further conversation without the presence of her lawyer. As she is now officially a suspect, she has to be made aware of her rights and cautioned that what she might say could be used as evidence against her. She is a formidable adversary, Mercedes. We are not going to be able to trick her."

"I can see that. I really thought we'd be able to make this work. Well, we're left with the DNA analysis from the clothes. We may not be done yet," Mercedes said.

After two days, the DNA extracted from the garments from El Corte Inglés revealed evidence of DNA from Victoria and Martina Muñoz, and several others, not identifiable.

"Mierda, mierda, mierda"—shit, shit, shit—said Mercedes when viewing the laboratory report. I can just see where this is going. Victoria tried on the clothes in the store and Martina asked to try them on when she got back to the SLT office—probably vice-versa. The other sets of DNAs could have come from salesclerks or other customers who tried them on before Victoria's—or someone's— purchase. Zero, we have zero," she lamented to Gino "She is always one step ahead of us."

"With DNA evidence out the window, I am at a loss as to where we go from here?" Gino said. "I was sure she'd admit her involvement after seeing the photo the FBI constructed, like she slipped with her white feather comment, but she was too smart for that. Same with the clothes. By having both Martina and Victoria try them on, we cannot disprove her presence in Madrid the morning of the attack on Naranjo. We know that Victoria was behind this, Pamplona and undoubtedly, the other incidents, but we cannot prove anything. Pamplona was our best chance and we couldn't get it done."

Chapter Forty-Three

Months passed an both the CNP and Interpol were engaged in stopping human trafficking operations that were plaguing Spain as well as other parts of Europe. This was their current priority.

On the animal rights front, two cities in Spain joined Barcelona in outlawing bullfighting and several towns no longer carried out their versions of the running of the bulls. There were outcries from the traditionalists who claimed that Spain's culture was being destroyed, but the anti-bullfighting fervor continued to spread.

In France, four horseracing trainers were suspended and their licenses revoked because of their use of performance enhancing drugs. New and more stringent anti-doping measures were adopted and there was hope for cleaning up the sport of thoroughbred racing in the country. What was happening in France was starting to be adopted elsewhere in Europe.

Six cities in the UK banned greyhound racing and strict, new regulations were enacted regarding the care and treatment of these animals. Heavy fines were imposed on promotors, trainers and owners who flouted the new regulations and several racetracks had their events suspended until there was proof of compliance. Bookmakers suffered from the loss of interest by the public and they had to curtail the afternoon races they sponsored, but they found other betting opportunities to cover those losses.

In the Netherlands and spreading throughout Europe, additional bans on the use of animals in medical and cosmetic research grew and the cosmetic industry was forced to find humane ways to test their products for use in humans.

Five violent deaths of individuals, so closely tied to animal abuse, was resulting in thousands of animals being spared from the horrors so traditionally associated with certain sports and the use of animals in research testing. "Never Again," became the mantra of these movements. Many, buoyed by the phenomenal increase in contributions and government backing, increased their attention to saving the whales and protecting elephants, with renewed diligence, worldwide.

* * *

Outside of the Las Ventas bullring in Madrid—still an active and popular venue for bullfighting—*Salvan Los Toros* and several others of the more active anti-bullfighting groups held a demonstration during the *Feria de San Isidro*, a nine-day cultural event held each May, featuring plays, concerts, parades, book fairs and art exhibits, including a series of bullfights with the finest matadors in the country. Victoria Valenzuela was chatting with her friend, Joseba Aguirre, from the *Partido Animalista de Bilbao,* while patrons filed into the arena on the first day of the San Isidro festival's bullfights, the most anticipated event of the bullfighting season.

Suddenly, a man, a portly man in a black and white stripped tee shirt and a black beret, broke from the line of people waiting to enter the arena and ran directly at Victoria. Brandishing a knife and screaming "*traidor*—traitor, *diablo*—devil" he crashed into her and repeatedly stabbed her as she fell to the ground. Aguirre and several others, including some on the patrons in line, plowed on top of the man, wrestled the knife away and subdued him. Almost immediately, police were dragging him away and calling for an ambulance, Victoria lay on the ground, blood seeping from the wounds in her chest, staring into the late afternoon sky.

The wounds were very serious and Victoria was taken to the Hospital Universitario del la Princesa, only eight minutes away. The Emergency Room immediately assessed her condition as critical. The knife used by her attacker—a lace knife—was of the type used in the bullring when a wounded bull refused to die. In these circumstances one of the *matador's* crew plunged a short, broad, and pointed blade—a lace knife—into the neck of the prostrate animal, severing its spinal cord and instantaneously ending its life.

Later, it was revealed that the attacker, a man in his fifties, had been part of a bullfighter's crew when he was younger and currently worked at the Ciudad Rodrigo bullring in Salamanca, in the north of Spain. He spent years as part of the *Carnival del Toro*, and event declared a National Tourist Interest, which included bulls running along the streets of the city and amateur and professional bullfights. The notoriety of the death of Naranjo in Pamplona spurred interest to curtail some of the bull-related events of the carnival. The attacker's—Diego Casado—devotion to bullfighting was not unlike many others who were bought up in what they viewed as the majesty of the sport. As bullrings closed and bullfighting became more and more unpopular, his grievances grew against those most active in trying to outlaw the sport. Victoria Valenzuela, *La Pluma Blanca,* was a well-known adversary and his rage against her could not be contained.

Gino visited Victoria at the hospital, where her condition was classified as critical. Her mother, Kim Watanabe, was constantly at her bedside, eyes reddened by tears and anguish. Throughout the day, members of the Valenzuela family came to comfort her and pray for her recovery. Attached to a multitude of tubes and beeping monitors, Victoria opened her eyes and smiled when she saw Gino. She asked her mother to give her a few minutes to speak with Gino alone.

"I'm so sorry, Victoria. I cannot say how sorry I am," he said softly to her.

"Gracias, my friend. Despite our situation, I still think of you as my friend, regardless of what you think of me," she said, her voice raspy and weak.

"Victoria, you should know that I think very highly of you. You know that I believe you were involved in these incidents, but your dedication, your passion for what you are trying to achieve, is amazing. You are a very special woman."

"Very special, but a killer, no?"

"Let's not go into that. Please know that I want only for you to recover. You beat me, and I admire you for that. I have never had such respect for an adversary."

"I thank you for that, and I compliment you—and your wife—for almost uncovering this plot. And, yes, I was the one who led Naranjo to his death, and I'm not sorry for that. As to the other incidents, they will remain a mystery to you. I will say nothing further, but I wanted you to know that you almost had me. So very close."

"No more about that Victoria. I just want you to get better to continue your magnificent work. But no more killings, please."

Victoria laughed, then coughed and the machines around her flashed red and beeped loudly. A nurse rushed in and asked Gino to leave. Doctors followed and the door to her room was closed. Outside,

Gino stood with Kim Watanabe and Vergilio Valenzuela, the uncle that showed him around the family's ranch.

Minutes passed in silence. Then a physician emerged from Victoria's room. He went directly to her mother and said, *"Señora, lo siento"*—I'm sorry. Victoria had passed away.

Chapter Forty-Four

Victoria was taken back to Extremadura to be buried in the family's plot at the ranch. It was a private ceremony.

However, Victoria had made friends all across Europe and even in the USA, recognized as one of the foremost advocates and protectors of animal rights, and almost singlehandedly, starting to transform public opinion in Spain. To celebrate her achievements and the esteem in which she was held, a special memorial was organized for her, using one of the ballrooms at the Melia Castilla Hotel, on Capitan Haya in Madrid. Hundreds of her collaborators traveled to Madrid to celebrate her life. Many went to the podium that was surrounded by arrays of red roses, her favorite flower. They spoke in Spanish, English, and French, saying words of friendship, respect, and sorrow.

Gino and Mercedes attended, with Gino especially affected by her passing and the way that she died.

"You liked her, didn't you, Gino?" Mercedes asked her husband.

"I did. Very much so, despite what she did, although no one will ever know what she said to me in that hospital room, except you."

"I only have seen photos of her alleged conspirators, but you met each of them. Do you know if they are here today?" Mercedes asked.

"Yes, I think all of them. I saw the Brits, and Camille Beaumont said a few words at the podium, and the Dutch stand out because of their height, almost a head taller than everyone around them. I see Max de Groot, who was close to her. I want to say a few words to him. Will you excuse me?" and he walked into the crowd.

Approaching de Groot, Gino said, "Hello Max. My condolences."

"Thank you. She was a very special lady, Chief Superintendent. More than you realize."

"Max, I am totally aware of the conspiracy she created and I am sure that you were an integral part of what transpired, but no one will ever know. Of course, I abhor what you did, but I have to recognize the talent and commitment she had to pull this off. All of you for that matter. An incredible operation that kept authorities in four countries guessing for many months. You got away with it and we have closed our investigation, but we know you were complicit—all of you—the Brits, the French, the Spaniards and of course, you and your colleagues in Holland. A brilliant operation. And Beekhof's management of the drugs used was impressive More than impressive."

"Speculation, Chief Superintendent, Pure speculation," Max responded, smiling.

"I trust this is now over, Max. You get to move on, and I strongly suggest that you keep it that way. You have to know when to fold them, borrowing a phrase from a Kenny Rogers song."

Max nodded his head in recognition.

"Know when to walk away, the song continues, so that is what I suggest you and your colleagues—conspirators—do. Walk away, Max."

"That is what we will do. We have accomplished a great deal and I'm sorry that Victoria cannot walk away with us. We are all devastated at what happened."

"Again, my condolences. What is it you say in Dutch, *Tot ziens*?

"Yes, goodbye, but sometime *tot ziens* is used to say, 'see you again.' I sincerely hope that doesn't happen."

Gino laughed. "I hope not also."

Rejoining Mercedes, Gino remained silent.

"Well, like your Strangers on a Train story, someone—actually many—walks away, free of the crime he was involved with."

"Yes, the tennis player never gets charged with plotting his wife's murder."

"Never thought you'd be living in an Alfred Hitchcock thriller, did you Gino?"

"No, and I hope this is the last time. Let's go home."

the author